Estelle Ryan

The

Pucelle Connection

The Pucelle Connection
A Genevieve Lenard Novel
By Estelle Ryan

First published 2015
Copyright © 2015 by Estelle Ryan

Acknowledgements

Most authors would tell you that writing is an isolating and lonely profession. I don't experience that. I am honoured to have the love, interest and unconditional support of amazing people. They pull me back into reality, make me laugh and definitely make me feel loved.

As always, Charlene, for your love and support. Linette, for always being there. Moeks, for being a pillar. Anna, for your support. R.J. Locksley for your astute editing. Julie, Kamila, Jola, Ania S, Alta, Krystina and Maggie for your continued interest and support. Jane, for your continued love and support.

A very special thank you to all the wonderful readers who have contacted me and who keep in touch through Facebook – thank you. Every email, every comment touches me deeply and is more appreciated that I can ever express.

Dedication

To Ania B

Chapter ONE

"This looks like an original Pucelle." Colin frowned as he turned the antique-looking book over. The moment Phillip had shown him the small book, Colin had covered his hands in his scarf and touched the book with reverence. "There are very few of his illuminated manuscripts on display. Even fewer artists would ever consider forging his works. Especially a book of hours. Where did you get this?"

"It was a gift." My boss, Phillip Rousseau, straightened his shoulders in response to Colin's accusatory stare. "You should know better than to look at me like that, Colin."

Colin Frey was a member of our team working on art crimes and other cases selected by the president of France. He was also a thief working for Interpol. And he was my romantic partner. His expression was contrite as he briefly closed his eyes and nodded. "My apologies. This is just... it's unexpected."

We were standing in our team room in the offices of Rousseau & Rousseau, Phillip's high-end insurance company in Strasbourg. It was three minutes past eight in the morning and as usual we were first in the office. Like many non-neurotypicals, I followed a routine every day and it was very important to me. It made me feel safe. It made me feel that everything was under control. I knew this was an illusion, but since I could control my routine, I insisted on it.

I understood that neurotypicals didn't have the same obsessive needs and I didn't expect punctuality from the rest of the team. Yet Colin insisted on driving to work with me every morning. He said it was no problem for him to fall in with my schedule. It was becoming a problem for me. He was becoming part of my routine and I dreaded the day he would be late. I didn't expect my reaction to be favourable.

I shifted the strap of my handbag still slung over my shoulder. Phillip hadn't given us time to settle in my viewing room. The moment we'd stepped into the team room, he'd been there, holding the book in cotton-gloved hands.

"Who gave the book to you?" I took my handbag from my shoulder and keyed my code into the glass door to my viewing room. I needed to finish my routine. The door whooshed open and I walked in, knowing the two men would follow me.

"It was sent by a new client," Phillip said. "Why they would send me a gift is beyond me. They are our clients. We are supposed to be sending *them* gifts."

"Good morning, all you beautiful people." Francine walked into my room. Today, she was wearing black leather pants, a white silk shirt and a lot of gold jewellery. Instead of looking tawdry, the four different chains around her neck, hoop earrings and noisy bracelets added a flamboyant finish to her outfit. She was one of the top hackers in the world, our team's IT expert and called herself my 'bestest' friend. She was also notoriously curious. "What are you looking at? Something fabulous?"

Colin lifted the book. "An illuminated Gothic manuscript."

"Ooh!" She stood closer and stared at the book. "Gothic like with vampires, black makeup and The Cure?"

Colin laughed. "No. Gothic like the mediaeval age just before the Renaissance period."

"Pah." She waved one hand, bracelets jingling. "Not as exciting."

"Looking for another scandal, supermodel?" Colonel Manfred Millard asked from the team room. He was the only law enforcement member of our team and, according to Francine, had a dry British sense of humour. Since my brain processed everything literally, I didn't understand humour and didn't know if Francine's assessment was correct. I didn't consider him comical. He dropped his coat on his desk and walked into my room. It was beginning to feel very crowded. This was why I preferred we had our meetings in the team room. There was a large round table and the room was two and half times the size of mine.

The soundproof viewing room was supposed to be exclusively my domain where I watched footage of interviews with clients and suspects. Analysing their nonverbal cues, looking for inconsistencies was not only my forte, but it gave me great pleasure. In the last two and a half years, I'd given up any hopes of being left alone for hours on end, losing myself in these activities. Nowadays, I'd become accustomed to constantly being interrupted by my team.

"Hey, you handsome beast." Francine blew Manny a kiss. "I'm hoping you will make a scandal with me. We can rock each other's worlds and make headlines at the same time."

Manny waved his forefinger at her. "One day. One day your big talk is going to come back and bite you in the…"

"In my sexy tush? Ooh, I didn't know you were into that." She pretended to shiver.

Manny sighed heavily, pointed at the book and looked at me. "What's happening here, Doc?"

"Phillip received a book from a client. Colin thinks it is an original Pucelle. Francine thinks Gothic art has some connection to vampires." I looked at Francine, my brow furrowed. "You're far too intelligent to entertain the silliness of vampires. Someone as well-read as you should know the myth comes from folklore, ignorance about the human body's decomposition process and mass hysteria."

"But they're sexy."

I recognised Francine's body language and facial expressions. She was baiting me. It gave her inexplicable pleasure to fluster me with her outrageous theories and beliefs in inanities. Colin bumped me with his shoulder, his smile soft. He enjoyed that the team was teasing me. I knew this indicated their affection. Yet after two years, I still wasn't comfortable with it. "No. No. I'm not being drawn into this. Tease Manny. He enjoys it. I'm not going to get into another debate with you. Not today."

"I do not enjoy supermodel's pestering." Even though the corners of Manny's mouth were turned down, his other micro-expressions belied his outrage.

"You do." I pointed to his eyes. "When Francine teases you, your eyes widen which is a sign of pleasure, your pupils dilate which is a sign—"

"Can we analyse this book, missy?" Manny only called me 'missy' when I'd done something irksome.

I thought about what I'd said, but couldn't find the reason his nostrils were flaring, Francine looked surprised and Colin was laughing. I returned to the neutral topic. "I will need to know more about this book to analyse it."

"Frey can start by telling us who this Tucelle was."

"Pucelle." I bit down hard to prevent myself from berating Manny for getting another name wrong. He was baiting me. Just like Francine.

"Jean Pucelle was possibly the most prominent artist of the first half of the fourteenth century." Colin's posture straightened. He loved talking about art. "His distinctive style influenced the future of French illuminations."

"And an illumination is what?" Manny lifted one eyebrow, his lips pulling to one side in a half-sneer. "Intellectual enlightenment?"

Colin closed his eyes and sighed. "Oh, you ignorant old man. Gothic-era illuminated manuscripts were Bibles, books of hours and psalters. Later on, the production of such works included more secular books like chronicles and other works of literature."

"And how were they illuminated?" Manny moved his hand in a rolling motion, hurrying Colin along.

"Like this." Colin carefully opened the book and lifted it for us to see. "See how the text is decorated, especially the first letter of the paragraph? This one also has marginalia, borders and miniature illustrations to accompany the writing. In the strictest definition, illuminated manuscripts are only those decorated with silver or gold. But today, this term is used for all decorated or illustrated manuscripts."

"And this book is suspicious why?" Manny reached for the book, but Colin pulled it closer to him, glaring at Manny.

"You don't touch an antique book with your bare hands. The pages are fragile."

"*Bon giorno!*" Vinnie's greeting boomed from the team room. "What y'all doing in there?"

"Out!" I motioned everyone out with my hands. "If we're having a team meeting, we should have it in the team room. Out. Go."

No one reacted to my annoyed tone. Instead they filed out of my room and took their usual places at the round table. Vinnie played an important role in our team with his connections in the crime world. When he wasn't helping us, he was maintaining his reputation as a ruthless criminal. But that was not the man I knew. Sharing an apartment with us, Vinnie was light-hearted, protective and had taken complete control of my kitchen. Now, he was unpacking pastries onto a plate, listening as Colin filled him in. Colin sat down next to me, reverently handling the leather-bound book.

"Someone gave you a mediaeval book as a thank you?" Vinnie nodded slowly. "I'd have gone with a bottle of rum."

"Who is the client?" Manny's attempt to make the question sound nonchalant failed. The concern was evident in his voice and on his face.

"ZDP."

"Who are they? What do they do?"

"They're an investment brokerage company." Phillip took the cotton gloves off and placed them on the table. "It's an old company, established by the current owner's grandfather ninety years ago. It survived the Second World War and numerous depressions and is still going strong."

"What is Rousseau & Rousseau insuring? Their assets? Investments?" Francine asked.

"Their art. The pieces in their head office alone amount up to over nineteen million euro." Phillip stopped as Tim, his assistant, entered the room with a tray filled with steaming coffee mugs.

Tim placed the tray next to the plate of pastries and glared at Vinnie. "These are not better than the ones I get."

"Dude, your little pastries are for metrosexuals. These pastries are for real men." Vinnie pushed an entire éclair in his mouth. I shuddered.

"You're an unsophisticated lug." Tim sniffed, turned on his heel and left the room.

"Why is this book suspicious?" Manny asked, his teeth clenched. He took his mug of milky tea from the tray. "I don't want to ask every question fifteen times, Frey."

"It's not the book per se," Colin said absently. He carefully turned another page, his eyes narrowing as he brought the book closer to inspect something that had caught his interest.

"It's odd that a client sends us a gift," Phillip said. "Not unheard of, just odd."

"So there's nothing to be concerned about then." Manny slouched in his chair. "Why all the excitement so early in the morning? Before my tea no less."

"I wouldn't say it's nothing to be concerned about, handsome." Francine turned to Phillip. "You said that the book was sent by ZDP. Right?"

"Yes."

"Well? Did anyone check it for electronics?" She lowered her voice. "We know that the CIA, FSB and many other alphabet agencies have devices small enough to hide in the pages of a book. They could be listening to us right now."

"Again with your conspiracy theories?" Manny slouched deeper into his chair. "Not everyone is out to get you, supermodel."

She leaned closer to Manny. "Just because you can't see them doesn't mean they're not there."

"Let's check this sucker." Vinnie got up, disappeared into my viewing room and returned with a small handheld device.

"Where did you get that?" My tone might have been a bit too harsh, but he had just come from my viewing room. My sacred space. "Did you store that in my room? It's my room. Not your office."

Vinnie chuckled. "I put it in Colin's desk drawer, Jen-girl. I would never dream of invading your space."

"Oh." I didn't know what else to say.

"Hold it up for me, dude." Vinnie waited until Colin lifted the book. He used the device as a wand and ran it around the book, spending extra time on the spine. No one spoke. After a second sweep, Vinnie straightened. "Nope. Nothing that can transmit or that has any power."

"That thing accurate, criminal?" Manny nodded at the device in Vinnie's hand.

"Better than any of the toys the agencies have." Vinnie lifted his chin. "I'm not telling you where I got this. Just be happy that I can clear these two rooms of bugs any time."

"If you didn't get as defensive as a teenage girl, I was going to ask how often you scan these rooms."

"Oh. Sorry." Vinnie shrugged. "I sweep both rooms every morning."

"Good."

"Hmm." Colin turned another page. His expression was no longer one of appreciation and focus, but rather of concern.

"What?" I leaned a bit closer. He was on the last two pages of the book. The text was slightly faded, the pages yellowed from age. Each page had five lines written in ornate letters. The rest of the pages were filled with lavish drawings. What appeared to be religious icons were coloured with rich blues and reds, with shades of yellow, pink and turquoise. I was so busy appreciating the intricate art of the written text that it took a few seconds to register that something was out of place. "I see it."

"What are you two talking about?" Manny leaned forward.

"This isn't Latin." Colin turned back two pages and pointed to the text. "Until this, the whole book is in Latin, as was usual for these books during that time." He turned to the next page. "The last three pages are not Latin."

"What is it then?" Phillip put his coffee mug on the table.

I leaned even closer and frowned. "It… it looks like a code."

"A code?" Manny glared at the book. "Does that mean the book is forged?"

"Most definitely." Colin put the book on the table. "It took only a few pages to see that it is a brilliant forgery. Whoever did this has an amazing skill. He used the correct type of parchment from that era. The text is in exactly the same style as Pucelle's original book of hours, *Jeanne d'Evreux*. The burnished gold dots, the *rinceaux*, this floral motif around the border, everything is as if Pucelle had come back to life and done this book again. The person who did this has mastered not only a unique skill, but also the ability to make an exact copy of Pucelle's work."

"Let me see." Phillip put his gloves back on and took the book from Colin. He chose random pages in the book, went to the last three pages and checked another few pages in the rest of the book. "Most peculiar."

"You see it?" Colin asked.

"Yes. I think Genevieve is correct." Phillip narrowed his eyes. "These are Latin letters, but I think some of them might be Roman numerals."

"A book cipher?" It had been my first thought. Book ciphers replaced the original words of the message or text with the location of the words from the book being used, the key book.

Phillip looked up. "You would know best. Codes are not my forte."

"Are you people sure it's not some strange language?" Manny's gaze went from me to Colin and back to me. "Just because you don't recognise it doesn't mean it is a code."

Colin shook his head. "I can't speak many languages, not like Jenny, but I recognise most modern and a few ancient languages."

I nodded. "It's true. I surmise it is a skill connected to his forging abilities."

"Thank you, love." Something in Colin's tone alerted me that his thanks was not one hundred percent sincere.

"Let me get this straight." Manny placed both hands on the table. "This is a gift from a new client. It is a forgery of some antique Gothic book with three pages in the back that don't fit."

"Give Millard a prize." Colin smiled when Manny scowled at him.

"I still think it is suspicious and should be treated as a danger to us all." Francine looked down her nose at Manny. "And don't tell me I'm being paranoid. A bit of paranoia can save lives."

"I agree. Pack that book up. I'm sending it to the labs for tests."

Francine's eyes widened and she slapped both hands on her chest. "Be still, my beating heart. Grumpy has just agreed with me."

Manny ignored her. He lowered his chin, his expression without any of the usual bantering. "Take photos of all the pages, Doc. But wear gloves. I'll get it to the lab to be tested and you and the thief can uncrypt the code."

"Uncrypt isn't a word." I closed my eyes and nodded. "We'll take the photos."

"Have you thanked this client for their gift?" Manny asked Phillip.

"Not yet. It was delivered a few minutes before Colin and Genevieve came in."

"Hmm." Manny took a sip of his tea. "Phone them. Thank them for this marvellous gift and all that BS they need to hear."

Phillip lifted one eyebrow. "And why should I use all that... BS?"

"If they didn't send this, they won't know what you're talking about." Vinnie took the last croissant from the plate. "If they sent it, you might be able to wrangle some more info from them."

Manny acknowledged Vinnie with a single nod. "Either way, we might get more info on this book."

"I'll phone them as soon as we're done here."

"Good. Now tell me how we're doing with that list of companies." Manny was talking about a case that we'd been following up on for the last four months. In summer, one of our investigations had brought Laurence Gasquet to our attention. He'd had contacts in Interpol, which had allowed him to conduct illegal and highly unethical business for more than a decade. The crime that had crossed our desks still affected my sleep.

His Interpol accomplices had been tried and were serving long sentences. Gasquet was still at large. The last four months we had been looking into his corporate security business in the hopes of finding him. We had not found him yet, but weekly we uncovered new bank accounts where he'd been funnelling money.

Since we hadn't found a client list anywhere, we'd been working our way through his many bank accounts to find his customers. Tracing payments into every account we discovered gave us new clients to investigate. Some had contracted Gasquet's security services for a few weeks, some for months. Some had shown many questionable business activities, some were completely legal in all their dealings. Francine had demonstrated the level of her skills by scrutinising each of Gasquet's bank accounts and finding links to more accounts which led us to more companies who had employed Gasquet.

"We found another two clients yesterday." Francine placed her empty mug on the table. "One of those was a data storage service. They hired Gasquet three years ago to run a systems security check. And went bankrupt last year."

"Anything interesting about that company?"

"Nah." Francine's shoulders dropped. "No scandal there. They were too small-time anyway."

I watched as Francine bit her bottom lip and pinched the skin under her chin. A very telling nonverbal cue. "You found something that is causing you concern."

"Is it the second client?" Manny asked.

"No." Francine shook her head. "No, they are an online clothing store. They specialise in designer pants for larger women. Their contract with Gasquet was for a project that lasted three months. I have their contact details."

"I'll speak to them today." Manny straightened out of his slouch. "Now tell us what is worrying you, supermodel."

"An hour ago, I found another bank account."

"We're now up to what? Eight?" Vinnie made a rude noise. "That ass has more bank accounts than you have shoes."

Francine laughed. "Impossible, Vinnie. He cannot have a hundred and seventy-three bank accounts."

"Bloody hell, woman." Manny's *corrugator supercilii* muscle pulled his eyebrows together. "Nobody needs that many shoes."

"Say that again and I'll never make you my grammy's Brazilian cookies." She glared at Manny until he waved her on. "At the risk of Genevieve shouting at me for speculating, I'm going to say that I think we've cut off most of Gasquet's funds. But the account I found yesterday has twenty-seven thousand euro in it. Well, it *had* twenty-seven thousand euro in it."

"He withdrew money?" I asked.

"Where?" Manny asked.

Francine swallowed. "From ATM's in Saint-Dizier, Void-Vacon and then Saverne."

"That's *en route* from Paris to Strasbourg." My heart rate increased. "He's coming here?"

"We don't know if he's even left Strasbourg, love." Colin took my hand between both of his.

The flare of excitement about the book of hours and the possible book cipher diminished, replaced by dread. Despite the time passed, I didn't feel prepared for another close encounter with a man as ruthless and, to use Francine's word, evil as Gasquet. "How did you find this bank account?"

"By seeing what looks like double payments. I don't know how else to describe it. So far, I've found two such transactions. Both were cash deposits and are untraceable." She swiped her tablet screen and bank statements appeared on the large screen against the wall. "This is the transaction history for May two years ago for two of Gasquet's accounts. Look at the third of this month."

"Ten and a half thousand euro was deposited into the first account. Four days later, twenty-one thousand euro was paid into the second account. Exactly double the amount." I wondered what this meant. If it had any meaning.

Francine tapped on her tablet and new bank statements appeared. "These are two other accounts. The statements are from August last year."

"On the seventh, eight thousand euro deposited, five days later sixteen thousand in the other account." Manny scratched his jaw. "Strange."

"Have you found more?" I asked.

"No." She shook her head. "I've just discovered this."

"We need to look for more such transactions."

Francine looked at her watch. "I've gotta go out for a while. I'll get back to this as soon as I return."

"Where are you going?" Manny asked. "You should be here. Working."

She lifted one eyebrow. "I'm taking Caelan some clothes I found online. He's going to love the three shirts. They're all the same style, but have different buttons."

Francine was talking about the young man who had helped us find some of Gasquet's illegal activities in the last case. Typical of someone on the autistic spectrum, he was socially unskilled and not well adjusted to society. In the last five months, Manny and Francine had made a point of visiting him, making sure he was looking after himself. Manny didn't like anyone knowing about it, but his micro-expressions revealed that he liked Caelan.

"He's not going to like the buttons," Manny said.

"He is. I asked him and even showed him the shirts online."

"Oh." Manny pulled his shoulders back. "I'll come with you."

Immediately they started arguing about whose car to take and who was to drive. I had also been spending time with Caelan. Most times, he came to visit me in my viewing room and we would talk. He was a highly intelligent teenager and I hoped to encourage him to start a university course within the next two years. Emotionally, he was not ready for it.

I returned my thoughts to the case that had brought Caelan to us. The four transactions might be a pattern that I'd missed in the months of looking through these documents. I wondered how many such transactions there were and where it would lead us.

Chapter TWO

"Doc? Doctor Face-reader. Oh, bloody hell. Where's Frey?" The worry in Manny's tone pulled me back into the room and into my own skin. I took a shuddering breath and stretched my neck. When I opened my eyes, Manny was sitting in the chair next to me, staring at me. "Please tell me you didn't go off on some tangent. Doc?"

I had shut down. Too much stimulation, or more often stress, would send me into a shutdown. Even though I would be awake, I had no awareness of my surroundings. Shutdowns could last minutes or hours and I did my best to prevent them. Controlling my emotional reaction to stress usually helped, but sometimes an event, or, like now, a discovery proved greater than my control.

I lifted my chin. "I'm fine, Manny."

"You didn't look fine." Manny leaned a bit closer.

"I wasn't fine. Now I am."

He fell back into the chair. "Good to know. Now tell me where Frey and that criminal are. And why did you zone out?"

"Vinnie took Colin to train with Daniel." It had been a surprise to everyone when Vinnie had put aside his deep distrust of law enforcement and started training with a GIPN team, the French equivalent of SWAT. He'd become friends with Daniel, the team leader. It gave him great satisfaction to outperform the team members and they enjoyed his sense of humour and lack of respect for authority. A few times he'd gone on raids with them, working well within that team dynamic. Recently he'd asked Colin to join them while training. Apparently Colin had skills he could share with them. Today's training was shorter than usual and included briefing Daniel's team on our current case. I glanced at the clock on my computer. "It's twenty-five past four and Colin said he'd be back before half past four."

"Talking about us, Jen-girl?" Vinnie leaned against the doorframe as Colin walked past him. They were both freshly showered, their skin still flushed from the training.

Despite the mystery of the books of hours, we had unanimously decided that finding Gasquet took precedence over studying the photos of the forgery. Colin had held the book and I had taken the photos as quickly as possible. We'd sealed it in an evidence bag Manny had provided and given it to him. Then we'd returned to searching for Gasquet.

After spending the whole morning going over the accounts of Gasquet's clients, Colin and Vinnie had lost interest and started interrupting my train of thought with inanities. I had been pleased when Vinnie had suggested a short training session with Daniel's team. It had given me the time and space to focus and I had made an important finding. Unfortunately, I had also shut down.

The moment Colin looked at me, he frowned. "What's wrong? Is Millard bothering you?"

"Nothing is wrong."

Colin looked pointedly at my legs. I had them folded under me like I always did when I went into a shutdown. I groaned as I lowered my feet to the floor, waiting for the painful pins and needles to announce the return of normal blood circulation.

"What happened, Jenny?" Colin rested his hand on my shoulder and kissed my forehead. "Did you find something?"

"Yes." I glanced at the monitors and immediately looked away. "I found dead people."

Manny straightened. "What the hell, Doc? Who's dead?"

"The competition." When I'd found the second such case, I had no longer considered it a coincidence.

"Love, you'll have to explain a bit more."

"Before you explain, Doc, tell me if this is going to help us find Gasquet. Or have you gone off on one of your side-investigations again?"

I deliberated my response. When Manny lowered his brow and glared at me, I still didn't know how to respond. "It's not related to finding Gasquet. But I do think he is involved in this."

"You think or you know?"

My shoulders dropped a fraction. "I don't have definitive proof."

"Hmph. Well, your thinking usually leads to something. I just hope it will lead us to this arsehole." Manny folded his arms. "Explain. In normal English."

It was hard work explaining my findings to my neurotypical friends. Every time, I had to organise my thoughts and share my conclusions with them with the right amount of detail. Too little and they said they didn't have context. Too much and Manny started complaining about not wanting a full lecture on financial data protection or whichever topic had to be explained. I tried, but didn't always find the right balance.

"I was looking into Gasquet's clients, the companies who hired his services. I only focussed on the companies who had been investigated and found guilty of financial crimes. A few showed curious growth patterns, but two made me look closer." I pointed at one of the ten monitors against the wall.

"This is the income over a three-year period of Laignes Société Anonyme."

"What happened in the first August?" Francine was standing next to Vinnie in the doorway. "That's some serious growth in one month. And that seems to set the pace for the next two years."

"That is a good question." I'd asked myself that. "Since Laignes SA is a personnel recruitment company, I compared their growth with similar companies to see if the summer season had any influence on their finances. I looked at a few other recruitment companies and none of them showed growth during August. Most of them stagnated or had a lower income in that month."

"Holiday month," Colin said. "People aren't looking for jobs."

"Is this a national company?" Francine asked.

"Yes. Not one of the largest nationally, but one of the strongest in Strasbourg."

"So what caused that growth, Doc?"

"Laignes SA's direct competitor in Strasbourg was DLC. It was a small company with a micromanaging owner who was also the CEO. Neither Laignes SA nor DLC would be a noteworthy company on a national scale, but locally they dominated the market and were both doing well." I pointed to a newspaper article on another monitor. "Until the owner of DLC died and Laignes SA bought them out—all within two months.

"When Monsieur Camille, the owner of DLC, died, nobody knew what to do without him. His company had an impressive annual turnover, yet he never had a CFO or even an accountant. No one had authority to pay bills, salaries or anything else. He also didn't have a last will and testament, so his entire estate was frozen while the government appointed an executor."

"How did he die?" Colin narrowed his eyes and read the article. "Wait, it says here that he suffered a head injury while rock climbing. It was declared an accidental death."

"Which could be convenient for Laignes SA, tragic for DLC's employees and not suspicious at all." Francine rubbed her hands. "But what if it's some huge conspiracy? What if—"

"I found another company with a similar growth pattern." I didn't want to listen to another one of Francine's flights of fantasy. It could last for hours. I pointed at another monitor. "This is their income over a two-year period."

"It has the same spike." Francine took a step into my room. "In January they tripled their income and it has continued to grow from there."

"Oh, hell." Manny pushed his hands into his pockets. "Did this company also buy their competitor after the owner died?"

This company's climb to success was more complicated, but I didn't know if Manny would be interested in the details. It was unbearably hard, but I answered with a simple, "Yes."

"Have you looked through all Gasquet's clients, Doc?"

"No. I've only looked at six companies."

"Two of which profited from their main competitor dying." Manny grunted. "Doc, are you saying that these guys are killing their competition?"

"No. I'm saying that their companies benefitted when they gained market share." I looked at Francine. "Did you find something else?"

"Did I ever." She turned towards the team room. "You'd all better come with me."

The blood flow to my legs had been restored, so I had no problem getting up and following everyone into the team room. We sat at the round table and Francine connected her tablet to the large screen against the wall. A website filled the screen. She gestured dramatically at the screen. "This is Saint-Florentin SA. I found this little gem while looking for more second payments. And just by the way, I found another three. All those second transfers were made into different accounts. Those accounts had immediately transferred the money to other accounts. Those accounts—"

"Supermodel!"

"Those accounts"—Francine spoke slower, looking at Manny—"did one more transfer before all the money was paid into the account for Saint-Florentin SA. It's a shell company, its seat in the Bahamas, but I'm convinced it is Gasquet's."

"The Bahamas," Vinnie said. "Tax haven for the rich and criminal."

"And a country that doesn't ask questions about the money they're holding." Manny rubbed his stubbled jaw. "More countries need to stop hiding all this black money."

"Pah! More countries need to respect their citizens' privacy." Francine lifted one hand, her palm towards Manny. "The most important thing right now is that the Saint-Florentin account has been drained."

"When?" Manny asked.

"Three weeks ago. Two hundred and thirty-three thousand euro was wired to a bank in Spain. I hacked the bank and saw that a Mister Bessette had personally collected the cash." She pointed her index finger with a manicured blue nail at Manny.

"Don't you dare look at me like that, you judgemental cop. I didn't steal anything. I just looked."

Francine and Manny started arguing about the methods used in our investigation, but I wasn't paying attention. A few things didn't make sense. "Why didn't he use the dark net? Why didn't he exchange the cash for bitcoins? It's untraceable."

The room went quiet. Our first encounter with Gasquet had been during a discovery of an auction site on the dark net selling human organs for transplantation. All transactions had been done with bitcoins. Combined with the use of the anonymous browser Tor, they had been protected for months, their heinous acts undiscovered.

"I have no answer for that." Francine shook her head. "Nope. Nothing."

"Not even a wild theory, supermodel?"

She gave a half-shrug. "There is the possibility that he needs cash."

"Some things can only be bought with cash," Colin said.

"Guns, explosives, drugs." Francine lifted her tablet. "He could buy those on Tor."

Manny thought about this for a few seconds. "I want you all to be careful. Watch your backs. Watch each other's backs."

"Francine, what can you tell me about ZDP?" I asked.

The expressions on everyone's faces communicated their confusion in the change of topic. Francine tilted her head back for a moment, then started tapping and swiping her tablet screen.

"Why are you asking, Doc?"

"I'm not comfortable ignoring that they sent a forged book to Phillip." The more I analysed it, the more concerned I became.

Francine leaned back. "As you know, ZDP was one of Gasquet's clients."

"Bloody hell. Why didn't you say anything? Why didn't Phillip say anything?" Manny looked towards the hallway. "Where is he? We need to get him in here."

"He's in a meeting with another client." I shrugged. "He won't be able to answer any of your questions."

"Then you'd better start talking, missy."

"ZDP didn't hide their association with Gasquet. The moment it became news that Gasquet was being investigated and was a fugitive, they went to the Financial Crimes Unit and submitted all their financial records. They'd been very insistent that they wanted no connection with Gasquet and would co-operate fully."

"They were cleared?" Manny asked.

"I looked at their books and didn't find any suspicious activities. The Financial Crimes Unit had a forensic auditor look at it and he also found nothing." But I could have missed something. My throat tightened.

"They are a brokerage firm, in business for the last ninety years." Francine read from her tablet. "The current CEO is Romain Proulx. He took over when his father died fifteen years ago. Their website says they pride themselves on their integrity and honesty in business. Like anyone would ever believe investment brokers are honest. Hah. Wait, let me look. Hmm. Their file here shows Rousseau & Rousseau insuring ten works of art to the value of nineteen million euro. Just like Phillip said."

"For the love of Pete." Manny's *buccinator* muscles pulled his lips into a sneer. "Why on God's green earth would anyone have such expensive art in an office?"

"Where else are they supposed to have it, Millard?" Colin huffed. "Hanging behind the toilet door? Locked in a safe?"

Manny ignored Colin and looked at me. "If they have this kind of art hanging in their offices, what is their yearly turnover?"

"Seventy-nine million euro," Francine said before I could answer, her eyes not leaving the tablet screen. "Since sonny-boy took over fifteen years ago, the company has grown quite a lot. But in the last five years, it's really grown. It is now considered one of the most reliable investment companies for the who's who."

"Any controversies? Court cases?" I didn't know what I was looking for, but the forged antique book alarmed me. I could blame it on my intense dislike of surprises, but this went deeper than that. My subconscious had registered something worth being concerned about, but this information had not yet travelled to my cerebral cortex, my thinking brain.

Francine was quiet for another minute, tapping and swiping on her tablet. Then a genuine smile lifted her cheeks. "A scandal. A delicious scandal. Ooh, this is making me such a happy girl."

"Stop swooning and tell us." Manny leaned closer to look at Francine's tablet.

She tilted it away from him. "I will forever remember that you used the word 'swoon'. Sometimes I think you time-travelled from another century."

"Supermodel." Manny's voice was low in warning.

"Okay, okay." She winked at him. "When Daddy Proulx died, the circumstances of his death didn't make the major newspapers. I can only imagine that the family bought this media silence. Why, you might ask? Well, Daddy Proulx died in the dungeon of a crossdressing dominatrix."

"Many men in powerful positions enjoy sexual games placing them in submissive positions," I said. "They find it arousing to give control over to someone who has their pleasure in mind."

"Doc, please." Manny rubbed his hand over his face.

Francine leaned over and whispered in Manny's ear, "I have a whip at home."

"Get away from me, Delilah." Manny's lips thinned even as a blush warmed his skin. "Stop talking nonsense and tell us more about ZDP."

Francine took a moment to enjoy Manny's discomfort. "ZDP is a family business. The company was named after the grandpa, Zacharie David Proulx, who gave his son those exact names. When the son, Zacharie David Proulx II, died, the business suffered for a full year. I can't say it was because of his naughtiness. It was most likely the investors' reluctance to trust the grandson with their money."

"How old was he when he took over?" I asked.

Francine's eyes narrowed as she scanned the tablet screen. "Thirty-eight."

"That's young to be in control of such a large corporation."

"Well, he proved himself." Francine brought up an article on the large screen. "The *Economic Review Magazine* interviewed him three years ago. There sonny-boy said a year after Daddy died, he updated their system, gave retirement packages to quite a few of the older-generation employees and made ZDP a pioneer in advanced technology in their field. But it took him almost a decade to bring back ZDP to the glory years of his grandfather's rule."

"Any other family members? What about the mother?" Vinnie asked.

"Hmm." Francine swiped the tablet screen. "Nothing. Nothing. Ooh, wait! The mother died, but... ah... there was a sister. Let me just check. There *is* a sister." She looked up. "Ooh, this is like one of the Brazilian soap operas my mother never wanted me to watch."

"Who's the sister?" I frequently became impatient with Francine's theatrics.

"Simone Proulx, but..." Francine's smile widened. "She goes by Simone Simon. A fabulous soap-opera name."

"That name is familiar." Colin stilled next to me. "Isn't she... oh, she is. Simone Simon is one of the most respected art restorers of this decade. Oh, Jenny, you must see her work. She's a genius in restoring mediaeval stained-glass windows to their original glory."

Manny lifted both hands. "You can gush later, Frey. Supermodel, tell us how she fits in with the Proulx men and their business."

"I don't know. Not yet. Give me some time and I'll give you her favourite shoe brand."

"I'm sure you will. Just don't break too many laws doing this." Manny turned to Colin. "Okay, tell us what you know."

"I only know her professional achievements. She was part of the restoration team of the cathedral here in Strasbourg six years ago." Colin put his hand on my forearm. "We have to go to the church again so I can show you exactly what she's done. She's one of the best restorers in Europe."

"Do that on your own time, Frey. Her ability to fix old windows is not going to help us find Gasquet. We need to keep our focus on that."

"We'll go tomorrow morning." Colin ignored Manny, his attention completely on me.

"No. Manny is right. We need to find Gasquet."

"Jenny, you only move between our apartment and this office. You need to get out more."

"No."

"You also need to break your routine once in a while to keep your mind challenged."

"No."

"We can have breakfast at our favourite café." His facial expression conveyed charm. "Tomorrow is Saturday and we haven't been in a while. You know how much you enjoy that café."

I hesitated. He was right about the café. He was also right that we hadn't gone for our Saturday breakfast in the last five weeks.

"Oh, for the love of all that is holy." Manny slapped his hands on his thighs. "Just go with him, Doc. I can't stand his nagging. Let him show you the church and then you can come search for Gasquet."

"So this is going to be another working weekend." Francine sighed dramatically. "There goes my plan for a wild weekend."

I frowned. "You told me you were going to clean your apartment and read the two books I gave you for your birthday."

"And those were my wild plans." A smile crinkled the corners of her eyes.

"It's settled then." Colin leaned back in his chair and squeezed my shoulder. "We'll go to the church before we come in tomorrow."

I straightened my back and tried to shrug his hand off. "I did not agree."

"You will. I know you want to have breakfast with me."

Vinnie chuckled. "This can go on for hours and I'm hungry. Are we done here for today? Can we go home? I want to make dinner."

Manny looked at his watch. "Go ahead. I have to make a few more phone calls, then I'm going home for an early evening."

"Shouldn't we stay?" I didn't feel comfortable leaving the office when we'd made the first significant progress in months.

"No, Doc. This is not the first time we've thought we had a lead on Gasquet's location." Manny rubbed the back of his neck, his jaw clenched. "It's bad enough that we're going to follow up on all this new info during the weekend. I'm not going to let us pull an all-nighter on flimsy links."

"Thanks, old man." Vinnie got up. "For that I'll even save you a plate of the biryani I plan to make tonight."

"One of Nikki's favourites." Francine turned off her tablet and went to her desk. "How is that girl? I haven't spoken to her in a few days."

Nikki was a second-year art student who had been living with us for the last sixteen months since her criminal father had died during a case we'd been working on. Her guilelessness had won everyone's affection in a very short time. At first, I had been deeply uncomfortable with her affection and youthful melodrama. Recently, I'd found myself missing her laughter and chatter whenever she went away for a few days with friends. She had moved past my intense dislike of intimacy and become an important part of my life.

"I think she's coming down with something," Vinnie said. "This morning she was complaining about a headache and chills."

All my attention was on Vinnie. "Does she have a fever? Did you check? Is she drinking enough fluids? We should take her to the doctor."

Colin laughed and took my hand. "Why don't we go home and check on her?"

Thirty-five minutes later, we walked into my apartment. Vinnie pushed past me and walked towards his and Nikki's side of the apartment. My apartment used to consist of three bedrooms and a large open space that included the kitchen, dining room, living room and reading area. Colin had bought the apartment next to mine and we'd combined the two. Now my part of the combined space had a large sitting area and dining area. The other part had the entertainment area where Colin and Vinnie frequently watched sport and intellectually numbing shows. Vinnie and Nikki's rooms were on that side, giving all of us enough space and privacy. A quick scan through my side of the apartment showed that no one else was there but us.

"Punk?" Vinnie yelled towards Nikki's bedroom. "We're home and I'm making biryani."

I put my handbag in its usual place on the second dining room chair and turned around when I heard soft footsteps. Nikki walked into the living area, dressed in yoga pants and an oversized sweater. Her hair wasn't in the usual untidy ponytail, but was hanging limp around her face. But it was the greyness to her skin and her listlessness that concerned me most. She was not well. I crossed my arms. "You know my rules about being sick."

"Hi, Doc G." She lifted her arm in front of her face and breathed into the crook of her elbow. "I'm not sick. Thanks for asking. I'm just feeling a little under the weather. Thanks for asking. I didn't have a good day at uni. Thanks for asking."

I pulled my arms against my body and frowned. "I didn't ask any of that. Why are you being sarcastic?"

She lowered her arm, walked to the sitting area and fell into one of the sofas. "Because I'm feeling like crap and you only care about my vicious little germs magically jumping on you and infecting you."

"Punk." Vinnie walked to the sofa and sat down next to her. "That wasn't nice."

Nikki and I had had disagreements in the past, but I'd never seen her behave like this. I closed my eyes and mentally called up an empty music sheet. After writing two bars of Mozart's Flute Concerto No. 2 in D Major, I walked to the sitting area and sat in the far corner of the second sofa. Seeing Nikki roll her eyes, I got up and moved closer. My fingers curled in to form a tight fist, but I breathed through my obsession with avoiding close proximity to any illnesses.

"You contradicted yourself." I ignored her glare. "You said you feel a little under the weather and that you feel like crap. You were lying about the first."

Nikki picked at her thumbnail, not even looking up when Vinnie bumped her with his shoulder, his brows pulled in and down in concern. "What's up, punk?"

Nikki pulled her sleeves down to cover her hands and tucked them under her arms. "Nothing. I just feel sick."

Colin sat down next to me, but didn't say anything. A quick glance revealed concern on his face as well. My work was to observe people. Sharing my home with these three people and spending most of my waking hours with Manny, Phillip and Francine had given me clear understanding of the dynamics of our group. Whenever Nikki felt vulnerable, the others' concern and sympathy was helpful, but she had an inexplicable need for my personal attention. It challenged me in ways I had always done my best to avoid.

"Nikki, look at me." I waited until she reluctantly looked up. Her body was turned away from me, her arms crossed and her brow lowered. I waited a few more moments until she stopped glaring at me and paid attention to the expression on my face. I made sure it communicated my emotions. "I'm sorry for not asking how you felt or how your day was."

She slumped deeper into the sofa. "It's okay, Doc G. I'm sorry I was being sarcastic."

"You really feel sick, don't you?"

"Yes." Her voice was thick with tears. "I don't want to have a cold."

"That's normal." I strongly disliked being sick. The twice I'd had rhinopharyngitis—the common cold—I had banned Colin from our room and had changed the bedding daily. He had slept on the sofa. When he'd had the flu, Nikki had moved in with Francine for a week and Colin had taken her room. I could not bear sharing a bed with a viral infectious disease and was not going to let him spread that in the communal area. It had caused tension between us, but I had been adamant. This was the first time Nikki had been sick. I didn't know how to handle this. "You should go to the doctor."

"It's just a cold. He'll tell me to take aspirin and phone him in the morning."

"Why would he tell you to…" I sighed. The slight lifting of the corners of Nikki's mouth indicated I'd missed a joke. "Is there something I can do?"

"I could do with a hug, but I know you will then go and have a scorching hot shower, so no. There's nothing you can do."

"Punk." Even though Vinnie's tone was reprimanding, he leaned closer and pulled Nikki into a tight embrace. "I'll hug you for all of us, including Jen-girl. 'Kay?"

Her answer was muffled in Vinnie's shirt. He whispered something in her ear that made her chuckle. When she looked up, her smile was genuine, but the longing in her expression when she looked at me was still there. I took a shallow breath and analysed my reluctance to physically comfort her.

Nikki sighed in resignation and got up. "I'm going to shower. I'll be out before dinner. If I'm allowed at the table."

I recognised the sarcasm for what it was. The hurt on her face affected me and I got up. "I'm sorry."

She stared at me and sighed again. "No, Doc G. I'm sorry. I'm being really bitchy. I'll feel better after the shower."

"You'll have dinner with us?" I would have time to prepare myself while she had her shower.

She smiled and nodded. "I'd like that."

I watched her go to the other side of the apartment. I always felt ill-equipped while dealing with Nikki. It was hard with my other friends, but she held a much more emotional challenge. I couldn't imagine my life without any of them in it, but in honesty, I acknowledged that my existence had been simpler when I'd been alone. And lonelier.

The rest of the evening was quiet. Nikki didn't eat much of Vinnie's delicious biryani, and went to bed soon after dinner. I indulged in a long, hot shower, not only in surrender to the compulsion to clean off any possible contamination, but to give myself time to ponder on caring for my friends. I was at a loss. As I dried myself I decided to invest in a few more books on friendship. As soon as we caught Gasquet.

Chapter THREE

"Some say that the word Gothic started as a derogatory term used for the artists who destroyed ancient buildings after conquering Rome, using trending architectural designs to construct new buildings." Colin took a sip of his coffee. We were in the café across from the Strasbourg Cathedral, having breakfast. For the last thirteen minutes, Colin had been giving Vinnie a detailed lecture on the intricacies of mediaeval art. All because Vinnie had asked what the difference was between Renaissance and Gothic art. Colin pointed at the cathedral. "Gothic architecture is characterised by the use of pointed arches, like you'll see in there. I'll also show you the rib vaults, rose windows, spires and flying buttresses, typical of that era."

"Dude, I don't understand half of what you're talking about." Vinnie broke a piece off his third muffin. The waitress' eyes had widened when Vinnie had ordered a full breakfast and three muffins. Soon there would only be crumbs on his plate. I'd had a croissant and two cups of coffee. Vinnie swallowed and smiled. "At least I can tell Francine I've seen flying waitresses' butts."

It was a beautiful winter's morning. At half past eight on a Saturday, very few people were outside their warm homes. It had snowed lightly last night, covering everything in a layer of white dust. I looked out the café window to enjoy the view of the Strasbourg Cathedral, also known as *Cathédrale Notre-Dame de Strasbourg*. Colin huffed in annoyance and continued his impassioned explanation of the characteristics of Gothic architecture.

"Dude, stop." Vinnie held up one hand. "It sounds like all the French churches are the same?"

"No, not at all. Stylistically, they are much more unified than cathedrals in England, for example. France is where Gothic architecture had its most distinctive roots. Some of the designs were quite complex and required great engineering and architectural knowledge."

"The mediaeval period was from around the fifth to the fifteenth century. The Gothic era is included in that time, from the mid-eleven hundreds to the fifteen-hundreds." I enjoyed history. It fascinated me to see how patterns emerged. And were repeated. "In that time the world went through numerous changes. The Crusades took place, Joan of Arc made history, the Black Death killed thirty-five million people in Europe alone and Leonardo da Vinci took part in a few of the earliest autopsies and created many detailed anatomical drawings."

"Seriously?" Vinnie asked past the muffin in his mouth. "Earliest autopsies, huh?"

Colin shook his head. "He's looking for disgusting detail to tease Francine with. You know how squeamish she can be. He'll wait until she's eating one of her favourite dishes and then he'll share these factoids with her."

"Oh." I thought about this and turned to Vinnie. "I'm not telling you anything."

"You should, Jen-girl." Vinnie moved his head in an exaggerated nod. "You really should."

Colin put his empty coffee cup down. "Did you speak to Nikki this morning, Vin?"

"I did. The little punk is not looking too good." Vinnie's narrowed eyes and frown showed his concern. "I made her promise to go to the doctor on Monday if she's not feeling better by then."

"Good." I'd seen Nikki briefly this morning and concurred with Vinnie's assessment. She had shown signs of a fever and had not looked well. I thought of all the infection trapped in her heated room and felt the sudden need to be outside in the crisp winter air. "Let's go."

"One more muffin and I'm done, Jen-girl." His mouth twitched when he noticed my expression. "Okay then. I can wait until we get to the office."

"I'll be outside." The heated interior of the café was pressing down on me. I grabbed my coat from the coat tree and left the café while still buttoning up. One of the things I loved about winter was that I got to wear gloves. Not only did they keep my hands warm, but I felt free to touch things I normally wouldn't. I had a wide selection of fleece gloves, allowing me to wear a fresh pair every day. I couldn't imagine people wearing the same pair of gloves for weeks on end without washing them. The horror of this thought sent a shiver down my spine.

"You should've waited inside where it's warm." Colin stopped in front of me and rubbed my arms. He wasn't wearing gloves. It wasn't cold enough, he'd said.

"I'm not cold. I was thinking about microorganisms."

Colin laughed. "Well, then. Let's go to the church and get your mind off… microorganisms. You could always call them germs like most people do, you know."

"I prefer the correct terminology. Did you know how many different microorganisms are on church pews?"

Vinnie joined us, pulling a knitted cap over his head. "Please, do tell."

I narrowed my eyes and pointed at his face. "Your micro-expressions are not kind, Vinnie. I'm not going to say anything else that you plan to use to torment Francine."

"Aw, come on, Jen-girl. It will be fun."

We walked to the front of the large Gothic structure. This was one of my favourite historical buildings in Strasbourg. At a hundred and twelve metres long and a hundred and forty-two metres tall, it was imposing.

"Did you know Goethe said that the more he contemplated the façade of the cathedral, the more he was convinced of his first impression that its loftiness is linked to its beauty?" Colin looked up at the intricate artwork above the door and the beautiful rose window above. A couple left the church, the man putting a camera in his backpack.

Colin's expression remained the same as it had been in the café—appreciative, awed. His love for art was evident. "This cathedral is the sixth tallest of its kind in the world and for two hundred years it was the tallest. Even today, it can be seen from the Vosges Mountains as well as the Black Forest on the other side of the Rheine. It's a landmark."

"A pink landmark." Vinnie snorted.

"It has this pink hue because it was built with Vosges sandstone. It makes it even more unique." Colin's nonverbal cues conveyed his irritation.

"Huh." Vinnie tilted his head. "It's a building. An old building, but a building."

"With thousands of years of history, Vin." Colin's lips pulled in a sneer. "If you can't appreciate the value of this, maybe you should go to the office."

Vinnie's eyebrows lifted. "For reals? Dude, you know I'm not into art like you are. No need to get snippy."

I didn't have patience for this. "Vinnie, think of this building as a museum. Everything outside and inside is of historic value."

Vinnie leaned back, staring up at the cathedral. "Hmm. That makes a lot more sense, Jen-girl. Kinda makes me less pissed off about all the money the Church spends on these places."

Colin stared at Vinnie for a moment before shaking his head. He took my hand and walked up the steps. We entered the huge interior, Vinnie's combat boots squeaking as we walked deeper into the church. A lot of people talked about feeling a reverent atmosphere whenever they entered a church. I didn't feel it. I had told Vinnie to view it as a museum because that was how I experienced these buildings. The history it contained within its structure—painted on the walls, depicted in the stained-glass windows—equalled that of well-preserved castles and palaces.

"The foundations of the current cathedral started as a Romanesque design and it was later finished in the Gothic style we see here." Colin looked up at the pointed arches and vaulted ceilings that soothed my mind with their symmetry. We were standing in the nave of the cathedral, the central part of this beautiful interior. Colin pointed his chin to the front. "That astronomical clock is one of the largest in the world."

"Is it accurate?" Vinnie whispered his question, following Colin's example.

"Yup. It even includes leap years." He walked to the left of the nave, his attention on the stained-glass windows. Along both sides of the church and in the front, tall windows allowed the winter light in. We stopped in front of a set of windows, each one colourful and unique. "I found details about the renovations last night. Simone Simon worked on all these windows. Some needed much more work than others. In places, she only cleaned the glass—"

"In other places, she repaired the glass or replaced it," a male voice said behind us. As one we turned around. A priest was standing next to one of the pillars, a small but genuine smile lifting the corners of his mouth. "You know quite a lot about this."

"Gothic architecture is one of my favourite eras in design." Colin returned the priest's smile, his gaze evaluating. "You also know a lot about this era."

The priest's smile widened. I had never been religious or attended any churches. My contact with clergymen had been sparse, but the man in front of me did not remind me of any of the priests I had met before. His English sounded native to the United States with a soft Midwestern accent and I wondered how much his American upbringing might have influenced his attitude. I estimated his age to be in the mid-forties. He had a slight receding hairline, but not a lot of grey hair. His body language was open and relaxed. Other priests I'd met had been distant, their nonverbal communication clearly conveying the message that they were separate from everyone else. Not this man. His interest was real.

He leaned a bit closer and lowered his voice. "In secret, I'm an amateur art historian."

"You studied art?" Colin asked before I could question the need for secrecy. I knew some priests had degrees not related to religion, yet they were very open about it.

"No." He laughed. "I'm a total amateur. When we were studying Church history, I got interested in the art side of it.

A wee bit less violent, if you know what I'm saying."

"The Church has a long history of violence," I said. "Despite advocating peace, the Catholic Church has been part of or started a great many wars. Only in the last century has the Church played a less territorial role."

Vinnie snorted, but covered it by pretending to cough. I frowned. Had I said something inappropriate?

"So you know about Church history. An art history buff, a Church history buff and you?" The priest looked at Vinnie.

"I'm the muscle."

The priest's laughter echoed through the church. "So you're just buff?"

Some of the tension left Vinnie's body. A small smile pulled at his lips as he nodded.

"I'm Father Nate. It's a pleasure to meet you."

"I'm Edward Taylor, this is Doctor Genevieve Lenard and the buff guy is Vinnie." Colin showed no sign of deception as he used one of his aliases—the name of a seventeenth-century poet.

The priest looked at me. "Doctor Lenard. Why does that sound familiar?"

"I don't know." How could he expect me to answer that?

He stared up at the pointed arches for a few seconds. Then his eyebrows shot up and he snapped his fingers. "I know! I read one of your articles on nonverbal communication in traumatised children. It was incredibly helpful, if you know what I'm saying. It's truly a pleasure to meet you, Doctor Lenard."

I didn't hesitate to shake his offered hand. I was wearing my gloves, a barrier that created a feeling of safety no matter what or who I touched. Tonight, these gloves would go into the laundry basket. Father Nate shook Colin's hand and turned to Vinnie. "Are you going to crush all the bones in my hand?"

"I could."

"I know." He made a fist and held it towards Vinnie. "Fist bump?"

Vinnie tried for two seconds, but then couldn't hold his laughter. Not only did he bump fists with the priest, but he also shook his hand. Father Nate's ability to win over Vinnie's respect was admirable, even more so with his lack of artifice.

"I take it you aren't here for spiritual reasons. Did you just come in here to look at the art?"

"Yes, but it is a bit more than that." Colin turned back to the stained-glass windows. "We came to look at Simone Simon's work. We know that she was part of the team who renovated the church six years ago."

"Hmm. Yes. That was before my time. Father Clément Vaugrenard was here before me. He took loads of before and after photos. It's in an album in my office if you would like to see."

Colin's eyes widened and I knew our visit was going to be extended. We followed Father Nate through a side door out of the main building to his office. It was a large room, but made much smaller by the two bookshelves, the large mahogany desk and three wingback chairs. The desk was covered in piles of papers, making me think of Manny's desk in the team room. I breathed past the compulsion to start organising.

Instead, I walked to one of the bookshelves and perused the collection. The priest walked to the other bookshelf to retrieve the album. Most of the leather-bound books on the shelves in front of me were Church-related. One shelf was dedicated to travel guides, favouring South American countries. I wondered if they belonged to Father Nate or the priest who had been here before him.

"Ah, here it is." Father Nate put a large album on a pile of papers on his desk. I walked closer and stood next to Colin. Father Nate pointed at the first photo. "Here you can see how much work it needed, if you know what I'm saying."

I reminded myself that meaningless sayings were part of most people's vernacular. Just because I thought it inane that he ended most sentences with 'you know what I'm saying' didn't give me any right to confront him with it. I took a deep breath and focussed on the photos.

It was clear from the photos taken before the restoration how needed the maintenance had been. The work was well documented, the photographs revealing the notable improvement. It was the work on the stained glass that stood out. The before photos showed that the perimeter putty that held the stained-glass windows needed to be replaced, the frames needed to be painted and the perimeter re-caulked. I couldn't be sure, but it looked like the wood and stone had also needed replacing. The after photos showed all that to be done with most impressive workmanship.

"Father Clément was so proud to be part of the restoration. It was such a pity that he died so soon after it was completed. He barely had three weeks to enjoy the new old church, you know what I'm saying?"

"Such a pity." Colin leaned in to study photos of the window to the right of the nave. "Was he ill?"

"Not at all. He had a bit of flu, but then he went and died of a heart attack. God's ways are mysterious, you know what I'm saying?"

I didn't know what he was saying, but something he'd said had caught my attention. "He died of natural causes?"

"Oh, yes. It was his time." Father Nate stooped slightly and rubbed the heel of his palm against his chest.

"How old was he?" I failed at keeping the urgency from my tone. Colin straightened and looked at me, then at the priest.

"Fifty-two." Father Nate must have noticed the change in our interest as well. "Why?"

I shook my head. A connection was looming in my subconscious, fighting to reach my cerebral cortex. I closed my eyes, trying to relax into the connection. It didn't work. I felt Colin's arm around my shoulders and leaned into his warmth. Experience had taught me that I could trust him completely in vulnerable moments like these.

"We need to get back to work." Colin's tone was polite, no longer as warm and friendly as a few seconds ago. He was concerned about me. I opened my eyes and tried to smile when I saw him looking at me. He squeezed my shoulder and turned back to the priest. "Father Nate, thank you so much for your time and this very interesting discussion."

"It was my pleasure, Edward." Father Nate lifted a few papers until he found a business card and handed it over to Colin. "This is my mobile number and email. Feel free to contact me any time."

Colin put the card in his coat pocket and took my hand. "It might be sooner than you think. Thank you again."

The priest was clearly surprised by our sudden need to depart. Speculation formed around his eyes. But I was only concerned with this overpowering urge to lose myself in Mozart's Piano Concerto No. 24 in C minor. Listening to the chromatic opening theme of one of Mozart's greatest works would allow my brain to bring to the fore whatever pattern it had recognised.

Colin's arm was still around my shoulders and he guided us through the church to the chilly morning air outside. After another attempt to gain my attention, Colin gave up and talked with Vinnie about their impressions of Father Nate. I stopped listening completely when we reached Colin's SUV. As soon as I was settled in the passenger seat, I mentally started writing the concerto.

Chapter FOUR

"Okay, Doc. Give it to us." Manny settled in his usual chair at the round table and took his mug of tea from the tray Tim had placed in the centre of the table. "What did your brilliant mind find now?"

It was thirteen minutes after eleven and I had found more than I'd expected. "When Father Nate mentioned the death of Father Clément, it reminded me of something we talked about yesterday. Francine got excited about the possibility that there was a conspiracy involved in the death of Laignes SA's competitor."

"The one who died in the rock-climbing accident?" Manny asked.

"Yes."

"Ooh!" Francine sat up. "What did you find? Is there a conspiracy? Was I right? Wouldn't that just be the best ever?"

I ignored Francine's enthusiasm. "On the eighth of June, Laignes SA had made a payment of thirty thousand euro to Gasquet's business account. On the twelfth, the owner of DLC—Laignes' biggest competitor—dies. On the thirteenth, Laignes transferred sixty thousand euro to one of the accounts Francine followed all the way to Saint-Florentin in the Bahamas. Then as we saw yesterday, in August, Laignes' finances spiked. That is because they bought DLC two months after the owner of DLC died."

"Bloody hell, Doc." Manny's eyes were wide.

I took a deep breath. "I confirmed this pattern with the other company I found yesterday and have found another one with the same transfer history. One payment made to Gasquet, a few days later their biggest competitor dies. A day or two after that, an amount double the first is transferred via other accounts to the Saint-Florentin account."

"Holy hell." Manny slowly put his mug on the table, his *corrugator supercilii* muscle forming what is called 'the thinker's brow'. "This is real. These guys had their competition whacked. Sometimes I think the corporate world is worse than the criminal underground."

"Which are the other companies you found, girlfriend?"

"Ribemont and Marmoutier. I haven't had time to look through the finances of all of Gasquet's clients."

"Oh, my God. You and I share a brain." Francine grabbed her tablet and started swiping and tapping furiously. "I had exactly the same idea as you. I found seven more companies that had one payment to Gasquet and exactly double the first to the Saint-Florentin Bahamas account. Two of those companies are Ribemont and Marmoutier."

"So we now have eight companies that made second payments after paying Gasquet," Colin said. "Did they all have some unfortunate event happen to their competition?"

"I'll look into it."

"I'll help." Francine's excitement was evident in all her nonverbal cues. "I was right. This is so cool."

"Not for the dead people." Manny lowered his brow. "If Doc is right and these other people have also been killed, it will send a huge shock through the business world."

Francine leaned back in her chair, staring at her tablet. "Do you think Father Clément was also a victim?"

"There is no proof whatsoever to connect his death to these businessmen." I didn't want Francine to create another, more elaborate conspiracy theory.

"Hmm."

I knew that sound. I was also familiar with the expression on her face. She was going to look for a connection between the death of this priest and the deaths of the businessmen. Francine seldom wasted time when there was an urgency to a case, so I decided to not confront her about her intentions.

"What I want to know is who did all this killing." Vinnie had been quiet throughout our briefing. I often found his input invaluable. He asked questions that were frequently overlooked in my—our—attempt at finding answers.

"Until six months ago, I would say Dukwicz did it all," Manny said. Dukwicz had been a murderer who'd taken pleasure in hunting his victims before killing them. He'd been killed during a confrontation in our last case, the same case that had brought Gasquet to our attention and that I was still recovering from. Manny looked at me. "If you find any more deaths, check if any of them were in the last six months. If not, we have our answer. While you guys are burning up the computers, I'm going to prepare a briefing."

We decided it was best for Francine to join me in the viewing room. Together we were faster at finding information. She had the IT skills and I analysed and processed information to find patterns. Vinnie and Colin mentioned what they planned to do, but I wasn't listening. I was thinking of how many more companies we would find that had managed a market advantage by eliminating the competition.

It was only when Phillip insisted that we took a break for the lunch he'd had delivered to the office that Francine and I moved away from my wall of monitors. Hyperfocus was the reason I would sit for hours, sometimes days, to find a solution to a problem. Francine's obsession wasn't born of hyperfocus. It was pure curiosity. The last four hours I'd observed her reactions to a new discovery and there was no other explanation for her behaviour.

After a quick visit to the washroom, I joined everyone at the round table. Colin and Vinnie were there too.

"Where have you been?" I opened the sealed container of Chinese food.

"I told you, love. We met with Daniel."

I broke the chopsticks apart and knew my expression was contrite. "I wasn't listening."

"Yeah, I thought so." He narrowed his eyes. "You didn't even miss me, did you?"

"No." I frowned at his silly question. My frown deepened when he clutched his heart, pretending to experience pain in his chest. He was in a good mood. "Did you embarrass Daniel's team again? What did you do? Pick their pockets again?"

The few times Colin had trained with Daniel's GIPN team, he had enjoyed shaming them by picking their pockets, breaking into places they had told him were impenetrable and scaling walls faster than any of them. After each such practice, he'd come home in a light-hearted mood. Like now.

"You shoulda seen it, Jen-girl." Vinnie shook with laughter. "He stole all Pink's electronic gadgets without the dude noticing. It was epic. Pink had a fit when he couldn't find his tablet. It's like he needs the thing to breathe. And my man did this in the first five minutes while he was telling Daniel about this new info we have on Gasquet."

Colin's shoulders moved back, his chest puffing. It was subtle, but there.

"Once a thief." Manny pointed his fork at him. He enjoyed the food from the Chinese restaurant we favoured for takeaway meals, yet he refused to even try eating with chopsticks. "What did you and supermodel find, Doc?"

"Give Genevieve time to eat." Phillip moved his left shoulder to the front, creating a subtle barrier between Manny and myself.

"The food is still warm. I'll share what we've found."

"I'll make sure she doesn't get it wrong."

I turned to Francine in surprise, but swallowed my argument when I saw the muscle contractions around her eyes and mouth. She was teasing me. I resisted a sigh and upended the container of food onto my plate. "We checked the other companies and found three more situations where these companies paid Gasquet some money, a few days later their competitor died and soon after they transferred more money. Added to Laignes SA, Marmoutier and Ribemont, we have confirmed six double payments with deaths connected to them."

"One payment goes into Gasquet's business account, and a second into the Saint-Florentin Bahamas account." Francine shrugged, feigning innocence when I lifted both eyebrows. "What? I was just making sure you add all the details. Just like Manny always wants."

This was going to be a trying lunch. "It will take more time to carefully go through the client list we have."

"If these companies paid Gasquet to whack their competition, it was a smart plan." Vinnie shrugged when

Manny glared at him. "What? It was. They wrote it off as a consulting fee and I'm sure Gasquet even invoiced them for it."

"Your idea of smart business is not legal, criminal." Manny scooped food onto his fork. "Tell me more about these companies you found, Doc."

"Together with Laignes SA, Marmoutier and Ribemont, they fit a specific profile. All six companies were founded less than four years ago. They have an annual turnover of between five hundred and seven hundred and fifty thousand euro. Not big enough to bring them to the attention of any major investors, but also not small enough to be dismissed." I picked up my chopsticks and put them down again. "All of them struggled in the beginning, started to show a profit, but were faced with strong competition."

"This competition," Phillip said. "Was it only one company that had the majority market share?"

"In these six cases, it was only one company. The other competition did not have enough market share to pose a real threat to their growth. Another interesting discovery is that in all six cases, the main competitor was owned by, run by or completely dependent on one person."

"So Gasquet could take one guy out and the business would close?" Manny asked.

"Yes. It's impressive that he found six companies and their competition fitting such a specific profile. Even though the demise of their main competitor would result in more clients for everyone, none of the smaller competitors were strong enough to outgrow Gasquet's clients."

"He must have researched them very carefully," Colin said. "I can't imagine companies know that there is a service provider they can hire to kill, literally kill, the competition."

"I agree." Phillip nodded. "I think Gasquet looked for companies that would benefit from this… service and approached them."

"But how is it possible that everyone agreed?" Manny asked. "Surely not all business owners are without an ethical backbone."

"Gasquet's profile is such that I agree with Colin and Phillip." I lifted one hand to stop Manny. "I'm not speculating. I'm working on the profile I'd created. Gasquet is strategic. He's also very thorough in his research, as we found out in our previous case. He doesn't leave anything to chance. Hence I agree that he would've searched not only for companies that could use his service, but for company owners who would have no problem disregarding ethical and moral standards."

Manny and Phillip started discussing the ruthlessness of business practices and I took this opportunity to eat my lunch. I contemplated the similarities and differences between Gasquet's clients, their finances, communication, tax payments. Then something clicked.

I looked up. Everyone had finished their meals, me included. I couldn't remember clearing my plate. "Why was there no contact between ZDP and Gasquet?"

"Context, love."

"Oh. Yes. Of course." I pushed my plate away. "All of the companies that employed Gasquet had frequent contact with him. There were emails and phone calls between them, especially during the first few days and weeks of their co-operation. If the service lasted only a few weeks, the contact was almost every day. The longer the contracts, the less frequent the emails and phone calls were, but they were there. It didn't matter whether those companies had been found guilty of some sort of white-collar crime or not. They all had contact with Gasquet. Except for ZDP. They hardly had any contact with him."

"Supermodel?" Manny turned to Francine. "Bring up everything we have on ZDP."

Francine frowned, swiped her tablet a few more times and nodded. "Give me a moment."

I noticed the alarm around Francine's eyes. Usually she would have had ZDP's information on the large screen a few seconds after I'd mentioned them. Not this time. She had been working on something else, something that was causing her distress.

"Here we go. Oh, my God. You're right, girlfriend. Look at that." On the large screen, she highlighted seven phone calls between ZDP and Gasquet. "These are the only records we have of calls between them. That is not possible. ZDP was Gasquet's client for five years. ZDP paid Gasquet a lot of money for numerous security projects. There should be more emails."

"How many are there?" Manny asked.

Francine changed windows. "Twelve. Including the two… no, four about the contract they signed."

"How many email exchanges did Gasquet have with his other clients?" Manny asked.

"Look for companies that were his clients for more or less the same period of time," I added.

Francine were busy for almost a minute. "As far as I can see, the average was almost two hundred emails and the same for phone calls."

"Any of them have significantly fewer emails and calls than the others?" Tension caused my voice to tremble.

Francine's mouth tensed. "Nope. Even the clients who had one-month contracts had more contact with Gasquet than ZDP."

"That makes ZDP an outlier. Why?"

"I'm having a really bad feeling about this," Vinnie said.

"We did a complete background and financial check before we signed them on." Phillip had lost some colour in his face. "Did we miss something, Genevieve?"

I felt an irrational ownership of Rousseau & Rousseau. Phillip was the father I hadn't had as a child and I'd never known I'd needed. Whenever he had doubts about a potential client and asked me to do a background check, I made sure he and this company would not be jeopardised in any way.

"I don't know. Your other team investigated them." When Phillip had asked me to give his new investigative team the space to investigate ZDP as a potential client, I'd respected his wishes. Maybe I shouldn't have even though I'd already cleared them after looking into their dealings with Gasquet. I had found nothing alarming in their data. Had I been wrong? "All I can say is that they don't fit the profile of the companies Gasquet had received those second payments from."

"Companies that killed their competition," Vinnie said.

I turned to Phillip. "Have you spoken to ZDP about the book of hours they sent?"

"I phoned Romain Proulx, the CEO, yesterday, but he was out of the office. Since the gift came from him, I didn't want to speak to anyone else about it."

"Phone him now."

Phillip looked at me until I wondered if I'd been rude. Then he took his smartphone from his jacket pocket. Even on the weekend, he dressed in a bespoke suit. He swiped the screen a few times before putting the phone on the table. He'd put on the speakerphone, the ringing an abrasive sound in the team room. On the fourth ring, a loud male voice answered.

"Proulx."

"Mr. Proulx, it's Phillip Rousseau from Rousseau & Rousseau. I hope I'm not interrupting your Saturday."

I admired Phillip's natural ability to soothe people, his behaviour, tone and words always professional.

"Not at all, Phillip. And please call me Romain." His words were slurred. I didn't think it was a speech impediment. Combined with his loudness, I surmised he was drunk. "To what do I owe this call?"

"Firstly, to extend my gratitude. The gift was most unexpected and is greatly appreciated."

There was a moment of silence. "What gift, my friend?"

The muscle tension of everyone in the team room increased. Phillip merely raised one eyebrow, but his disquiet was evident in the *depressor anguli oris* muscles tightening around his mouth. "The lovely antique book of hours you sent on Friday."

"I didn't send any book. There must be a mistake." There was laughter in Romain Proulx's voice. "I wish I could take credit for sending you an antique book, but I don't even know what a book of hours is."

"Oh, dear. My assistant must have made a mistake reading the attached card. Romain, please accept my apology for disturbing you at the weekend."

"Ah, no problem at all. I'm just glad you didn't phone with bad news. That thing with our security company a few months ago really put me through the wringer. I was terrified that it would leak to the press and we would have to prove that we're not guilty of our consultant's crimes. Good thing you came so highly recommended. I know now our reputation is safe with Rousseau & Rousseau."

"Of that you can be sure, Romain. We take pride in our history of insuring our clients' interests to the highest standard. That is why we rely so heavily on word of mouth as our advertisement." Phillip was using the tone he reserved for charming information from unsuspecting clients. "How did you come to hear of us, if I may ask?"

"Well, uhm." Romain cleared his throat. "You will not believe it, but it was our security expert who mentioned you."

Phillip's eyes widened, then narrowed. "Laurence Gasquet? The same person who put your company at risk?"

"The one and only. That's why I said you won't believe it. A few days before that whole scandal broke, he phoned me and told me that I deserved the best. He recommended you." There was a short silence and a sound like ice clinking in a glass. "Well, then the shit hit the fan for him and everything went belly-up. But that ass got me thinking, so I looked you up. I asked around a bit and within a month I fired my old insurance company."

"We are honoured to have you and your business, Romain." Phillip closed his eyes, shaking his head. "I hope you have a lovely weekend."

"You too, my friend. You too." Romain had barely said the last word when Phillip tapped the screen to end the call.

When he looked at me, I cringed at the disquiet and regret in his micro-expressions. "I made a mistake, Genevieve."

"Based on the information you had, you made the right decision." But there was always so much more to a decision, to a person, than facts. "Regret is an unproductive emotion. We can't change our past choices, but we can make wiser decisions based on the new information we now have."

"Listen to you being all guru-like, Jen-girl." Vinnie's teasing tone brought a slight smile to Phillip's mouth. "Okay, so how is this asswipe involved in all this malarkey?"

"We don't know if Romain Proulx is involved." I chose to ignore Vinnie's figures of speech. "All we know is that he became a client because Gasquet mentioned us."

"Then why do we think we made a mistake?" Vinnie looked confused.

"He said that Gasquet phoned him a few days before Gasquet's business dealings were exposed." I nodded at the large screen. "The last phone call recorded between Gasquet and ZDP or Romain was four months before that."

Francine nodded. "Right on, girl. Four months."

"And that is why I am suspicious of Romain."

"And of that book." Colin looked at Manny. "Did you send it off to the labs?"

"Unlike you, I don't play cops and robbers with GIPN all day, Frey. Of course I sent it to them. Since there was no urgency to it, I didn't mark it as such. That means they'll only start working on it after the weekend. Bloody hell. Doc, should I get them to check it out now?"

I thought about this. "I can't see any reason to. We have the photos we've taken of the pages, so we can look at them if we need to."

"You don't think we need to?" Colin looked eager to study the pages of the book.

"No, I don't. I think it's more important for me to look into ZDP's business history." My expression softened. "However, you can study those photos and take note of anything out of the ordinary."

"You know just how to make my day, love." He leaned in and kissed my temple.

"Oh, for the love of Pete. Get a room." Manny got up and walked to his desk. "Or even better, go investigate. We can have double weekends when we put this thing to sleep."

"We need to find out if having ZDP as a client has in any way compromised us." Phillip also got up, his lips thin. "I'll get some guys in to help with that."

When I'd started at Rousseau & Rousseau eight years ago, my role had been as insurance investigator. When Colin, Vinnie and the rest of the team had entered my life and my work, Phillip had decreased my workload, but I had insisted on continuing. Despite his disapproval, I frequently spent my personal time investigating insurance claims and looking at the video footage of interviews with clients suspected of insurance fraud. Phillip had been the first person in my life to treat me with respect. That had won him my unquestioning loyalty and unsolicited help.

Three months ago, Phillip had used his stern tone with me. He had ordered me to help him find suitable candidates to do the work I'd been doing. It had taken a month and fifty interviews before Phillip had employed three experts. Two had been highly decorated detectives and the third was a respected body language expert. As a team, they worked well together. I knew this because I'd asked Phillip to give me full access to their computers to monitor their work. I was satisfied with their competence.

I hoped they would be able to find out if Rousseau & Rousseau's reputation was threatened by the association with

ZDP. I didn't trust them to find Gasquet though. I walked to my room, barely hearing Manny asking Francine what was troubling her. I was more concerned about what approach I was going to take looking for a further connection between ZDP and Gasquet.

I settled at my desk and Colin sat down next to me. His laptop was open and the photos of the book on the screen. Both of us were going to be very busy for the next few hours.

Chapter FIVE

The stress of finding illegal activity in ZDP's accounts caused such tension in my abdominal area that I felt nauseous. It had taken me two and a half hours to uncover a suspicious transaction. ZDP had been good at covering their online tracks. Had I not taken a more aggressive interest in this company, I would never have found any of this. I sat back in my chair, then leaned forward again.

"What have you got, Jenny?" Colin's soft question startled me. He chuckled at my reaction. "Sorry. You forgot I was here, didn't you?"

"You've been very quiet."

"Well, this is interesting stuff." He nodded towards his computer. "But first tell me what has you shifting in your seat."

"ZDP has been involved in insider trading or market manipulation. I'm not sure which."

"What the bloody hell?" Sounds of movement came from the team room. Two seconds later Manny appeared in the open door between the two rooms. "You'd better get in here and debrief us, Doc."

"I'm not finished with my research yet."

"Don't care." Manny lowered his chin and stared at me. "Unless you want all of us to come in there and crowd you."

I reeled back. "That is extortion."

"Maybe." He straightened and stretched his neck. "It's time for us to wrap this up for the day. It's six o'clock and it's Saturday."

"I'm not finished yet." Did he not understand that I could not leave after finding such key information?

"Still don't care, Doc. Now get your butt in here. You too, Frey."

Manny and I glared at each other for a few moments until his micro-expressions registered in my mind. He was not only tired, but concerned. Manny was one of the most hard-working and dedicated people I knew, but he always fought with us to slow down and rest. This realisation brought an awareness of my own tight muscles. A debrief to end our day was a prudent suggestion.

I nodded and got up. Colin followed me into the team room, his laptop balanced on the palm of his right hand. Vinnie was at the table, reading a gun magazine. Francine was at her desk, her eyes riveted on her computer monitor. The *depressor anguli oris* muscles pulled the corners of her mouth down. She was distressed.

"Come on, supermodel. You can continue playing Solitaire when you're at home."

Her head snapped up, her eyes narrowed. "You're just sour because you will never beat my score."

"Hmph." Manny sat down and looked from Vinnie's face to the magazine in his hands and back. "Did you find anything that will bring us closer to finding Gasquet or are you shopping for more illegal weapons?"

"Suffering from PMS, old man?" Vinnie put his magazine down.

Manny grunted and turned to me. "Tell us about this insider trading or market manipulation, Doc."

"I first looked for spikes in their finances." I noticed Francine's attention kept drifting to her tablet. Not in the way she did when she researched a topic we were discussing, but rather because something on her tablet was worrying her. "Since the father died, the company's growth had been gradual but slight until five years ago. Something changed to make ZDP show a sharp incline in revenue."

"How sharp?" Colin asked.

"Francine, can you bring up ZDP's finances?" Usually she would've had it up already. We waited a few seconds until the graph showed up on the large screen against the wall. "See it?"

"Oh, my God." Francine pointed at the screen, her attention now completely on the current topic. "That is quite a change."

"But not big enough to attract too much interest. We hadn't considered it suspicious. A lot of companies have an increase in income because of a marketing campaign, new products, new premises or something similar. Also, ZDP presented a very good reason for their growth. I read that magazine article that Francine had found about ZDP and Romain. There, he attributed the recent success of his company to the new staff he had hired."

"New staff? Got any names?" Manny asked.

"I looked at their employment records, but didn't see any key people employed in the last six years. They replaced a few personal assistants, but nobody who would have had an impact on their financial results."

"And now you're going to tell us what you found. Right, Doc?"

"Yes. I looked for new clients that were added five years ago. Most of those clients were legitimate. A few corporate clients didn't have any physical addresses or additional information on file. I checked those companies' financial profiles." I took a breath to continue, but stopped when Manny held up his hand.

"Doc, please just tell me what you found, not how you found it."

I took a few moments to consider my answer. "So far I have found three shell companies that were operational for only a short period. All three were registered as venture capitalists. All three invested in only one business venture by becoming shareholders. All three sold their shares a few months later at spectacular profits. All three companies still have their accounts open, but have not shown any activity since they sold their shares.

"These three shell companies invested in products and companies highly recommended by ZDP. At the time of investment, ZDP had encouraged some of their other clients to also invest in these products or companies."

"What kind of products and companies?" Manny asked.

I counted on my fingers. "A pharmaceutical company releasing a new drug, an app developer launching a new app and a software developer also launching a new product. I haven't had enough time to find out how, but the evidence leads me to the conclusion that Romain registered each shell company with the sole purpose to invest in an upcoming company or product about to be launched.

"I don't know how he had inside information on these events, but the judicious investments just before these three events netted him over nine million euro. His ZDP clients who invested in the three companies also benefitted, but he wisely never got everyone to invest and never with amounts that would draw attention."

"But it was enough to gain the trust of his clients, grow his business and get even more clients because of these successes." One corner of Colin's mouth lifted in a half-smile. "Clever bastard. This is a long con. Only the best of the best can pull something like this off without being caught."

"Eventually, everyone is caught, Frey." Manny's expression suggested there was more to his words.

"Or some arsehole agent gets lucky because someone calls him." Colin was referring to Manny arresting him many years ago after a long pursuit. A guard in the museum Colin had broken into had suffered a heart attack and Colin had called Manny. No sooner had Manny brought Colin in than Interpol had taken him and gotten him to work for them. For many years Manny had searched for Colin, not knowing that he was stealing back art and other valuable items for Interpol. It had taken more than a year of working together in this team for the animosity between them to subside. But they still bickered a lot.

Manny made a rude noise and turned to me. "Anything else, Doc?"

"Not yet. I need more time to find more shell companies and connect those to investments and other events on the market."

"I think we need to shelve that one for now. It's not getting us closer to finding Gasquet. Where the hell is that bastard? Frey, did you get anything from your pretty photos?"

"I got a lot of beautiful art. I've glanced at the pages, but only managed to work my way through two thirds of the photos. I haven't found anything strange yet. Of course, this is not an authentic Gothic book of hours, but it is an amazing replica. The person who did this has incredible skills."

"There's nothing suspicious in there?"

"Oh, there's plenty suspicious on those pages. I mean, who has the skill to so expertly copy Pucelle's work? But that code in the back is the real worrying factor. Why create such a beautiful forgery only to deface it with a code? And why send it to Phillip? Why target him?"

My throat tightened. Colin was right. Phillip was professional in all his dealings, well respected in the corporate, art and insurance industries. What was the motive for sending this book? And to what end?

"What are you doing about the code, Frey?" Manny asked.

"I haven't spent much time on it. As far as I can see, Jenny was right. It looks like a book cipher." Colin lifted his hands while shaking his head. "We'll need the key book to decipher the code."

"Doc?"

I frowned. "I haven't looked at the book yet. You told me to look at ZDP's finances. I've only had three hours."

"I didn't mean for you to have solved every single mystery we have. I want to know what you think about those last three pages."

"Then why didn't you say that?" It frustrated me when neurotypicals weren't clear in their communication. "My answer is the same. I haven't looked at those photos, so I don't have an informed opinion."

"Finding the key to such a code is always easier when we know who wrote that code," Colin said.

"He's right," Francine said. "The same is true for computer security. If you know a person well enough, it's easy to guess their passwords for their online accounts. People use their kids' names and birthdays, their pets' names, their own birthdays for everything including their online banking. So irresponsible. And so easy to hack."

Francine's tablet pinged and she picked it up from the table.

"Okay, I'm beginning to think I might need to put a rush on processing the book. Doc?"

"I concur." Earlier I hadn't considered the book to be urgent or important. Now I didn't know what to think. Was it a threat to Phillip? To us? Was it related to Gasquet?

"I'll get the lab to start with fingerprints," Manny said. "Who knows? Maybe we'll get lucky."

I wasn't listening to Manny any more. Francine pressing her fingers hard against her parted lips had my full attention. "Francine?"

She didn't look away from her tablet. She was slowly dragging her finger up the screen, reading something that was causing her great concern. Manny turned towards her, a frown pulling his brows together. "Supermodel, what have you got there?"

Still she didn't respond. Manny's lips tightened and he grabbed her tablet.

"Hey!" She reached for it, but Manny had turned his back on her, holding the tablet out of Francine's reach.

"What the hell is this?" His frown intensified as he squinted at the tablet. "Why are you reading articles about deceased priests?"

I'd known Francine would not have abandoned her suspicion about Father Clément's death. It had been in all her nonverbal cues. "What did you find?"

"A serial killer."

"Say what?" Vinnie straightened. "We haven't had one of those in like ever."

"How do you know this is a serial killer?" I asked. Francine was prone to being hyperbolic.

She pulled her shoulders back, studiously avoiding Manny's glare. "I found six murdered priests."

"This here says Father Allais died from natural causes." Manny waved Francine's tablet at her. "There's nothing here that says he was murdered."

"He was murdered." Francine's tone and body language communicated conviction. "He and the five others I found this afternoon."

"You were looking for dead priests while we're searching for Gasquet?" The supratrochlear artery on Manny's forehead became pronounced. "God rest their souls and all that, but what the bleeding hell do their deaths have to do with this case?"

"I don't know. Yet." Francine straightened even more. "There is something not right about all these deaths, Manny."

It was not often that Francine called Manny by his name. His expression softened and he handed her tablet back. "Explain."

"Apart from Father Clément, I found another five priests in France who died in the last four years." She put her hand on Manny's. "Please just hear me out before you hit me with your sarcasm."

Manny lifted an eyebrow as he looked at her hand resting on his. Then he looked at her. "Speak."

She pulled her hand back. "I did a very elementary search. I compared the list of deceased priests from the National

Death Index to any articles written about these men. It's crude, but it gave me five more names. For example, Father Gounelle died at the age of forty-two after a short illness. He had been in great health before he got sick out of the blue."

"What was the cause of death?" I asked.

"Heart failure."

"The same as the other priests?" If the murderer used the same method killing them, I would take this allegation more seriously.

"No." Her shoulders dropped. "Two others died from complications after they got flu and one died from an exotic disease."

"Where is your evidence then that this is a serial killer?" I asked.

"I don't know, all right?" She sighed heavily. "I have a gut feeling about this. I know you hate it when we talk about gut feelings, but this is real, Genevieve. I feel it."

I didn't respond. The micro-expressions on Francine's face told me that she needed my support. I couldn't give it to her. How could I support a theory that was built on circumstantial evidence?

"Lass." Manny waited until Francine focussed on him. He very seldom called her anything but 'supermodel'. "I know this is important to you because of your mum and your dad."

"Leave my parents out of this." Francine crossed her arms tightly against her chest. "This has nothing to do with them."

"*Au contraire*, my dear. I think it has everything to do with them." Manny's expression was gentle. Francine's father was a priest and her mother a nun. Both lived and worked in Brazil. They'd had her before they'd entered their individual callings and she had been raised with much love. "I know you have a soft spot for the Church, but you can't let it take your focus away from our present investigation."

"We will help you look into the priests' deaths as soon as we have Gasquet," Colin said. "Jenny will help you work through the data and Vin and I will do the legwork."

"Right on." Vinnie nodded slowly. "We've got your back."

"Oh, bloody hell. Fine. I'll also help with this flight of fancy." Manny shook his index finger at Francine. "But first we find Gasquet. Got it?"

The tears forming in Francine's eyes prevented me from voicing my reluctance to waste time on a baseless case. It clearly meant a lot to her. She swallowed with difficulty and blinked a few times. "Thanks, guys. For real. Thank you."

"Let's pack it in for the day. We can continue this tomorrow." Manny took time to look at everyone, but his gaze lingered on Francine. "Go home. Rest. I want you all fresh tomorrow so we can find Gasquet."

Chapter SIX

It was the third sneeze that pulled me away from the new shell company I was looking into. I glanced at Colin sitting next to me, but he was scrolling through the photos of the book of hours on his computer. Another sneeze caused my back muscles to tighten and I turned around to face the person who was spreading their microorganisms in my viewing room.

"Hi, Doc G." Nikki was sitting on the floor between two of the three antique-looking cabinets at the back wall.

"What are you doing here?" My tone was a bit harsh and Nikki flinched.

"Sketching." She looked at the sketchpad on her lap.

"You can sketch at home. In your bedroom."

"I was getting cabin fever." Her nonverbal cues fluctuated between defiance and insecurity. "I needed to get out of the apartment and my feet brought me here."

I frowned. "Your feet are not separate from your brain or the rest of your body. The whole of you came here."

She laughed and sneezed again. I was pleased to see that she was sneezing into the crook of her arm. At least she was minimizing the airborne spread of whatever she was suffering from.

"How long have you been here?"

"An hour?" She looked at Colin, who had also turned around and was watching us. It was eight minutes past twelve. We'd been in the office for the last three hours.

Colin nodded at Nikki. "Yup. You came in about an hour ago. And she's been real quiet, Jenny."

"I didn't want to disturb you, Doc."

"But?" I'd heard the unfinished sentence and also saw it in her expression.

She looked me straight in the eye. "I didn't want to be alone anymore."

One thing I had admired Nikki for from the first time I'd met her was her emotional openness. She was never scared to make herself vulnerable by admitting her needs. I knew that her desire not to be alone was only half of her need. She needed to be with me. I still marvelled at this strong, intelligent young woman's need for my presence.

More often than not, I erred by saying and doing things that would be extremely hurtful for most neurotypical nineteen-year-olds. Not for Nikki. She'd accepted my non-neurotypical behaviour and never hesitated telling me when she didn't understand me or when she considered my responses rude. In turn I appreciated her emotional openness and worked hard to respect it. I never wanted to cause her to become more closed. It was refreshing to find someone with so little guile. It was for these reasons and more that I forced a Mozart etude into my mind and nodded tightly.

"Just make sure you continue to sneeze into your sleeve."

"Yes, Mom." She drew out the two words while rolling her eyes dramatically. Then she winked at me. I could see that this exchange was taxing for her. Her blow-dried hair and makeup did not effectively hide how weak she was feeling.

"Why are you wearing makeup? Are you trying to hide the rings under your eyes?"

"No." She folded her arms, rolled her eyes again and unfolded her arms. "See? You're making me defensive. I just wanted to feel better. Having greasy hair and seeing my pasty face every time I went into the bathroom was making me feel even sicker."

There was nothing indicating deception, only annoyance. She was telling the truth. I nodded. "Okay."

"So what are you guys working on?" Her tone and expression gave her tactic away. She was trying to take the attention off her. She pointed at Colin's laptop. "That looks interesting."

Colin shifted it to give Nikki a better view of the photo on the screen. "These are photos of a book of hours."

"It looks kinda mediaeval-like." She tilted her head. "We just started looking into that period. So far I'm not finding it awesomely interesting."

"Then you haven't seen the right works yet." Colin zoomed in on the photo. "The books of hours are the most complete record of Gothic painting. Each book was made with great care. Many books of hours were made for women, sometimes even given as a wedding present from a husband to his bride. The most richly illuminated books were ordered by those who could afford it—royalty, the elite. That is why these books were so individualised. Some books would even incorporate small portraits of the owner into the illustrations."

"Huh." She nodded. "That is supercool. Those figures make me think of Gothic architecture—elongated and very detailed. You know, it actually reminds me of a noteb…"

"Why aren't you in bed, punk?" Vinnie walked into the viewing room and stopped in front of Nikki. Standing up, she looked petite next to him. Sitting as she was now, he towered over her. He stood with his legs apart, his hands resting on his hips. "This morning you looked like death warmed up. You should be in bed, sleeping. Did you eat the soup I left with you? Did you take your meds?"

"Stop!" She winced at her loud voice and rubbed her temples. "I already have a headache and you're making it worse. I swear, you are worse than a mother hen. Cluck, cluck, cluck."

Vinnie leaned forward, his frown severe. "I care about your scrawny little punk ass. You should be resting and getting better."

"I've already been through this with Doc G." Nikki waved towards me. "Care about me by not fighting with me anymore."

Vinnie glared at her for a moment before nodding. "I'm going to make you some tea. You need fluids."

"Actually"—she lowered her eyes and sighed—"could you please take me home? I think the walk here might have been a bit too much too soon. My hands are shaking too much to draw anything decent."

"Of course I will." Vinnie waited until she gathered her pencils and pulled her up. "You're a stubborn punk, you know that?"

"Pfft. Like everyone here. Would you stay in bed if I ordered you to?" She didn't wait for him to answer. "No, you wouldn't. None of you would. That's why I fit in here so well."

Her voice had lost all its strength and she was leaning against Vinnie. He put his arm around her, making her look even more vulnerable. My chest tightened with concern and affection— two emotions I'd come to associate with Nikki. She was in no way related to me, yet these emotions overwhelmed me at times to the point where I found it hard to focus on anything else. I could not imagine how parents felt about their own children facing the dangers of modern society.

"Let's get you home, punk."

Vinnie turned her towards the door, but she stopped him and looked at me. "Will you be home tonight? Will we still have our girls' night?"

For three weeks, Nikki had been asking me daily to have a girls' night with her. She explained it included doing each other's nails, braiding each other's hair and watching romantic comedies. I'd been horrified at the prospect of anyone touching my nails and had told her so. She'd laughed and told me that she just wanted to hang out with me and didn't care what we did together.

After consulting Colin, I'd proposed watching an art film and sharing a pizza. Vinnie was to make the pizza for us, which would allow me to enjoy it without obsessing about the cleanliness of fast-food restaurants. She'd agreed on watching an art film as long as she got to choose it. The last week, she'd mentioned the girls' night frequently. I thought of all the work that I still wanted to do, but it lost importance compared to the expectation on her face.

"I'll be home at six." I nodded at the genuine happiness relaxing her features. "We can eat early and you can get to bed if you're still feeling weak. I do think that you should consult a doctor tomorrow."

"I think so too." She rested her head against Vinnie's chest. "I'm feeling crappy, but I looked really hard for that movie and really want to watch it."

"Come on, punk." Vinnie kissed the top of her head. "I'll make you some more soup and beat you at *World of Warcraft*. There's not much for me to do here in any case."

I watched them leave my viewing room and sighed. "She's sicker than she's showing."

"I know." Colin took my hand. "We'll get her to the doctor tomorrow. She'll be fine. It's just a bad cold."

"I don't want children." As I said it, I realised how true it was. "Never."

Colin's eyes narrowed as he studied me. "Why not?"

"I'll never be able to work. All I'll do is obsess about their emotional and physical safety." I shook my head and couldn't stop. "No. I won't be able to do it. I'm not strong enough."

"Hey." Colin cupped my cheek, which helped me stop shaking my head. "You are one of the strongest people I know. Having kids is not proof of strength or weakness. Although I've heard it makes you stronger."

I started shaking my head again. "I can't. I just can't."

For a few seconds I focussed on the warmth of his hand against my cheek. It was enough to change my focus from my own fears and register Colin's micro-expressions. "Why are you disappointed? Did you think you were going to have children with me? I don't want children. I know one should never say never, but I can't see it changing in the near future. Then I'll be too old to bear children. You should find someone else who can give you children."

"Whoa there, love." Colin laughed softly and kissed me until I relaxed into his embrace. He pulled back and tapped me on my nose. "Are you sure you saw disappointment?"

I thought about the expression I'd seen. I frowned. "It was sadness. Why were you sad?"

"I was thinking that you would be a great mom. It made me sad to think that there will be no children to experience your love and care."

"I'd damage them emotionally."

"No, you wouldn't. You haven't hurt Nikki in the year she's been with us. As a matter of fact, you've made her stronger, happier, healthier."

I found it hard to accept that Nikki's growth had even partly been my doing. "I still don't want children."

"Neither do I, so we are a perfect match."

I stilled. This was a significant statement and I didn't want to take it at face value. I analysed Colin's face, recalling every muscle movement when he'd spoken. As usual, he leaned a bit back and waited for me to read his expression until I'd reached a conclusion.

"You're telling the truth."

"Yes."

"Why don't you want children?"

"My life isn't the one of a daddy." He shrugged. "And I've never had the need to immortalise myself through a continued bloodline. My life, our life, as it is right now is a perfect fit for me."

He was still telling the truth. Until a few minutes ago, I had not given any thought about Colin's need to procreate. On the one hand I worried about being so self-absorbed that I hadn't thought about his desires. But on the other hand, I experienced immense relief. I didn't want to lose him. My life had become rich and nuanced with him and the others in it. But Colin was the one who'd anchored me.

"Thank you." My words came out as a whisper.

"For what?"

"Being an uncommon neurotypical."

"Are you two at it again?" Manny walked into the room, his top lip curled. "I wish you'd keep this for... for when I'm not around."

"Deal with it, Millard." Colin kissed me lightly on my lips and leaned back. "What's up?"

"That's what I want to know. Have you got anything? Wait." Manny half-turned to the team room. "Supermodel, get in here."

Francine said something very rude, but joined us, her tablet in her hand. She sat on the third chair in my room, leaving Manny to stand. This was the maximum number of people I could have in my viewing room without feeling crowded.

"Okay, Frey. Talk."

"With all that charm, I'm surprised that you don't have women standing in line for you, Millard." Colin's expression and tone indicated sarcasm. He turned to his computer and zoomed out of the photos he'd shown Nikki. "This is the work of a very gifted artist."

"You said this before. Have you come across anything like this in your... work?" Manny spat out the last word.

Colin shook his head. "Not this calibre, not for this era. This person must be a closet savant."

"I have never heard of such a savant." How curious.

Colin looked confused. Then a smile lifted his cheeks. "An expression that I'll explain later. It just means this person is hiding his or her expertise."

"Why would someone hide a skill as proficient as this?"

"I have no idea. Maybe this person is finding forgery more profitable than creating his own works. Although I know of at least two Parisian art galleries that would snap up original works of this quality."

"Isn't there some way to identify this artist?" Manny waved towards Colin's computer. "You know, with that brush stroke uniqueness and bollocks."

"Firstly, it's not bollocks. And secondly"—Colin's smile was the one he used when he was baiting Manny—"you've been paying attention in class, haven't you. Little Manny gets a gold star."

Francine giggled and held up both thumbs to Colin.

"And little Frey won't get bailed out by me next time he gets arrested. I'll just leave your sorry arse to rot in jail."

"I have the details of seven shell companies investing only once, later selling those shares and the profits going straight to ZDP." I was much more comfortable discussing the investigation than trying to follow their banter. "I have the businesses and products they invested in. I have the exact amounts invested. And I have the information on the profits made each time the shell companies sold their shares. Most importantly, I think I have the connection between ZDP, the shell companies and Gasquet."

"Bleeding, holy hell, Doc." Manny's eyes were wide. "What's the connection?"

I winced. "It's circumstantial."

"Doc, call it what you want, just tell me."

"Five years ago, ZDP started showing impressive growth. It happened because of these timely investments into companies and products that ZDP should not have known would've made such a profit."

"Somebody tipped them off." Francine looked happy.

I nodded. "The shell companies are all registered here, but their profits have been paid into a numbered bank account in—"

"Ooh!" Francine clapped her hands. "The Bahamas? Please let it be the Bahamas."

"It is." I leaned away from her when she did a strange wiggle in her chair, waving her arms. "I've not been able to identify the owner of the bank account, but I posit that…"

"Don't stop now, Doc," Manny said when I hesitated.

"I posit that Gasquet met Romain Proulx five years ago and somehow helped him regain ZDP's position in the market. It makes sense that Romain would advise Gasquet to open a bank account in the Bahamas."

"And tell him how to route money from a local account to another account somewhere to another until the trail ends in the Bahamas. The more places the money has to go through, the more difficult it would be to trace." Francine leaned forward, excitement lifting her features. "And what do you want to bet Romain has been getting inside information about who and what to invest in from Gasquet?"

"How do you know this?" Manny asked.

"Um… I guessed." She lifted one eyebrow. "My guesses are usually right, you know."

"She might be correct." I suspected this, but would never have stated it as a fact. Not with the same confidence Francine had done. "I looked at Gasquet's client list and in every case, he had a client in the market that had experienced an event that had changed the market into their favour. Gasquet had clients in the pharmaceutical, software, financial, science and technology fields."

"Ooh!" Francine moved to the edge of her chair. "If he was working on their security, he would've had full access to their data. That would've given him the inside scoop on what's hot and what's not in that company's trading or research and development. I was right. How cool is that? Huh? So... Gasquet is feeding Romain info on possible changes in the market. Romain gets his shell company to invest in them, waits for the event and boom!"

"A lot of people make a lot of money," Colin added.

"And some people die." Manny's tone was sombre.

"I haven't found any deaths connected to these shell companies." I had been quite thorough in my search. "It would appear that only Gasquet's clients had the competition eliminated by assassination. The shell companies had simply created a competitive edge. Investing in a small software company three months before they launch a patent that was greatly anticipated is evidence of business acumen."

"A skill most conmen have," Colin said.

"Have you got anything else for us, Doc?"

"Not yet. I will look for more shell companies, but this is already enough evidence that Romain has been manipulating the market."

"Right." Manny thought about this for a few seconds. "I think we should leave Romain to his vodka this weekend. I'll bring him in tomorrow or Tuesday for questioning. Let's first see what else we can find on him. Such a high-profile businessman will come with seven lawyers and will stonewall us before we even ask him if he had a nice weekend."

Three pings from Francine's tablet drew me out of my thoughts. She looked at the screen, reacted and immediately tried to hide the distress by replacing it with a false interest.

"You're usually better at deception," I said. "What is on your screen that perturbed you?"

"Bloody hell, supermodel. Are you still looking for dead priests? I thought you agreed we'll look into it after this case."

"She never agreed to that. Everyone committed themselves to helping her after the case. She didn't say she would stop looking."

"Thanks, girlfriend. Kinda makes me feel better that you were the only one who didn't promise to help."

I shrugged. "Why would I promise to waste my time? Unless there is sense in launching an investigation, I would rather spend my time more wisely."

"Well, I'm hoping you'll think this is time spent wisely." Francine looked at her tablet and sighed. "My search has just produced another three dead priests. I think only two of those qualify, but one of those I think is very interesting."

Manny sighed. "Pray, do tell. Why is it damned interesting?"

"He's local and he died eight months ago. But the cherry on the cake was that he was a priest at the church in the village close to the farm Gasquet owned."

"The farm he and his buddies had used to hunt humans?" Manny's lips thinned. Our last case had had a huge psychological impact on all of us.

Francine nodded.

"Well, hell." Manny rubbed his face. "I guess we're going to church, then."

"What? Now?" Francine stood up. "You'll go with me? We're not waiting until after the case?"

"We're all going. If we can learn anything about Gasquet from the church, it will be worth it."

"I'm not going." I crossed my arms. "There are all these shell companies to look into."

"They'll still be there tomorrow, Doc."

"The church will also still be there tomorrow." I didn't like eye contact, but understood neurotypicals' need for it. I stared at Manny, but he didn't look away or lower his gaze.

"Finding Gasquet trumps arresting Romain for white-collar crimes, Doc. Come on, get your handbag. I want to be home before six. There's a movie I want to watch."

Manny continued to insist until Colin eventually asked me to go. I was not happy. I told them so. Repeatedly.

Chapter SEVEN

The smell in Colin's SUV challenged my control. We were still another five minutes' drive from the church and I couldn't wait to stand in the fresh winter air. It was too cold while driving to open any window. I focussed on Mozart's Clarinet Quintet in A major to take my mind off the aroma of deep-fried potatoes.

It was taking us much longer than it should have to reach the church. First, we'd had to stop for fuel. But then Manny had said he was hungry and would love real English chips, none of the *frou frou* fries. Those had been his words. Colin had mentioned a place he knew that made great deep-fried chips and before I had the chance to complain about the waste of time, we had been on a detour.

Not even when I had told them the ice served with the soft drinks in such establishments contained more bacteria than the water in the toilet bowls from the same establishments did they reconsider their unhealthy lunch. I had to admit that the interior of the shop had been clean, but I'd only bought a bottle of water. I would eat when I got home. I hadn't lingered in the shop for the same reason I found it hard to breathe at the moment. The smell of heated oil.

When I had seen Manny's micro-expression of genuine pleasure when he ate the first chip, I had stopped reciting the health risks involved in eating fast food. Francine had moaned and said it was better than the chips she'd had in any of London's restaurants and pubs. I had taken over the driving, since Colin had also bought a large order of chips and was eating with as much enjoyment as the other two. I suppressed a shudder when I glanced over and saw his shiny fingers.

I turned right into a narrow street and focussed on reaching the church. Another two streets and the large Gothic structure was up ahead, to our left. I found parking a hundred metres from the church. As soon as the car was neatly parked, I jumped out and inhaled deeply. I reached into the SUV for my coat and scarf, breathing in the cold air.

Soon, everyone was dressed against the below-zero temperature and ready to walk to the church. Manny was holding a plastic bag with the remnants of their lunch, amiably discussing religion with Francine. How they could talk about a controversial topic with such tolerance but argue about inconsequential things was something I planned to analyse at a later stage.

"I grew up in Anglican England." Manny dropped the plastic bag into a rubbish bin on the pavement and pushed his hands into his coat pockets. "The military healed me of any notion of religion. I respect everyone's religions and wish them the freedom to practice it, but have no interest in it."

"Why not?" I had never thought about Manny's spiritual needs. Or anyone else's.

"As a teenager, I suppose it was rebellion more than anything else. Now? I simply don't have the time to think about such things, Doc."

"Maybe you should," Francine said. "We are not just physical beings. Everyone has a need to believe in something."

"I don't." I frowned. "I don't have that need, so you can't say that everyone does."

"I know you've said this before." Francine had once spent an entire lunch questioning me about my beliefs. "But I still don't get how you can't believe that there is something, someone bigger than us out there."

"Is that what you believe?" Manny asked. "Aren't you Catholic?"

"Well, kinda. Because of my parents, I still say I'm Catholic, even though I'm not practicing. I would rather say I'm a deist."

"A what-ist?" Manny scowled. "What on earth is that?"

"It's actually quite an appealing philosophy." I had researched most religions in order to understand people's need to connect to a mystical being they had no evidence of. "Deism is the belief in a deity. Most deists don't try to quantify this deity since they believe that it would attribute human qualities to it."

"Hmm." Manny nodded slowly. "Makes sense."

We reached the church and stopped outside the doors. It was a beautiful building. Similar to the Strasbourg Cathedral, the artwork around the doors was elaborate, drawing attention to the rose window above and between the two doors.

"See the pointed arches?" Colin pointed at the decorated arches framing the doors. "It's a perfect example of Gothic architecture. What is not as well known is that these pointed arches were part of seventh-century Islamic architecture. It is believed that the Crusades brought the Western world into contact with the Muslim world, which may have influenced the mediaeval adoption of this arch."

We stood in silence.

"It's stunning," Francine said softly after a while. "Majestic."

Colin nodded. "Such magnificence can make anyone believe in God. Or a god."

"What do you believe, Frey?"

"That karma is a bitch." Colin's answer was fast, but truthful.

I frowned. "Believing in karma is comforting for most people. It also helps them justify being kind and polite when they least desire to do so. And it gives victims peace of mind when they fall prey to something bad, whether it be a crime or an illness. In their next lives they would have better luck. Why would you need to believe something like this? You are far too rational for such fantasy."

Colin closed his eyes briefly. Blocking behaviour.

"Love, you need to be careful saying such things. Even though you mean no offence, it does come across extremely intolerant."

I gasped and leaned back. "I'm not intolerant."

"I know that. Millard and Francine know that, but someone who holds their beliefs dear might not know that."

As he was speaking, I considered his words and what I had said. He was right. "I apologise. But I still want to know why you believe in karma."

"I don't believe in it in the traditional sense, Jenny. Rather that in most cases people get what they deserve."

"That makes no sense at all. How does a three-year old child deserve cancer? Or to be molested? Or how does anyone deserve to be born into a war-torn country? Or…"

Colin held up his hands. "I said in most cases. But you are right. There are many unjust situations in the world that cannot be explained by any religion."

Manny pushed open the doors. "Come on, children. Let's find out what we can and go home."

We followed him into the church. It was considerably smaller than the cathedral, but the high vaulted ceilings created a sense of space. The interior was not heated and cold seeped from the floors through the soles of my boots.

Since it was Sunday, it was no surprise to find a few people sitting in the pews. Some were praying, some staring into space. In the second row from the front, three elderly ladies sat close to each other in silence.

I sighed. I could not let go the remnants of our conversation. I elbowed Colin lightly and lowered my voice. "Do you really believe in karma? It doesn't make sense. How do you justify it?"

Colin stopped in front of an intricately carved wooden pulpit and stared at it for a few seconds before looking at me. "I suppose I don't believe in it as much as hope for it. It would be nice to know that good people will be rewarded for their good deeds and bad people will reap the fruits of their behaviour."

I relaxed. "Oh. Okay."

Colin's comment about me appearing intolerant was most unsettling. As someone who had been discriminated against for most of my life, I didn't have patience for people not accepting the differences in others. Yet the idea that Colin might believe in something I could not rationally explain had caused stress and disappointment. It weighed heavily on me to know that I'd expected Colin to think like me and believe like me. Why was it that I often expected people to be more accepting and tolerant than I was willing to be?

"Hey." Colin touched my forearm and waited until I looked at him. "What's wrong?"

"If you want to believe in karma and reincarnation, I accept it."

Colin blinked a few times. "Okay. Um. Thank you."

I could see he wanted to say more, but his eyes narrowed as he focussed on something behind me. I turned around. An elderly priest was walking to the left of the nave. Colin squeezed my forearm and quickly walked towards the priest. Manny must have also seen the man. He reached the priest at the same time as Colin did. I joined them in time to still hear the quiet introductions. Colin was speaking with a heavy German accent, introducing himself as William Strode. Another seventeenth-century poet he sometimes used as an alias.

"We would like to ask you a few questions about Father Sidney Larousse, if you don't mind." Manny was at his professional best. His approach to the priest wasn't the same as his typical pretence of being absentminded and unfocussed. He was even standing straighter than usual. I wondered if it had anything to do with the building we were in and the person we were talking to. Cultural heritage such as religion was sometimes so tightly woven into our psyche that people didn't realise how it altered their daily actions.

"There isn't much to tell you." The micro-expressions on the priest's face weren't welcoming. He looked towards the elderly ladies sitting together and sighed. "It might be better if we take this to my office."

Without waiting for a response from us, he turned around. His cassock billowed as he made his way to the front of the church. Francine had joined us and together we followed the priest. He waited until we went through a door to the left and closed it behind us.

"It's the second door on the right," he said as he turned an oversized key to lock the door. An uneasy feeling caused me to look down the corridor, looking for an alternative exit. There were three other doors in the corridor, but only one was open. Further down, a beautiful stained-glass window allowed coloured light to brighten the hallway. In an emergency, I was convinced Manny would break the window to lead us to freedom. I wasn't so sure if Colin would allow him to destroy that beautiful work of art. But I was sure that I would appreciate Manny's action.

Colin looked at me with concern and I realised that I'd taken his hand. I tried to pull it back, but he held on and winked. I frowned at the silliness of my unfounded concerns as we entered a small room. Unlike Father Nate's office, this one was spartan in its décor. A pinewood desk faced a small window, a small bookshelf to the left of it. Above the doorframe, a small crucifix was the only decoration on the off-white walls.

If it weren't for the lack of colour and furniture, I might have felt more claustrophobic. I estimated the room to be half the size of my viewing room. Five adults in this small space was not comfortable for me, but I needed to be here to read the priest's nonverbal cues. I didn't know whether the irritation I had noticed earlier was because of our presence or because of another reason.

The priest walked past us to his desk and leaned against it. "Why is Interpol interested in Father Sidney's death?"

"Unfortunately, we can't talk about an ongoing investigation, Father Mason." Manny leaned against the doorway, his body language open, his expression friendly. "Anything you can tell us about Father Sidney will help."

The priest, Father Mason, sighed. "Our congregation is a tight-knit family. We were hit hard by two events this year. First, it was the shock of that old man's property being used for those horrid activities. What kind of evil person hunts other people? What makes it that much worse is that it was so close to us and we never knew anything about this. For weeks, our village was overrun by law enforcement people. A lot of them were not too kind to my people."

His lips contracted into a thin line. If anything, the priest was understating his horror at the activities that had taken place on the piece of land Gasquet had inherited from a man who had treated him like a son.

"Then Father Sidney died." The corners of Father Mason's mouth turned down in grief. "He was a dear friend. We had served this congregation together for seventeen years."

"I'm so sorry for your loss." This was the first time Francine had said anything. The sympathy on her face was genuine. "My dad is also a priest and I know how much he values the friendships he has with his colleagues."

Father Mason tilted his head. "Your father is a priest?"

"And my mom is a nun." She smiled at his raised eyebrows. "It always makes for a great conversation starter. They had me before they decided that they were not meant to be together and would serve God better by going into His service."

"They got divorced after you were born?" His brow lowered in censure.

"No. They were never married." Francine crossed her arms. "Don't judge them. I had a better childhood than almost everyone I know. They are wonderful people."

The priest nodded slowly. I hoped he wasn't going to pursue this topic. Every time Francine told me anecdotes from her childhood, it greatly pleased and entertained me. My own childhood had been one of constant pretence. Only when I'd pretended to be happy, to fit in socially, to smile insincerely, had my parents stopped taking me to all kinds of doctors in an attempt to make me 'normal'.

"Was Father Sidney sick before he died?" Manny's question was a bit louder than needed. The look of concern he'd given Francine, followed by anger, had been brief, but I'd noticed.

"Not for very long. He had the usual aches and pains that come with our age, but there were no warning signs." Father Mason sighed heavily. "He had the flu. The simple flu. Then I found him in his room one morning. Dead."

When we were overcome with grief, our throat muscles constricted, creating the need to swallow away the feeling of thickness. Father Mason was quiet for a moment while swallowing hard, trying to regain composure. I walked to the bookshelf to look at the few books displayed there.

Unless Father Sidney's immune system had been compromised, having influenza should not have killed him. Adding his death to the others from a similar cause made it much more than a mere coincidence. As reluctant as I had been in the beginning, I was now viewing these priests' deaths with the same suspicions Francine had.

Manny was asking the priest about Gasquet's involvement in the community and Father Mason gratefully grabbed onto the change of topic. He was genuinely relieved that Gasquet had never been a part of this congregation. He repeated how much his congregation was like a family. I grew bored when he started going into the details of parishioners' friendships and turned my attention back to the books.

Most books appeared at least twenty years old. I looked for a cover that looked new, but found something much more interesting. I leaned a bit forward. The back of one of the books looked familiar.

"What are you looking at?" Colin's thick German accent startled me. He stepped closer to stand next to me.

I never liked it when he used aliases. It caused anxiety to build in me until the fear of mistakenly revealing Colin's true identity overwhelmed me. I forced these thoughts away with an irritated sigh. Pointing at the leather-bound book, I looked at the priest. "May I look at this?"

"Sure. All those books were Father Sidney's. My books are in my bedroom. I read for two hours every night."

Glad that I was wearing my gloves, I took the book from the shelf. Colin gasped and reached for it, but I didn't hand it to him. "You're not wearing gloves."

"What you got there, Doc?"

"It's another book of hours." Colin leaned closer. "Go to the back of the book."

I paged to the last three pages. "Just like the book we got."

"What the h… What on earth?" Manny glanced at the priest before walking over. "Speak to me, Frey."

Colin was leaning right in, studying the strange lettering. To my eye, it looked like exactly the same coded words as the book of hours delivered to our offices. Colin straightened. "Same artist did this."

"Are you… of course you are sure." Manny turned to the priest. "Do you know anything about this book, Father Mason?"

"I've never seen this before. Father Sidney and I didn't share the same passion for reading." Father Mason lifted his chin towards the bookshelf. "As you can see, he never had much of a collection. He only read what he was required to. Frankly, I'm quite surprised to see something so beautiful among his books."

"You don't know where he got this from?" Manny asked.

Father Mason only shook his head, the corners of his mouth turned down.

"Did Father Sidney have a secretary, or anyone who might know anything about this book?"

"We're a small parish. We don't have secretaries. Father Sidney handled all his own administration." Father Mason clasped his hands together. "I can ask the people in the congregation and our other staff if it's so important."

"It is very important." Manny took a business card from his coat pocket and gave it to Father Mason. "Anything you find out about this book, no matter how small, please phone me."

"What is it? Why is it so important?" Father Mason's expression intensified. "Does it have anything to do with that evil man?"

"Laurence Gasquet?" Manny's eyes narrowed marginally. "Why would you ask that?"

Father Mason lifted both hands. "No reason. I just... I don't want my friend's good name, his good work to be in any way connected to the evil that happened in those woods."

"Would you mind if we take the book with us?" Colin asked.

"Please take it." Father Mason had no reason to associate the book in my hands with anything negative, but he was glaring at it. "I don't want it here."

Francine searched through her oversized handbag until a soft rustling sounded. She pulled out a plastic bag and handed it to me. Long before they had entered my life, Francine, Vinnie and Colin had learned how to avoid leaving evidence. That also meant they knew how to preserve evidence. I put the book in the bag and wrapped the excess plastic around it.

Father Mason was relieved when, after a few more questions he couldn't answer, we turned to the door. Some of the tension in his shoulders left when he accompanied us to one of the three doors in the hallway and opened it to reveal the backyard of the church. He said a short blessing in Latin and closed the door the moment we were outside.

"Not one of the friendliest priests I've ever met." Francine sniffed. "Brazilian people are much warmer as well."

"Don't let that old man get to you, supermodel."

Manny and Francine became involved in a discussion about the scandalous behaviour of spiritual leaders. The earlier respect they'd shown for each other and everyone else's beliefs was no longer evident. By the time we reached Colin's SUV, their voices were raising in tone and volume. It was the sarcasm, however, that made me lose interest. When I could no longer discern between sarcasm and sincerity in someone's speech, I felt powerless to ascertain their true communication.

Colin opened the SUV door and I stepped back. "Please let the car air for a few minutes. I simply cannot spend another hour in that smell."

"It bothered you? Why didn't you say anything, Jenny?"

I looked away and lifted one shoulder. "You were enjoying it."

Colin opened the other doors before pulling me into a tight embrace. He kissed me on the top of my head before leaning back to look down at me. "That was very sweet of you, love. To suffer through that for us."

"I'm not sweet." Especially not after the realisation that I was intolerant.

"Yeah, you are." Francine got into the back of the SUV, but didn't close the door. "You're going to suffer through crunching popcorn and watching a movie with Nikki because you love her. That's sweet."

Colin nodded his head. "It is."

I punched him lightly on the chest. "You're teasing me. I'm not sweet. Don't tease me."

Everyone laughed and my lips lifted in a half-smile. It was good to have neurotypical friends in my life. They prevented me from taking myself too seriously.

Colin tightened his arms around me before letting go. "Tell us if the smell is okay now."

I leaned my head into the SUV and inhaled. The smell still lingered, but it was no longer overwhelming. A few minutes later we were on the main road back to Strasbourg. I watched the wintry scene speed by, wondering if the book of hours we'd found was important. Did it have any connection to Gasquet? To Rousseau & Rousseau? To ZDP?

"Jenny?" Colin's tone warned me he'd been calling me for some time.

I turned to him. "I was thinking."

"I know." His smile was wide and genuine. "We were talking logistics while you were thinking. I'll first drop Manny and Francine off at the office, then I'll take you home."

I glanced at my watch. It was only twenty past five, so there was enough time to still be home before six. I nodded. "Are you going directly to your male-bonding evening or are you coming up?"

Colin was meeting Vinnie and the GIPN team in one of the few places in Strasbourg with pool tables. Vinnie had been proud to take credit for this initiative and then took offense when I'd called it male bonding. Colin chuckled. "I'll go straight there. Vin is taking this very seriously. According to him this is not male bonding, it's a playoff to the death."

I glanced at him to see if he was joking and relaxed. "It's male bonding."

"If I have to play against Vinnie, I'll tell him that. He'll be so insulted, he'll miss his shot."

"That's cheating." I thought about this. "Is it? Or it that a strategy allowed by the rules?"

Laughter filled the car. Even if it were at my expense, it pleased me that the atmosphere in the car was light-hearted.

"What do you make of this book of hours nonsense, Doc?" Manny asked after the laughter stopped.

"I don't know. I'm not willing to speculate."

"Frey, what messages are behind these books? Were these books ever used to send secret messages with plans to topple kingdoms?"

"Ooh, I like how you think." Francine's voice was excited.

"No," Colin said. "As far as I know, books of hours were not used to send secret spy messages."

"That would've been fabulous though," Francine said and spent the rest of the journey presenting us with various conspiracy theories. When she mentioned aliens, I stopped listening and hoped Vinnie had made the pizza he'd promised. I hadn't had lunch and was hungry.

Soon Colin dropped Francine and Manny in front of the office and we were on our way to my apartment. Another thirteen minutes later, Colin left to meet with Vinnie and I was in the elevator to my apartment, relieved that it was three minutes to six. I liked being punctual, but preferred being early.

I opened the door to the smell of pizza and popcorn. One thing I disliked about winter was having to seal the windows against the cold. Not only did it keep the heat in, it also kept all odours in. And Nikki's virus. I locked the five locks, left my boots on the designated mat and went to put my handbag on its usual place by the dining room table. That was when I saw her.

Nikki was lying on the floor in the kitchen, popcorn spread around her. Her pallor was that of the wall in Father Mason's office.

I froze, clutching my handbag to my chest. Dark panic rushed in on me, threatening to shut me down completely. Only the knowledge that Nikki needed me kept me from giving in to that safe place. Without taking my eyes off her motionless body, I pushed Mozart's Violin Concerto No.4 in D major into my mind. It took three lines to send adrenaline to my limbs.

Still clutching my handbag, I rushed into the kitchen. Popcorn crunched under my socked feet, but I was focussed only on Nikki. Her chest moved as I knelt next to her and held my hand above her forehead. It took me a moment to dismiss all my concerns about contamination and lower my hand. Her skin felt cold and clammy against my palm.

"Nikki." My voice was hoarse. I cleared my throat. "Nikki. Wake up. Nikki?"

Panic crept into my tone and I forced myself to calm down. I could give in to all the thoughts about viruses, bacteria and all the other horrors threatening to limit my ability to help Nikki at a more appropriate moment. When Nikki was awake. And healthy.

I sat down on the popcorn, reluctant to move her in case she had injuries I didn't know of. I reached into my handbag for my smartphone and phoned Colin. He would know what to do.

I pushed Nikki's clean hair off her face, my heart contracting.

"Nikki. Please, be well. I'm getting help."

Chapter EIGHT

"Doc G?" Nikki's whisper accomplished what Colin and Vinnie had not been able to do in the last eleven hours. It brought me out of my frozen state in the chair next to Nikki's hospital bed.

I stood up, not taking my eyes off her. Her micro-expressions showed no evidence of pain, just confusion and fear. "I'm here."

"What happened?" She closed her eyes on a groan, but opened them again, waiting for my answer. I didn't know what to say. Did she want to know that she'd been unconscious for eleven hours and eight minutes? Should I tell her that I hadn't been able to get up from the kitchen floor to open the door to the EMT's no matter how hard they had banged on my front door? That I had cradled her until Vinnie and Colin arrived minutes after the paramedics? That letting go of her and allowing the paramedics to do their work had been one of the hardest things I'd ever done?

It had been a traumatic experience I had not foreseen, even though logic dictated that at one point a loved one might become gravely ill. I had been on the verge of a meltdown when the strangers had told me I could not go with Nikki in the ambulance. In recent years, I'd had only experienced one meltdown. That had happened last year when I was being kidnapped. The severe stress of the situation had caused my mind to shut down, but I had attacked my kidnappers and screamed until I'd had no voice. Such an uncontrollable meltdown would not have helped Nikki. Colin had convinced them to allow me to accompany her.

I had not left her side in eleven hours, not even to relieve myself. Apart from the physical effects of not sleeping, I was mentally and emotionally exhausted.

The only way I had been able to prevent completely shutting down was by watching Nikki's face for the slightest hint of waking up while mentally writing Mozart's compositions. I had worked through my favourite opera, *Die Zauberflöte*, two concertos and seven smaller works. It had taken a significant amount of energy not to give into all the obsessive thoughts and panic that accompanied me whenever I was in a hospital.

Colin had ordered the EMTs to bring Nikki to the hospital that had previously treated Francine. The five-star hotel-like quality of the furnishings in the room made being here marginally more bearable. The spaciousness of the room also helped. On the other side of the room was a private washroom and small lounge area.

"You've been out for the count the whole night, Nix." Colin put his arm around me and reached for Nikki's hand. He'd been in the chair next to mine most of the night. "Jenny found you passed out on the kitchen floor, lying on a bed of popcorn."

Nikki groaned. "Sorry, Doc G. I'll clean up."

"Wait! What?" Vinnie jumped up from the chair in the far corner of the room where he'd fallen asleep. He rushed over to the other side of Nikki's bed and grabbed her other hand. "You're awake? Howdy, little punk."

"I messed up Doc G's kitchen."

"I'll clean it, punk. You just get better."

"I don't care about my kitchen." My tone was harsh. A prickling started in the back of my throat and tears burned my eyes. "I don't care about my kitchen."

Nikki pulled her hand from Colin's and held it out to me. I stared at her hand, amazed that the most dominant thought was not all the diseases I could get. No. I was concerned that I might hurt her if I held onto her hand with the powerful need I had to reassure myself that she would be all right. But she was the one who held very tight when I took her hand.

"What's wrong with me, Doc G?"

"The doctors don't know yet." I put my other hand over hers. At this point I wasn't sure who needed more reassurance. "They've taken blood and are doing a lot of tests. We're waiting for the results."

"I'm going to tell them you're up, punk."

Nikki's eyes widened slightly, her expression pleading. "Not yet, please, Vin. Just give me another minute."

Vinnie squeezed her hand, his smile gentle. "Sure thing. Do you want some water?"

She nodded and took a few sips from the straw when Vinnie held the glass to her. Her head dropped back on the pillow, the small physical activity taking its toll. She looked around. "What is this place? It looks like the Ritz."

"The best hospital with the best doctors, Nix." Colin's smile was encouraging. "They'll figure out what's making you sick and we'll have you home in no time."

"You don't kno…" I stopped, realising he was lying to appease her. Promises like these were given to calm, reassure and comfort. I wondered if I should give Nikki these false promises, but simply couldn't form the words. I bit down on my lips.

Nikki's smile was resigned, but with good humour—a smile she always gave me when I failed to be socially correct. Soon her smile faltered and her hand tightened around mine again. "Doc, promise me that you will tell me whatever it is the doctors find. Promise me."

I didn't have to consider my answer. "I will be completely honest with you."

"Thank you." She relaxed against the pillows.

"Is she awake?" Manny asked from the door. He walked to the foot of the bed, the rings under his eyes darker than before. I didn't know when Colin had phoned him, but Manny had been in and out of the room a few times during the night. He touched her covered foot and squeezed. "How're you feeling, lass?"

"Like the wrong side of an elephant after he ate a tonne of fermented fruit."

The men snorted. I still stared at her, studying every micro-expression. I'd had a lot of time to think while waiting for Nikki to regain consciousness. There had been many unconnected incidents in the last few days. I was wondering if they really were unconnected.

"What do you think is wrong with you?" Often doctors relied on a patient's body-awareness and instinct to help them reach their diagnosis.

"I just feel like I have the mother of all colds, Doc G."

"When did you start feeling poorly?" Manny frowned. Was he also suspicious?

"I don't know. Maybe Wednesday?" Nikki lifted one shoulder in a half-shrug.

"It was Tuesday morning you first showed symptoms of being unwell," I said. "You came into the kitchen for breakfast and complained that you didn't sleep well. You also said that the central heating was too high. It wasn't. You must have had a fever already."

"Oh. Yes, now I remember. Monday evening I felt, like, really tired and went to bed early, but I didn't sleep well. It sucked."

"What happened on Monday?"

"Um…" She looked up and to the left, accessing memories. "Nothing strange happened. I went to university, had two lectures and one long session in the art studio. The smell of paint is always strong there, so maybe it could be that?"

"Was it stronger than usual?" I asked.

"Not that I recall." She closed her eyes. The conversation was tiring her.

Manny must have seen her exhaustion as well. "Has the doctor been to see her since she woke up?"

"No." Vinnie stepped away from the bed. "But I'm getting Doctor Fancy Pants now."

Doctor Paul Vasseur was a friend of Andrew Marvel—one of Colin's aliases. When we'd brought Nikki in, I'd registered the speculative look he'd given us. He hadn't said anything and had been completely professional.

I looked at Nikki's pale face. I didn't want to push her when she was feeling so weak, but anything she said might help Paul diagnose what was wrong with her. "Did you eat anything strange on Monday?"

"I can't remember." Nikki frowned. "Why all the questions? I feel like I have a cold. I don't have a cold, do I?"

"The doctors don't know what's wrong, Nikki." Maybe she hadn't heard me the first time. "They're still doing tests to find out exactly what caused you to lose consciousness for such a long period."

She stared at me. "Are you worried?"

I considered my answer. "Not about the diagnosis. You might have contracted some form of food poisoning. There are so many possibilities that it will take the doctors a while to eliminate the obvious and find out what it is." I straightened my shoulders and took a deep breath. "But I am worried about you. I don't like you being here. I don't like you being sick."

Paul and a nurse entered the room ahead of Vinnie and the next fifteen minutes were focussed on Nikki's health. Paul ordered everyone out, but Nikki begged him to allow me to stay. I was glad when he agreed. It stopped the dark panic from closing in on me. I was not yet ready to leave Nikki's side. After checking all her vitals and adjusting her medication, they left.

"Doc G?" Nikki held out her hand and this time I took it without thinking. "I know how you need your routine, but do you think you could stay with me today? I know it's Monday, but... please?"

Not letting go of her hand, I pulled the chair closer and sat down. "I'm not going anywhere."

"Except to shower." Francine walked into the room with an overnight bag in one hand. She dropped it on the sofa and walked to Nikki's other side, smiling. "Hey, chickadee. I'm not going to ask how you are. I can see you're feeling like crap."

"Gee, thanks, Franny."

"Touché, you little wench." Francine's smile softened the words. She hated it when Vinnie called her Franny, which he only did when Francine was frustrating him. Nikki had only used this name twice, both times when Francine had insulted Nikki's fashion sense. "Clearly you haven't lost your sharp tongue."

"And I'll still beat you at *Deus Ex*, old lady." Nikki's voice was weak, her breathing shallow. Yet she was joking with Francine. It brought a feeling of warmth to my chest.

They smiled at each other until Francine looked at me and nodded towards the sofa. "I brought you fresh clothes. Colin said you haven't even peed all night. What's up with that, girlfriend?"

"He said that?" How dare he discuss my bodily functions?

"Of course he didn't. He said you've not moved from that chair at all." Francine waved me out of the chair. "Why don't you have a quick shower in that fancy, super-clean bathroom over there? I'll sit right here and keep an eye on Nikki while you're freshening up."

I didn't get up. "Where's Colin?"

"The guys went to the cafeteria to find coffee." She waved again. "Come on. Move your butt. A quick shower and you'll feel better."

Nikki squeezed my hand. "I'll be okay, Doc G. Francine can sit very close so I can see if she's developed any more wrinkles in the last week."

It was clear that Nikki was trying very hard to appear stronger than she felt. I'd also seen a glimpse of guilt when Francine mentioned I'd been next to Nikki's bed all night. I didn't want her to feel guilty. I got up. "I was here all night for myself as well as for you. I needed to see that you were okay."

"I'm okay for now." She pulled her hand from mine, her eyes watery. "Thank you, Doc G."

I nodded stiffly and went to the bathroom. Francine was right. There was not a speck of dust or a water-spot to be found anywhere. The smell of disinfectant further assured me that it was safe to use the facilities. I opened the bag Francine had brought and exhaled in relief. She had packed sensible clothes—a pair of comfortable jeans and one of my favourite tops. She'd even packed my makeup and hairdryer.

Ten minutes later, I exited the bathroom, feeling refreshed, my short hair styled. Colin and Manny were back in the room, both sipping from steaming paper cups. Francine was still in the chair I'd been in all night, teasing Manny. Nikki was lying with her eyes closed, a small smile around her mouth.

"There you are." Colin held out a cup. "I brought you some coffee. It's not half bad."

I frowned at the cup. "What does that mean? If it's not half bad, is it half good? That's not an endorsement."

"It means it's quite good, Jenny." He pushed the cup towards me again. "Not as good as our coffee, but almost."

"It's a silly expression." I took the cup, removed the cover and looked at the dark liquid. "Did you...?"

"Yes, I made sure no one touched the rim of the cup and I used your disinfectant wipes before I put the lid on." The first time Colin had been with me when I'd bought a coffee to go, his eyes had widened in shock. I didn't care that people thought my behaviour odd. I didn't want to expose myself to unnecessary bacteria.

"Ready, old man?" Vinnie walked into the room.

"Let's do it." Manny gave Nikki a quick smile. "Tell her we'll be back soon."

"I'm awake," she said softly and opened her eyes. "Just dozing."

"Well, then." Manny winked. "We'll be back soon, lass."

"Give 'em hell, punk."

Manny and Vinnie left before I could say anything. I turned to Colin. "Where are they going?"

"To get all Nikki's personal things from the university and samples of all the paints from her class."

Francine got up. "I'm also going. Nikki needs you here, so I'll go into the office and work on finding more links between everything. And I'm going to see if I can decrypt those pages in the two books."

A feeling of great discomfort tightened my throat. Francine had brought to my mind all the work waiting for me. I glanced at Nikki. She was watching me intently. Her lips were trembling, her blinking increased. She was scared. It caused a strong emotional response in me. The need to soothe someone's fears was unique to my relationship with Nikki. I did not experience it with anyone else. I purposefully walked to the chair Francine had vacated and sat down, barely controlling my need to cross my arms over my chest. Instead, I held tightly onto the cup of coffee.

"Keep us updated," Colin said as a greeting. "We'll do the same."

"Cool bananas." Francine pointed a manicured finger at Nikki. "Get better or I'll start fooling around with your apps."

"You wouldn't." Nikki's jaw dropped a little. "That's… that's…"

"Evil. I know." Francine looked proud of herself. She wiggled her fingers in a wave. "Toodles. See you guys later."

Colin sat down next to me and we sipped our coffee. He was right. The coffee was not as good as the coffee from my machine at home or the one at work. It also wasn't bad. But I would never describe something as half bad.

Nikki was resting, her eyes closed, but she didn't have the complete lack of expression she'd had while unconscious. Colin shifted next to me and put his hand on my arm. It took me a few seconds and three bars of a Mozart etude before I looked away from Nikki. An unfamiliar expression on Colin's face caught my attention. I studied him. "Why are you uncomfortable?"

"Because I don't know how to phrase my thoughts."

I shrugged. "Just say it."

"I know how much you value your independence, love." He inhaled deeply before taking the coffee from my hands and placing it on the table next to Nikki's bed. Then he took both my hands in his. "Nikki's situation has made me realise that we have nothing formal binding us. We're already a family. I think we should get some paperwork done to make it more formal."

"Oh, my God. You're getting married?" Nikki's eyes shot open and she rolled onto her side. Excitement brought colour to her face for the first time since I'd found her on the kitchen floor. "When? Can I be the bridesmaid? No. Francine will be the bridesmaid. I'll be the flower girl. It will be so supercool."

I jerked my hands out of Colin's and stared at Nikki in shock. "No. No. No. No. No."

Colin started laughing and couldn't seem to control himself.

"Doc G." Nikki looked devastated. "You can't say no. Not like that. You must say yes. Colin loves you."

"No. No." I couldn't find anything else to say. I wrapped my arms around my torso.

Colin seemed to have calmed himself, but was still chuckling. He cupped my face in his warm hand and shook his head, his laughter building up again. "See? This is why I should've spent more time thinking how to phrase my thoughts."

"Then maybe you should do that now." My tone and body was stiff. Still Colin chuckled.

"Firstly, I didn't ask you to marry me." He turned to Nikki. "Thanks for jumping to shocking conclusions, Nix."

"Sorry." The excitement was replaced by lowered eyebrows, the corners of her mouth drawn down. "You're not getting married?"

"Not yet, anyway." Colin turned back to me. "What I should've said was that we had some difficulty with legalities last night."

"You say 'difficulty', but your expression implies greater problems." Why did people always have to be vague?

"We have no legal right over each other. If it wasn't for Millard's law enforcement status, we might not have been able to make any decisions regarding Nikki. If something happens to me, you won't have any right to make decisions about my treatment, love."

The tightening around my chest felt like one of Vinnie's too-strong hugs. "You can't let something happen to you."

"I'm not planning it, love. Just like Nikki didn't plan to pass out on the kitchen floor. But we have to be smart. In our jobs, it might be a wise decision to get some paperwork done that gives us legal rights in situations like this." He leaned closer until his nose touched mine. "I would like to know that you'll be the one making wise choices when I won't be able to. You're my family, love."

I shook my head, my nose bumping against his a few times. He was right, but I didn't like this line of thinking. Again the emotional upset made itself known through my uncontrollable head-shaking. I focussed on taking three very deep breaths until I could control my head movement.

"Okay. But Nikki must also sign such a document."

"If she wants to," Colin added quickly before looking at Nikki.

She was lying on her side, staring at us. I sat straighter, glaring at her. "You *will* sign that paper. If I have to sign it because Colin calls me his family then you have to sign it because... because I'm calling you my family."

This had been the least rational argument I had ever presented in my life. Yet the effect was immediate and strong. Colin inhaled sharply. Nikki's eyes filled with tears and soon they were running down her cheeks. She wiped at them, her micro-expressions fluctuating between affection, gratitude and happiness. "I love you, Doc G."

I nodded tightly. "I know."

Colin took one of my hands in his and waited until I looked at him. He tilted his head towards Nikki. He frequently reminded me that Nikki needed to be reassured of my love. He said he knew I loved him and that I didn't have to tell him every day, but Nikki needed to hear it more often.

"I love you too, Nikki."

She laughed a little and wiped more tears from her cheeks. "It's kinda funny when you say it after Colin elbows you into it."

"It doesn't make it any less true." I frowned. "And Colin's elbow has nothing to do with my affection for you."

"I know." She still looked ill, but there was deep happiness on her face. "And I would love to sign anything that makes me your family."

"We don't need to sign anything to be family, Nix." Colin rubbed her arm. "We're already family. We're just going to make sure that we're legally connected."

"What about Vinnie, Francine and Manny? They are also family." I'd been excluded from so many things in my family. I didn't want to do it to my new family.

"Millard has family." Colin's top lip curled.

"Like you and me, he's not close to them. We have to include him."

"Hmm." Despite Colin's noncommittal grunt, I knew he would agree.

Nikki's eyes drifted closed. She was tired and needed to rest. I took my coffee from the table and leaned back in my chair, watching Nikki fall asleep. For almost an hour Colin and I sat in silence. I had no interest in doing anything but watching Nikki. Colin had taken out his smartphone and was tapping and swiping the screen.

"Is she sleeping?" Francine's whisper was loud, her steps urgent as she walked to us. "We should talk outside."

"I'm awake." Nikki's voice was sleepy, but her eyes alert. "What's happening?"

Francine looked at us, looked back at Nikki, indecision visible in the tension around her eyes. Francine took her tablet from her large red handbag and thrust it at me. I took it, Francine's micro-expressions causing my breathing and heart rate to speed up. "What did you find?"

"Not me. Vinnie." The corners of her mouth turned down. "And he found it in Nikki's room."

Chapter NINE

Some people rushed into danger without a thought for their own safety. Others ran away. And some froze. I fitted into the latter group. Unable to move, I stared at the electronic device in my hands.

"What did Vinnie find?" Colin asked.

"Where in my room?" Nikki asked immediately after.

"He found a book." Francine pushed Nikki's feet until Nikki made space on the bed. Francine sat down, looking like she was posing for a fashion magazine. "Manny took a hazmat guy with him to the university. They haven't found anything suspicious, but took all the paints Nikki used in for tests just in case. Vinnie went to your apartment to check out Nikki's room."

"Please tell me he didn't go through everything." Nikki put one hand over her eyes.

"I don't know where he looked. What do you have that is so bad?" Francine drew out the last word.

"Francine." Colin's tone was sharp. "What did Vinnie find?"

"Take a look." She nodded at the tablet I still clutched.

Colin pried my fingers loose and took the tablet. I rolled my shoulders and took a deep breath as Colin swiped the tablet screen a few times. "Shit."

I leaned closer and Colin turned the screen for me to look at the image that had caused me such panic. It was a photo of an empty page in a notebook. A beautifully decorated notebook. Colin touched the screen and enlarged the picture to have a clearer view of the detailed paintings framing the page. "It appears to be the same as the books of hours from the church and our office."

"Not exactly the same, but"—he swiped the screen to look at another photo—"it looks like it is the same artist."

"What are you talking about?" Nikki stretched her neck to see the tablet.

Colin turned the tablet for her to see. "When did you get this notebook?"

"Oh, that? It's pretty, isn't it?" She relaxed against the pillows. "I got it last Monday."

"From whom?" I asked.

"I don't know. It was waiting for us in class on Monday."

"Us? How many people got one?" If this was the cause of Nikki's illness, all her classmates could be in need of medical care.

"All of us. There's only nine of us in that class, so... Oh, my God. Do you think this is what's making me sick? How can a book make me sick?"

The sound of a lion roaring filled the hospital room. Francine started digging in her handbag. "It's Manny. He must be in your apartment now."

She found her phone and a swipe of the screen stopped the roaring lion. "Hey, handsome. I'm putting you on speakerphone. I'm with Nikki, Colin and Genevieve."

"Who gave you this book, Nikki?" Manny's tone was tight and I was sure a deep frown pulled his brows together. There was some argument in the background. "Oh, for the love of Pete. I'm also putting this call on speakerphone. The criminal doesn't want to be left out."

"Howdy, y'all." Vinnie's voice boomed over the phone. "How're you feeling, little punk?"

"A bit better. Hi, Vinnie." She was lying. I didn't need to see all the deception cues to know that Nikki was not feeling better. Not even a bit. The circles under her eyes were darker than before. I wished we didn't have to ask her any questions.

Manny cleared his throat. "I'm glad you're feeling better. Now tell us who gave you this book."

"I don't know." Nikki told Manny what she'd told us. "We didn't think anything of it. It was just a notebook. We thought it was cool because it was personalised."

"What do you mean personalised?" Manny asked.

"Mine had my name on it."

"I didn't see your name, punk. Where is it?"

My mind was reeling with this new information. "You shouldn't touch the book, Vinnie. If it has some contaminant—"

"It's too late, Jen-girl. I… er… already paged through it quite a bit before I made the connection that it looked like the book from the office and the one from the church."

"You were snooping?" Nikki's tone was high, outraged. "Please tell me you didn't snoop through all my things."

"You're talking about the bottom drawer, right?" Vinnie's tone indicated teasing. "I must say, I didn't see that coming, little punk. Nearly had me a little heart failure."

Nikki groaned, her eyes shut tightly. "Did any—"

"No, punk. No one else saw it. I will protect that drawer with my last breath." The lightness in Vinnie's tone relaxed me. If he wasn't worried about whatever Nikki had in that drawer, neither was I. "Anyhoo… I managed to take photos of all the pages before the old man and his space cadet arrived here. The book is now sealed in three bags and has been sent off for testing."

"They're rushing the testing as we speak," Manny said. "These books are becoming more than suspicious. They are a threat. Nikki, where is your name on this book?"

"My notebook was wrapped in thin paper with my name on it. The others were the same."

I had to ask. "Who is the space cadet? And what is a space cadet?"

"He's talking about the incident commander of the Hazardous Material Incident Response Team." Francine smiled. "Their protective suits make them look like astronauts. Hey, Vin. Is this space cadet at least one of the sexy ones?"

"I don't know. I don't look at Dom like that." Vinnie sounded offended. "I don't look at men like that."

Francine snorted and even Nikki smiled. I understood that people made jokes to deal with difficult situations, but I felt very uncomfortable with the light-heartedness of the conversation when this was such a worrying situation.

"Who is this Dom?"

"Doctor Dominique Robiquet is the on-site incident commander for the hazmat team," Vinnie said.

"Only it's not called a hazmat team here in France, Vin." Francine rolled her eyes. "They use the abbreviation HMRT for the Hazardous Material Incident Re—"

"Don't you get sick of all the abbreviations?" Vinnie interrupted. "ZDP, GIPN, HMRT, FBI, CNN, BBC. Too much!"

Everyone laughed. Again we were digressing.

"You need to make sure Nikki's classmates are all in good health." I looked at her. "Give Manny the names of everyone who received a book. We need to make sure everyone is okay."

Nikki didn't know everyone's surnames, but Manny assured her he would find her eight classmates. While they discussed ensuring everyone's health, I thought about the book in my apartment. We had no proof the book caused Nikki's health problems. Yet I considered it a reasonable conclusion. If this was the case, why had it not affected Vinnie, Colin and myself in the week it had been in Nikki's room? Did one have to touch the book to be affected? Was it airborne? I wondered what disinfectant I needed to use to make me feel safe in my own home again.

"You need to be tested." I blurted the words out while Manny and Nikki were talking about her professor.

"Who needs to be tested, love?" Colin put his arm around my shoulders.

"Vinnie." I leaned towards Francine's phone. "You need to be tested. You can't get sick."

"Not that I agree with you, Jen-girl, but what are they going to test me for? The doctors don't even know what's wrong with Nikki. Or have they figured it out?"

"No, they haven't." Panic flooded my system. Not only was I worried about Nikki's undiagnosed state, but now Vinnie's health was also in jeopardy. Colin pulled me closer to him and I allowed the warmth of his body to anchor me, calm me. I took a deep breath. This was hard. "I need you to be well, Vinnie. I need you to admit when you're not feeling well so we can make sure you get whatever medical help you need."

For a few seconds no one spoke. A few grunts and inaudible but angry whispers came through the phone.

"Fine." Vinnie didn't sound pleased. "For you, Jen-girl. For you, I promise to be a wimp."

I decided not to argue with what I assumed was his sarcasm. "Thank you."

"I'm getting hazmat to check your apartment, Doc." Manny's voice was all business. "The criminal is here to make sure they don't destroy your place. He'll clean up after them."

"And I'll clean up the little punk's room."

"Please don't." Nikki closed her eyes again. "I suppose you have to."

"Don't worry, punk. I've cleaned up after Francine. Your room is a breeze."

"Hey!" Francine scowled at the phone. "I'm not that bad."

Colin and Vinnie snorted. I agreed with their reaction. For a short while, Francine had stayed with us. Her room had given me panic attacks. Just like her basement workspace did at the moment. Nikki's room was messy, but at least she didn't let clothes and shoes accumulate on the floor until the only visible floor space was a path from the door to the bed and from the bed to the cupboard. Terrifying.

Manny asked Nikki a few more questions about the notebook, but she didn't have any more information. Her answers came slower and her speech started slurring. She was tired, but didn't want to give in to the need to sleep.

"Nikki needs to rest." I shook my head when she inhaled. "You have dark rings under your eyes and your eyes are bloodshot. You need to rest."

Her smile quivered. "I feel like I could sleep for a month."

"Doc is right. You need to rest, lass." Manny also sounded tired. "Doc? You need to do your Mozart thingie. We need to figure out what the hell these books mean. You need to find us a connection between Nikki, Phillip and Father Sidney's church and book."

"We have a connection." I frowned at the phone. "Gasquet is the one common factor between all three."

"And you are sure this is the only connection?"

I considered this. "No. I'll have to think about it."

"So do your Mozart thing and get back to me. Frey, you need to get your lazy arse in gear and give me something useful about these books. You've had more than enough time to study those pretty pictures."

"Illustrations," Colin said.

Manny ignored Colin's interruption. "I need to know whatever you can tell me about the art, the artist, and what the hell those last pages are."

"I've uploaded the text from the church book and the ZDP book into a program to see if it can crack the code." Francine wrinkled her nose. "So far no luck."

"If it's a book cipher, we'll need the book to give us the key." I was repeating myself, but sometimes I wondered if they paid attention. "Unless we have the specific book this person used when creating the code, we'll only be wasting time. We need to find the person who made the books."

I glanced at Nikki. She was lying with her eyes closed, but I didn't think she was sleeping. Her curiosity would override her fatigue. She would only rest if we weren't talking. Or weren't here. Manny and Francine were arguing about one of her outrageous theories. Nikki's smile pulled at her lips.

The fact that Nikki's notebook was addressed to her meant she was specifically targeted. Also, she was not given a book of hours, but something that would be of use to her. The book of hours was sent to Phillip. Why? Did that person know

Phillip would appreciate the value of the antique manuscript? And what about Father Sidney? Was that book of hours also given to him specifically? If he had been targeted, why would Gasquet want to kill a priest?

My thoughts about Father Sidney's bookshelf and the sad lack of any other books was interrupted by a much more important realisation. "There might be another book."

The room quieted. Manny sighed over the phone.

"I love it when you interrupt our conversation with your statements." A glance at Colin's face assured me of the truth in his statement. I didn't understand why he would love my rudeness.

"Well, I don't love it." Manny sounded like he didn't. "Doc, what the hell do you mean by another book? Where is it?"

"When we were in the Strasbourg Cathedral, we went to Father Nate's office. He had a lot of books there. He'd said that Father Clément died of a heart attack, but that he'd had flu before that."

"So?"

I organised my thoughts. "Another Gothic church, another priest who died from something related to the flu, but more importantly, there were a lot of books in Father Nate's office. I recognised a few of the books on the shelves. Books that were written in the Gothic era."

Colin's eyebrows raised. "There might be a book of hours amongst those."

I nodded. "There was a shelf filled with Gothic literature."

"If Nikki is sick because of this notebook, and Father Sidney got sick because of the book of hours, it stands to reason that Father Clément also got sick because of a book. It might be worth going back to the cathedral and looking through his library."

"You're not going there alone." Manny's tone brooked no argument. "Do you hear me, Doc? I'll meet you there and bring Dom along."

I looked at Nikki. She had opened her eyes and was staring at me. The need to follow up on my suspicion was strong. But the need to ensure Nikki's emotional and physical wellbeing overrode that. She held out her hand and I took it.

"I'll be okay, Doc G. I feel better. You should go and find out what is making me sick."

"Don't lie to me. I know you are not feeling better."

"I just need to sleep a little. You can go find that other book while I rest."

I pulled my hand back, crossed my arms and shook my head. "You're trying to placate me. Don't. Manny, I can't leave Nikki alone."

"I have an idea," Vinnie said. "Why don't we get Tris to stay with the punk?"

"Tris?" It took me three seconds to recall who that was. "Tristan Mazet? The new member of Daniel's team?"

"Yes. He's a trained EMT. He's also one serious dirty fighter when it comes to hand-to-hand combat. Ask Colin, he paired up with Tris during our last training session."

Colin nodded. "That's a good idea, Vin. Tris said last night he's just a call away. He'll make sure Nikki's safe."

I looked at Nikki. She was following the conversation with wide eyes. "You think my life is in danger?"

"We don't know what's going on, Nix." Colin took her hand and rubbed it gently. "I think it's better if we play it safe. Tris can make sure no one bothers you here. Jenny and I will see if we can figure out if it's the book that's making you sick."

I didn't know Tris. It took mentally writing four lines of Mozart's Piano Concerto No. 27 in B flat Major before I agreed. I only did so because I trusted Colin and Vinnie's assessment of Tris. They would never leave Nikki under the care of someone they didn't trust.

When the average-looking man arrived ten minutes after Colin phoned him, I studied him with an intensity that bordered on rudeness.

"You won't allow anyone but Nikki's doctors to alter her medication." I knew my statement came out as an order, but I didn't care. I was watching Tris' micro-expressions. I read nothing worrying in his expressions. He was uncomfortable with my scrutiny, but seemed resigned to it.

"They were right about you." Tris' smile was genuine and caused one dimple to dent his left cheek. "There's no lying to you, is there?"

I got up. "No. I'll see it immediately. And if you ever lie about the safety of Nikki—"

"He'll answer to me, Jenny. And to Vin. Tris might have a mean right hook, but we're both bigger than him." The lightness in Colin's tone belied his expression. He was presenting his sincere threat under the guise of jesting.

I turned to Nikki. We should never have kept her awake for this long. Her skin appeared grey, her eyes sunken. I swallowed against my need to sit back down and watch her like I'd done all night.

"Go, Doc G. I'll be fine."

I leaned towards her. "Phone me. Or Colin. Or Vinnie. Any time."

"Got it." Her smile was weak. "Go get 'em, Doc G."

I nodded stiffly and followed Colin from the room, leaving behind the sound of Tris chatting to Nikki. Francine had already gone back to her messy basement to check on the numerous searches she was running at the moment. Vinnie was still in my apartment, overseeing the HMR team's search, and Manny was going to meet us at the church.

Traffic through the city centre at eight o'clock on a Monday morning slowed us down. For the twenty-seven minutes it took us to reach the old town I used Mozart to calm my mind. My obsessions had not lessened with new people in my life. They had in some aspects worsened. My neurotic concerns about my own health and safety had been transferred to these people. When it had been only me, I had had more control of those two factors.

With what Colin called our new family, I had no control. Vinnie was very physical and often came home with minor and not so minor injuries. Colin had not stopped his work for Interpol, reappropriating important and valuable items. Sometimes it was art, but most times he was required to enter secure premises to acquire information of some sort. It frequently placed him in danger. The deeper I allowed these people to enter my life, the more obsessed I became about their safety. Till now I had been successful not letting them see how their lifestyles troubled me.

Too soon Colin parked his SUV and we walked three blocks to the Strasbourg Cathedral. Manny was waiting for us at the front door. Next to him stood a slightly overweight man. His long black hair was in a neat ponytail, his glasses giving him an educated appearance. In one hand he held a protective suit, in the other a large bag.

"Doctor Robiquet, this is Doctor Lenard and this is—"

"Edward Taylor." Colin held out his hand and greeted the leader of the HMR team. "Pleased to meet you, Doctor Robiquet."

"Dom, please." Dom held out his hand to me and I took it only because I was wearing gloves. "Such a pleasure, Doctor Lenard."

I didn't detect any deception and nodded.

"I phoned Father Nate." Manny rubbed his hands, then tucked them under his arms for warmth. "He's agreed to meet with us. He said he'll be waiting inside for us."

"Hopefully it's warmer in there," Dom said. "It's colder than a loan shark's heart out here."

I frowned at the strange expression, but didn't waste any time attempting to understand it. Manny held open the door and I walked into the cathedral. I'd been in this building two days ago and many times before that, yet the beauty of it grabbed my attention. There was something about the symmetrical designs that appealed to my non-neurotypical mind. It made sense to me.

"Doctor Lenard, Mister Taylor." Father Nate stood close to the door, arranging pamphlets on a table. He finished and stepped closer. "And which one of you is Mister Millard?"

"That would be me." Manny held out his hand. "Thank you for meeting us, Father Nate."

"No problem at all. I must admit that this has me very curious, if you know what I mean. You mentioned a book?"

"In your office." I lowered my voice so it didn't carry too far into the church. "I saw a few books dating from the Gothic era."

"Yes, those are Father Clément's books that I kept. I haven't had time to read any of them yet."

"Would you mind if we look at them?" Manny was in character. His shoulders were slumped, his hands pushed into his trouser pockets—the absentminded detective that people underestimated. "It might help us in an ongoing investigation."

"You mentioned you're from Interpol. Can I ask what this is about?"

"Unfortunately, we can't talk about an ongoing investigation." Technically it was the truth, since we couldn't divulge any details during an investigation. In this instance, Manny didn't want to share any information. "If you don't mind?"

"Of course. Of course." Father Nate led us to his office, chatting about the weather, the changing seasons and how different it was from the United States. He opened his office door and made a sweeping motion with his hand. "Please go in. Um… do you need me to come in or stay out here?"

Dom put down his bag, shook out his protective suit and started getting dressed. "I would prefer if everyone stayed out here for the moment. I'm just going to check if there are any bogies flying about."

I turned to Colin. He smiled and said, "He's going to check if there is anything in the air."

"How are you going to do it?" I asked Dom.

Dom took a square device from his bag. It was the size of four reams of paper and looked quite heavy. Dom held the device close to his chest. "This baby is going to tell us all kinds of secrets in five minutes."

"How accurate is it?" Five minutes seemed a very short period to identify possible toxins.

"Lucy is the top of the range in bio-detection technology.

We got her two weeks ago and I've been dying to use her outside of the lab. So far, she's picked up all twenty-seven pathogens we've sent her way. And some of the samples were really diluted."

"Only twenty-seven pathogens?" Manny asked.

"Twenty-seven is a lot. It includes Ebola, the Marburg virus and Dengue fever. The worst of the worst in viruses, bacteria and toxins." He pulled the protective headgear over his head and his eyes lost focus. I assumed he was doing a check to ensure he was fully protected when he absently pointed to different places on his body and finally nodded. He stepped into the room. "Give us five minutes."

I still had a lot of questions, but Dom closed the door, leaving us in the hallway. We waited in silence for almost six minutes before Dom called out that it was safe. Manny usually waited for me to enter a room ahead of him, but this time he opened the door and pushed in front of me. He did a visual sweep of the room before he stepped away from the door. I walked straight to the bookshelves, only vaguely hearing the conversation between Colin and Dom. Father Nate was leaning against the doorframe, watching us with interest.

It didn't take me long to find it. There were two shelves with books dating from the mediaeval and Gothic eras. I recognised the other two books I also had. I tilted my head when I noticed a familiar-looking spine next to an old copy of Gottfried von Strassburg's *Tristan*. I reached out towards it.

"Stop!" Dom was next to me within two seconds. "Tell me which one."

"I think it is the book between *Tristan* and *The Romance of the Rose*." I pointed, but kept my hand close to my body. "On that shelf."

"I think we need to double-check if this book is clean." Dom exhibited so many indicators of deceptions that I took a step back.

"You just want to play with your toy." Colin looked amused.

"I think he should test it." Manny pointed to the doorway. "Come on. We'll wait outside in case that book releases something."

I had no argument against Manny's reasoning and walked past Father Nate into the hallway. Father Nate's expression had changed from curious to concerned, but he didn't speak.

We waited another five minutes until Dom called us back. I followed Manny and Colin to stand next to Dom as he opened the book on the first page.

It was beautiful. The colours were faded as if the book was indeed four hundred years old. Dom turned the page. Along the margin were similar elongated figures depicting religious scenes. By the fourth page, the tension in Colin's body was visible from his fisted hands to the tense muscles in his jaw.

"It's one of them." He spoke through his teeth. "These illustrations are from the same artist."

"Holy…" Manny grunted. "Get that thing sealed, Dom."

Dom closed the book, put it in a container and sealed it with a twist of his wrist.

"We need photos of the book." There was no longer any doubt that I needed to analyse every page. I needed to find a pattern, I needed to find out what these books meant.

"We'll take the photos, Doctor Lenard." Dom looked at the container. "But we need to do it in a contained environment."

"Pathogens? Contained? What's going on?" Father Nate no longer sounded friendly. I looked up and saw concern contracting the muscles around his eyes and mouth. "I'm in this room every single day. What is wrong with that book? Is it dangerous? What about the other people who come into this room? Could this have spread to the church?"

"We don't know what we're dealing with, Father Nate," Manny said. "I wish I could tell you more, but at the moment it is all guesswork. Dom? Do you think Father Nate needs to be worried?"

Dom took a few seconds before he shook his head. He winced and removed his headgear. "It might be a good idea to get tested though."

"Tested?" Father Nate's voice was a few tones higher. "For what?"

The silence in the room was accompanied by a variety of nonverbal cues. The anger, frustration, but mostly concern visible in Manny and Colin's body language reflected how I felt. We didn't know what these books meant. We didn't know what danger they posed. We didn't know for what Father Nate should be tested. But most importantly, we didn't know what was wrong with Nikki.

Chapter TEN

"Outside of the girl's room, we didn't find anything else." Elisa Flynn, a short HMR team member, looked at Dom. "Seriously, that place is immaculate."

We were in the large conference room at Rousseau & Rousseau. It was unimaginable to have the HMR team as well as ours congregate in the team room. The HMR team consisted of five members. We were comfortably seated around the conference table and they were reporting back on their search through my apartment.

"What did you find?" I hoped we could give Nikki's doctors the reason for her ill health.

"A mystery." Elisa, the only woman in their team, lifted both shoulders, shaking her head. "We found nothing in the girl's room."

"Nikki." My tone must have been too hard. Elisa leaned a bit away from me. I sighed and lowered my voice. "Her name is Nikki."

She nodded. "As I said, Nikki's room was without any detectable biohazard. We took the contents of the drawer the notebook was in to also be tested."

"Could it be a poison?" Colin asked.

"The list of all the things it could be is long, Edward," Dom said. "The lab is testing all three books, but put priority on Nikki's. They're testing everything—the paper, the ink, the paint, the glue. Everything. As soon as they find anything they'll let me know."

"Good." Manny slid lower in his chair. His stubble was at least four days old, his skin lacked its healthy, rested appearance and his eyes were bloodshot.

"We are scientists." One of the quieter HMR team members shifted in his chair. "Not investigators. Do you think this is a terrorist attack?"

"I'm not ruling anything out." Manny rubbed his hand over his eyes. "But at this moment, I don't think so. If they are terrorists, they are unlike anything we've seen. There are no mass casualties, no public claims that they are responsible or any demands. They've also been doing this over a long period, one priest at a time. I can't see the hand of any terrorist organisations in this, can you?"

"No, I suppose not."

"Why are we here?" I wanted to get to my viewing room. This was unproductive and wasting precious time.

"I asked for this meeting," Dom said. "I would like to impress upon you to be extra cautious."

Manny nodded. "From now on, no one here opens any package or touches any book without calling one of the HMR team first. We must treat all of them as potential threats."

"That's preposterous." I crossed my arms. "Why can't I open a book in my office that's been there for the last seven years?"

"He means any book that you don't know, that is a gift or something like that," Colin said.

"Oh." I glared at Manny. "Then you should say that. Be specific. Sweeping statements using words like 'all' and 'any' are confusing. And inaccurate."

"Fine, missy. How's this for a sentence: Be suspicious of any and all books." Manny was sarcastic. I had annoyed him.

Vinnie snorted, Francine laughed and Colin kissed my cheek. The HMR team members' reactions ranged from surprise to amusement.

I sighed. "Have you checked on Nikki's classmates?"

"We sent out another team," Dom said. "All of them are well. A few had been using their notebooks since they got them and they aren't showing any symptoms. We did take their books in for testing as well. We've also taken blood samples from them to check for anything out of the ordinary."

"You should also give us blood samples to test." Elisa looked at my arm and I immediately pulled it tight against my torso.

"No." I shook my head, my breathing harsh. "Until you know what to test for, I see no rational reason for me to submit myself to any such thing."

"What she said." Francine pointed at me. "And I'll just add that it will be a cold day in Hades before I willingly hand over my DNA to the likes of you. I know you people. You will store my blood somewhere, do some unethical testing on it. Movies have been made about this, you know."

The HMR team looked at Francine with incredulity. One member of the HMR team even lost muscle tension in his jaw, his mouth slightly agape.

"Are you for real?" Elisa asked.

"Honey, you have no idea." Francine got up. "If you'll excuse me, I'm going to find out who's behind this conspiracy."

Everyone watched Francine walk out in her red, high-heeled boots. Dom blinked a few times, his pupils dilated—a sign of arousal. "Who *is* that woman?"

Manny turned to answer, but stopped when he noticed Dom's expression. Manny's lips thinned and his nostrils flared. "Nobody. You will not go near her."

Dom lifted both hands and leaned away. "Just asking."

"You'll do better to ask the lab if they've got any new results."

On any other day, this possessive behaviour would've interested me and I would've studied it. Not today. I found it tedious and irrelevant compared to the concern for Nikki that would not release its hold on my mind. I got up. "I'm going to work. Don't disturb me."

I registered the shocked expressions from the HMR team, but it was not important. I needed to be alone. I needed to be in my soundproof viewing room. And I needed Mozart.

I left and was grateful when no one followed me. I didn't even turn on my computer, but immediately settled in my chair, closed my eyes and surrendered to Mozart's Clarinet Quintet in A Major. Instead of mentally writing it, I replayed it, feeling every note soothe my mind and untangle the flood of information we had.

My eyes shot open with excitement and I glanced at my watch. An hour and fifteen minutes had passed. As usual, I had tucked my legs under my body. I lowered them to the floor and rushed into the team room. Francine was at her desk, squinting at her computer monitor. Vinnie and Colin were at the round table, looking at Colin's laptop monitor. He was squinting at his computer, angrily typing. But it was Francine I needed.

I stopped in front of her desk. "How many dead competitors have you found?"

"We already had Laignes SA, Ribemont, Marmoutier and those other three." Francine clicked with her mouse and stared at the monitor. "I've found another five."

"How many of those died in accidents?"

"Like the rock-climbing accident?" Francine frowned. "Four."

"How did the other seven die?"

"Flu, heart failure or respiratory complications." Francine's eyes widened. "All could be related to flu."

"Holy hell!" Manny pushed away from his desk.

I lifted my hand to stop Manny from asking more questions. First, I needed more information. "When did they die?"

"The flu guys?" Francine looked back at her computer monitor. "Oh, my God. All of them died within the last eighteen months. No one had any more accidents in this time."

"What does this mean, Doc?" Manny asked.

"It means you have to phone their families or companies."

"And why should I do that?"

"To find out if they received books. Notebooks, books of hours, any kind of book with illustrations on it. If Gasquet got the illustrator to make a book especially for Phillip and Nikki, he might have also had books specially illustrated for those people who'd died."

"Hmm. Supermodel, do you have phone numbers for those people?"

Francine flicked her hair over her shoulder, her expression sultry. "It's gonna cost you, handsome. But it will be totally worth it."

"You know what else will be totally worth it?" Manny lifted one eyebrow. "Giving your hairbrush to the hazmat team."

Francine jerked back. "You wouldn't. Giving my DNA to those government lackeys? It's a low threat, handsome. Low."

"But it would give me such pleasure." Manny straightened. "Give me the numbers."

"You're no fun. I already emailed them to you." She twisted until he could clearly see her sneer. "A minute ago."

He turned to his computer and clicked with unnecessary force until his eyebrows lifted slightly. "Is this *the* Martin Delisle?"

"Right?" Francine got up and stood next to Manny. "At first I thought I was totally wrong. I triple-checked, but the results stayed the same."

"Who's Martin Delisle?" I had not heard of this person before.

"Only the sexiest photographer ever." Francine pinched Manny's cheek. "You're still my fave hero, handsome."

"Leave me alone, woman."

"He's just jealous." She winked at Manny. "Martin Delisle was voted the most eligible bachelor by a magazine four years ago. At that time he had just started his studio, so that wasn't what got him the attention. He comes from old money. Really old money. Before he opened his studio, he was a playboy and landed in jail a few times. Something happened to make him go straight and he started doing photo documentaries for a few charities. The eligible bachelor status was great PR for his studio and that's when it took off."

"Yup, sometimes life's a real bitch." Vinnie sniffed. "From most eligible to dead bachelor in four years. Maybe they wanted Gasquet to eliminate him because his business got good PR."

"At first, everyone said he'd died from an overdose," Francine said. "With his history of DUIs and drugs, no one was surprised. But the autopsy later found that he'd mixed different types of prescription flu medication, which didn't mix well. He passed out in the bathtub and drowned. It was huge news and quite sad."

Manny picked up his phone. "Holy Mary, this is a mess. Let's see if we can find any more books from these people."

For the next forty minutes we listened in silence to Manny's side of a few conversations. I sat next to Colin, unable to return to my viewing room without knowing the outcome of these calls. It was not a prudent use of my time, but I sat unmoving, learning about each case by listening to and watching Manny.

He was unable to speak to family members or work colleagues of three of the seven names Francine had uncovered. Of the other four, Manny spoke to close family members after numerous calls and an impressive display of diplomatic skill. When Manny put his smartphone on his desk after the last conversation, he pressed both fists hard against his eyes.

"Holy fucking hell."

During the conversations with the victims' families, I had seen the emotional toll it had taken on Manny. Even over the phone, someone else's grief had the power to affect us. Empathy and sympathy were human traits, needed by most people to cope with difficult situations. There was nothing as comforting as a friend willing to listen, or even better, someone who was able to understand what you were going through because of their own personal experience.

I'd known Manny for two years and considered myself to have an in-depth insight into his psyche. Yet I didn't know if the empathy he'd shown the families had been from a traumatic personal experience or from his professional training.

The familiar obsession about my lack of friendship skills threatened to pull my attention away from Manny's discoveries. I forced my mind back on topic. "We found three more books."

"Give me a minute." Manny phoned Dom, giving him the three addresses for the HMR team to collect those books. The fourth family member had given all her brother's belongings to charity and could not recall any antique book being amongst his things. I was pleased when Manny remembered to remind Dom to send us photos of each book as soon as possible. He ended the call with a heavy sigh and looked at me. "What do you think about this, Doc?"

"Those books were made to very specific orders." Even listening to only one side of the conversation, it was easy to come to that conclusion. "Tell us more about each book."

"Martin Delisle loved D.H. Lawrence's poetry. He got the book as a gift. Of course, his mother has no idea who gave him that book, only that he loved it. Apparently, he read from it every night. She said she didn't have the strength to look at it, so she'd put it in a box and has not taken it out since. Rainier Lahage's book is an illustrated compilation of jokes. His wife said he loved 'Yo Mama' jokes. Someone had made a book filled with them and beautifully illustrated them. He used to bring the book out all the time to read from it."

I leaned towards Colin. "Do I need to know what 'Yo Mama' jokes are?"

Colin smiled. "No, love. You don't need to know."

"But you should, Jen-girl. Some of them are the best. Like, 'Yo momma is so fat, when she sat on Wal-Mart, she lowered the prices.'"

Everyone laughed, but I looked at Vinnie in horror. "That is impossibly unkind. And not funny."

"Aw, Jen-girl. I think it's funny." He tilted his head. "You know, I've never heard you tell a joke. Ever."

Non-neurotypical people seldom found comedy humorous. In that aspect I was no exception. A few times we'd watched a comedy during one of Francine's movie nights. Nikki had laughed until tears streaked down her cheeks, joined by everyone else. As hard as I'd tried, I could never find the same humour, the same enjoyment in those ridiculous situations.

"Yeah, girlfriend. Do you even know jokes?" Francine's question was sincere.

"Yes, I do." My sense of humour was not non-existent. I'd read a few jokes that had made me laugh. I thought of my favourite joke and cleared my throat. "An infinite number of mathematicians walk into a bar. The first orders a beer, the second orders half a beer, the third orders a quarter of a beer and so on. After the seventh order, the bartender pours two beers and says, 'You people need to know your limits.'"

There was a stunned silence in the team room for a few seconds, then Vinnie cleared his throat. "Um. Yeah. Well."

"Sorry, honey." Francine's laugh was without ridicule. "That's so not funny. At all. But don't worry. I'll teach you a few jokes."

"No. Doc, don't let that Delilah teach you jokes."

Francine pressed both palms against her sternum in mock surprise. "Don't you think my jokes are funny? No, wait, you do! You even blushed a little when I told you that fabulous joke about the ceiling—"

"Can we please stay on topic?" I enunciated each word slowly. "What about the third book?"

"The same, Doc. Apparently Andrien Crevier loved writing haikus. His book is a notebook, each page laid out perfectly for a haiku."

"A hai-what? Is it some kind of recipe?" Vinnie frowned when Colin and I stared at him. "What?"

"A haiku is a very short form of Japanese poetry. There are four books with haikus on the bookshelves in my apartment—"

"Our apartment," Colin mumbled.

"—that you should've seen by now."

"Um. I don't really spend a lot of time reading your books, Jen-girl. I prefer some kickass action to some book about contemplating my navel."

I tried. I knew Vinnie's tactics and therefore tried even harder, but I couldn't. "None of my books are about the contemplation of one's navel."

Vinnie's smile was beautiful. "I know. I just wanted you to tell me again."

Again we had strayed from the topic. I turned to Manny. "If these books have been created with each target in mind, it only confirms Gasquet's involvement. Father Sidney's death I can include, but not Father Clément. As far as I could determine there was nothing connecting the Strasbourg Cathedral and Father Nate to Gasquet or any of his clients."

"Yes." There was no more teasing on Francine's face. "What about the six dead priests I found yesterday?"

"Hellfire. Of course." Manny's eyebrows lifted. "Yeah, there must be some kind of connection. Supermodel, send me the addresses of those churches as well. I'll get Dom and his team to go around there and collect any books they can find."

"They don't…"

"They will, Doc." Manny interrupted me. He knew me well. "They will know what to look for because you and Frey are going to give me a very precise description of those books. There is no way that any of us are going on our own to churches anymore."

Francine inhaled, then exhaled and shook her head, her smile wide. "Nah. It's too easy."

I didn't know what she was referring to, but didn't want another distraction. "Remind the HMR team to send us photos of every page in relevant books they find."

Manny's phone rang, another interruption. I should have been used to the lack of focus by now, but I still found every deviation hugely irksome. Manny scowled at the screen before answering. He grunted a reply and I got up to leave. I didn't want to listen to another one-sided conversation. Manny shook his head sharply and pointed at my chair. I sat back down, not pleased, but curious.

The four-minute conversation was truly one-sided. Manny's concerned expression intensified and he mumbled a few monosyllabic answers. Whatever news he was receiving was not positive. I hoped it would help us solve the case. Manny ended the call with a promise to confirm clearance and then to keep the person updated.

"Well, hell." Manny put his phone down. "That was the ECDC."

"The European Centre for Disease Prevention and Control?" Francine's eyes were wide.

"Yes. It was the head of the whole bloody place. They're joining in. The head is personally coming to oversee Dom's team while they're dealing with this."

"What else did she say?" I asked.

"How did you know it was a she? Oh, never mind. Doctor Eduard said that she was alerted to the situation when the third book was given to the lab this morning. She requested to be copied in, but I first need to check with the president about this."

Working directly for the president of France kept Manny in close contact with the leader. My contact was more frequently with the first lady. Manny and the president spoke weekly.

My thoughts returned to the question bothering me the most. "It's clear that Gasquet is not responsible for creating the books. Also it's highly improbable that he's been killing the priests. We need to find the person working for or with him. We need to find the connection between them."

"And why are they working together?" Francine asked.

"I don't know if they've been working together for long." I thought back on the information we had. "The priests who died unexpectedly go back as far as nine years. The deaths of the competition of Gasquet's clients only go back as far as eighteen months."

"I only looked with those parameters in place," Francine said. "Maybe both go back much farther. I'll get on it."

"And send me the priests' church addresses, supermodel."

Francine lifted one eyebrow. "Already done. I'm not just a pretty face, handsome."

"Hmph."

I got up. "I'm going to look through the photos of the books."

"Hopefully, you'll get more than Frey did. Sometimes I wonder why the thief is even here."

"To keep your blood pressure elevated, Millard." Colin also got up. "It's my life's only purpose, my dream come true."

From experience I knew that their sarcasm, insults and odd arguments were without malice. Sometimes I tried to make sense of it. Not today. I'd spent time on the companies, on Gasquet and on the priests. Now I needed to analyse the books. The key to Nikki's illness might be hidden in there.

Chapter ELEVEN

I stared at the photographed pages on the ten monitors in front of me. Dom's team had sent photos of the book of hours Dom had taken from the Strasbourg Cathedral. Including Nikki's notebook, I had photos of four books. I had looked through the photos of each book twice. A few illustrations had caught my attention and those were now displayed. Throughout the two-hour process, Colin had been sitting quietly next to me.

I shifted to tuck my feet under me. Keeping my eyes open, I mentally played one of Mozart's many minuets. After three lines of the harmonious composition, I rearranged the order of the photos. Nikki's notebook and the book of hours sent to Phillip were the newest. I put two pages from Nikki's book and three from Phillip's book on the first five monitors.

Father Clément from the Strasbourg Cathedral had received his book of hours six years ago, making it the oldest of the four books. Three pages from that book went to the far right monitors and two pages from Father Sidney's book next to it. Father Sidney had died eight months ago.

"Can you determine exactly when each book was made?" I asked Colin.

"You want the date the forger sat down and painted the illustrations?"

"Yes. Can you do it?"

"I can't. Forensic scientists might be able to analyse the paper, paints and ink of the books to determine the age, but that would be an approximate."

I nodded and continued looking at the illustrations on the pages. They were of a similar theme. Some pages had vines, some had animals, some flowers. On the monitors were only illustrations with people on them.

"What do you see, Jenny?"

I shook my head. "No, tell me first what you see."

"Expert illustrations in line with the Gothic era." He didn't hesitate. "There are elements of Pucelle as well as some of the earlier illuminators, but none of the illustrations are copies. This artist developed his own style. You see that headdress the woman on the third monitor at the bottom is wearing? It's in most of the illustrations with women. When I inspected Phillip's book of hours earlier on, I noticed it. It made me wonder and I checked all the major Gothic illustrators. None of them had that specific headdress in any of their works. It's unique to this artist."

I made a mental note of it. "Do you think the headdress has any significance?"

"Hmm. I can't see it having any helpful significance."

"What else do you see?" I was hoping for a specific answer, but didn't want to influence Colin's observations.

"You've arranged these pictures in chronological order and the ones with people in it." He tilted his head. "The newer illustrations show an increased level of skill. Six years is a long time if the artist has been prolific. The newer illustrations are more detailed, but…"

"But what?" I asked when he didn't continue.

"They display more aggression. It's not the colours. Those are the same."

"It's in the people's nonverbal cues." I zoomed in on one of the pages of Phillip's book. "See how the king's elbows are pointing away from his body, the front of his arms visible? It's in direct contrast to this one."

I zoomed in on a page from Father Clément's book. A young man was herding sheep, his arms tucked tightly against his body. It was a sign of submission, in extreme situations, an indicator of fear.

"Interesting. Do you think this means the artist is becoming angrier?"

"Possibly. The artist stayed true to the style, the colours, but these are the changes I've seen. It might help us understand the artist, but it's not going to help us find this person." I noted down the pages on the monitors before replacing them with the last pages of the four books. "Do you know if Francine has been able to decrypt this?"

"Let's ask." Colin phoned Francine. The conversation lasted less than a minute. "Her computers are still working on it, but she's more concerned with the priests at the moment."

"She's strongly affected by this because of her parents."

"Yeah, this is a hard one." Colin was interrupted by his phone. He looked at the screen and nodded. "Have to take this."

I was familiar with his shuttered expression accompanied by his neutral tone of voice. I nodded and watched him leave my room. He was going to one of the conference rooms where he could lock the door and speak in complete secrecy. He'd told me once that these calls were from the President of

Interpol. Colin's work for this and other agencies was highly secretive. I respected the need for confidentiality and never insisted on more information.

I turned back to the monitors and located four pages that had caught my attention for different reasons. Once I had them on the centre monitors, I locked my gaze on them and flooded my mind with Mozart's Horn Concerto No. 3 in E-Flat Major. I was almost at the end of the second page when I lowered my feet to the floor and stared at the illustrations in admiration. This artist was much better than even Colin had thought.

"What's up, love?" Colin was sitting next to me again, but he was working on his own computer. I had not heard him come back.

I didn't answer him. I didn't want to lose the pattern now so clearly visible to me. The four pages I had chosen didn't have the same theme. Some showed animals, some people and others just a nature scene. A commonality they did share was a night sky. I zoomed in on those parts of the illustrations. Still I wasn't satisfied. Using a favoured software programme, I cropped out those specific sections until only stars filled the monitors. Colin got up, left the room for a few seconds and returned with Manny and Francine.

"Whatcha got, girlfriend?" Francine sat down in Colin's chair. "Starry skies?"

"No." How could she not see it? "Look."

It took only three seconds.

"Oh, my God! Oh! Wait!" Francine jumped up, ran to the team room and returned with her tablet. "The security on this baby will protect us from whatever these might throw at us. Whoever said tablets are not secure has not yet met mine."

"Doc." Manny's voice was low, a sign of irritation. "What are these dots? Why do we need security?"

"The dots are QR codes." Francine sat down, aimed her tablet at the monitor with the photos from the book of hours sent to Phillip and took a photo. "I can't believe it. This is too cool."

"What the bleeding hell is a QR code?"

Colin's head was tilted, his eyes narrowed. "How did you see it?"

"People!" Manny's voice boomed through my room.

"A QR code is short for Quick Response Code," Francine said absently. She swiped on her tablet, frowning. "It's kinda like a barcode, but it's usually dots and not lines. Huh."

"Where did it take you?" I asked.

"Here." She tapped on her tablet, connected it to my system and filled the first monitor with a webpage. It was a simple dark green background with only one image. An elongated figure of a soldier dressed in mediaeval battle gear stood in the centre of the screen. There was nothing identifiable on his shield, his outfit or even his sword.

"Someone better start explaining to me what we are looking at." Manny scowled at the monitor. "And don't bloody tell me it's a soldier."

"A QR code has all these square dots or black modules arranged in a square grid with a white background. It usually contains information about a product or service, but sometimes it will open a website." Francine pointed at the first monitor. "This code took us to this website."

"So each code will take us to a different site?" Manny asked.

"Let's see." Francine aimed her tablet at the image from Nikki's notebook and took a photo of it. Soon we were looking at another website page. As the first one, it had a solid background, this one blue. The soldier on this page was just as fierce-looking as in the first. That and the Gothic style were the only similarities they shared. Their clothes and weapons were different in every way. Francine took photos of the QR codes from the churches' books of hours and those webpages opened up on the monitors.

"They're different." I was sure there was significance in this. "The QR codes from Phillip's book and Nikki's notebook lead to images with a simple background and the soldier."

"But look at these amazing illustrations." Colin didn't look away from the monitors with the last two websites. "It's outstanding work."

Each monitor displayed an illustration complex in its design and colours. They shared similarities though. Both had a border in the corner created from an intricately twisted vine. In Father Clément's book, the border was in the left-hand corner, in Father Sidney's book the vine border was in the right-hand corner. Next to both vines were a person and a small animal at their feet. The backgrounds were pastoral scenes, but unique in each illustration.

I would need a lot of time to study these works of art. I could not imagine the artist putting these codes, these messages in books he or she'd illustrated and not leaving a message on the websites the codes led to.

"We only have four books to compare, but this divides the books from the churches from Phillip's book and Nikki's notebook. Right, Doc?"

"As soon as we have more books, more data to compare, I would be more comfortable concurring, but this would appear to be the case." This might also explain the contradictions I'd noticed in this case.

"Would you concur"—Manny emphasised the word and I didn't understand why he was sarcastic—"that Gasquet is the one using the non-church books and someone else the church books?"

"Not at all." I frowned. "That is a gross assumption with many flaws in the reasoning. The books were all created by the same artist, which means we cannot separate them. So far the only real proof of division we have are these websites."

"What can you tell us about the websites, supermodel?"

Francine was tapping and swiping on her tablet. "Not much. There's only one page on each site. The sites can have unlimited pages, but I've only found one."

"All four websites?" Colin asked.

"I'm fast, but not that fast. Give me a minute." She tapped and swiped for more than a minute while we silently observed. Eventually, she sat back in her chair. "Nope. I'll double-check with my other computer, but all four sites have only one page—the page we are looking at."

"When were these pages created? Can you tell?" I asked.

She lifted her index finger and again worked on her tablet for a short while. "Okay, Nikki's site was created two months ago. The same as Phillip's site. It must have taken him a whole five minutes to get these sites up and running."

"How do you know he's a man?" This might help us find the artist.

"Oh." Francine looked up. "I don't know this. I suppose I just assumed that he's a man. He could be a she."

"What about the other two sites?" Colin asked. "When were they created?"

"Let's see. Father Clément's site was created six years ago and Father Sidney's site eight months ago."

"Do you have more specific dates?" An idea was forming in my mind and I needed more information.

"I have the exact hour." Francine tilted her tablet for me to see the dates and times. I grabbed my notebook and wrote down each date. Then I sighed. "I need more data. I need the photos of the other books."

Manny took his phone from his jacket pocket and phoned someone while looking at me. His eyes narrowed slightly before he spoke. "Dom, how many books do you have now? Uh-huh. Yes. Photos?"

The call lasted another minute, but I wasn't able to glean any information from Manny's side of the conversation. He ended the call and pointed at the monitors. "Dom said his team already sent another book's photos. They've been able to get all three of the books from the competitors. So far they got another two books from churches and will send us photos as soon as possible. They first have to secure the books before they take the photos. Dom said he can promise us the photos early tomorrow morning."

I wasn't pleased with this, but accepted the care Dom and his team had to take with each book. I rearranged the displays on the monitors. From left to right, I placed Father Clément's QR code illustration next to the website it led to, then Father Sydney's, followed by Nikki's. I leaned back and focussed on the illustrations and websites from the two priests' books of hours. "What do you see?"

"Who are you asking, love?"

I looked at Colin. "You."

His lips twitched with a smile. "Okay. Let me see. Firstly, I'll state the obvious. The webpages for the churches have much more beautiful and colourful illustrations than those two soldiers on Nikki and Phillip's sites. Secondly, the illustrations are definitely by the same artist. The woman in Father Clément's site has a headdress like in the books. Definitely his work."

"You don't know he's a man."

"Or a woman." Colin shrugged. "I'll just use he and him to make it easier for now."

I wanted to argue, but nodded tightly. Colin winked at me and took his time to study each illustration.

"Seriously, Doc. I don't see anything spectacular in these paintings." Manny's brow was furrowed in concentration, his mouth pulled in a squint. "It just looks twirly and pointy to me."

"That's why she didn't ask you, handsome." Francine's whisper was loud enough to be heard in the team room.

"The mood." Colin nodded his head as if agreeing with himself. "In the illustrations of Father Clément's book of hours that we assume is six years old, the mood in the illustrations is fearful. Angry, but fearful. The same with the illustrations in Father Sydney's books of hours. In Nikki's notebook and Phillip's book of hours, the illustrations are much more confident and aggressive. But the corresponding websites? The illustrations on these two priests' websites are happy."

"Look at the body language of the woman." I pointed to the illustration from Father Clément's website. "Her shoulders are back, her head tilted back, her smile far more than polite happiness. She's celebrating."

"I see the same in Father Sydney's illustration," Manny said. "That kid looks like he's just won a prize. What do you make of this, Doc?"

"I need more data."

"Doc." Manny sighed. "Do we really have to do this dance every time? Please just humour me and speculate."

"No. I will analyse the photos we'll receive tomorrow and then I'll give you a more informed opinion."

"Then I'll speculate." Colin's smile was playful. "The difference between the mood of the books and the mood of the websites tell me that the artist was angry when he painted the books. Maybe angry with the people he was targeting with his books or angry about something else. But he was definitely happy when he created the illustrations for the websites. Since these websites went up around the time of the priests' deaths, I think he was happy the priests died and this was his victory march."

"But what about Phillip and Nikki's books and websites?" Francine asked. "I don't see mood changes there."

She was right. I pointed at Nikki's QR code illustration. "This and its website soldier exhibit similar levels of aggression. There is no significant different in emotion portrayed here or with Phillip's book and site."

"Doc?" Manny lowered his chin and stared at me. "Speculate."

"Pure hypothesis?"

"Whatever works for you."

"The artist experienced annoyance, anger or a similar emotion while painting the non-church illustrations."

Manny straightened. "So his real beef is with the church?"

"I don't—"

"Millard means his real problem is with the church, love."

"Oh. Well, that is an assumption I'm not willing to make."

Colin took my hand. "When we get Dom's photos tomorrow, you can work on turning your hypothesis into something more concrete."

"Is this necessary?" Phillip stood in the open doorway leading to the team room. "Do you need to work through each night and each weekend?"

"We don't work each night and each weekend." I was happy to see him. Phillip often brought a voice of reason to our team meetings.

"When was the last time you slept, Genevieve?" There was no censure in his expression, only deep concern.

I calculated. "Thirty-eight hours ago."

Phillip clenched his teeth and closed his eyes for a second. When he opened his eyes, he looked at Manny. "Do you need to work now? Can this wait until tomorrow morning?"

"It can wait. We'll get those photos then."

"There's a lot we can do until then." There were still so many other aspects that needed our attention.

"Or you can go visit Nikki, then go home, have dinner and sleep. You know that you'll function much better after time away from the office and a good night's rest."

It wasn't his rational arguments about work that convinced me. "Yes. We'll visit Nikki."

"Then we'll go home." Colin stood behind my chair and rested his hands on my shoulders. "I agree with Phillip, love. All of us need to get some rest."

It was another thirty minutes before we left the office. Once I'd acknowledged my need to rest, exhaustion overwhelmed me. My muscles felt heavy, my eyelids heavier. The order of priority was a visit to Nikki, getting an update from her doctors, dinner at home, a hot bath and sleep.

Chapter TWELVE

The next morning, I was disproportionately delighted to open my email and find the photos of eight more books in my inbox. It would focus my mind on something neutral.

It had not been an easy night. Visiting Nikki had done nothing to appease my mind. Her health was declining even though she pretended to feel better. Paul and his team were still no closer to a diagnosis. This had heightened my concern and I'd refused all attempts to get to me to leave Nikki's bedside.

Only when Colin had shown true anger had I given in and returned home. The fear that exhibited itself as anger was the same I'd seen in Manny, Vinnie, Francine and even Phillip. It was a fear that might have given me another sleepless night had I not been as exhausted.

When I'd woken up at four o'clock, Vinnie was already in the kitchen making coffee. He'd not slept much either. Colin had joined us half an hour later and we'd sat in silence for ten minutes until we'd decided it best to get ready and come into the office. It was still dark outside, the office silent. Vinnie had left to find a bakery who had fresh croissants and pastries at this hour.

Colin came into the viewing room with two steaming mugs in his hands. "Fresh coffee."

"Thank you." I took the mug he offered and inhaled the aroma. "Dom's team sent the books."

"Great." He sat down and put his mug on my desk, using the coaster I insisted he used. "Love, are you okay?"

I pulled my shoulders back, not looking at him. "We need to analyse these pages."

Colin took the coffee mug from my stiff hands, put it on the table and turned me to face him. "You haven't said anything about Nikki since we left the hospital last night."

I stared at him and didn't respond. There were no words to accurately describe the pain I experienced in my chest. Rationally, I knew these were emotions—messengers, telling me something was amiss in my psyche. Yet it felt like a physical pain. It felt like my sternum was being crushed by a vice, pushing down on my heart. I resisted the urge to rock and keen.

"Love?"

I shook my head. "I can't. I just can't. I will… break."

He blinked slowly and his brow lowered, intensifying the concern that had not left his face since Nikki went into the hospital. He nodded and turned to the ten monitors against the wall. "Let's get those pages up and see what we can find. What do you have?"

"Eight new books. The three from the deceased competitors and five books of hours Dom's team were able to locate in the churches."

"But didn't Francine say there were nine more churches?"

"She did, but—"

"Dom's team wasn't able to get the belongings of all those priests." Francine walked into my viewing room. She was wearing tight black jeans tucked into knee-high red boots and a red mohair sweater. Her hair and makeup were perfect, but didn't hide the signs that she'd spent another evening working and not sleeping. "Some of them died a few years ago, their belongings given back to their family or donated to charity. This was all the guys could find."

"Been here all night?" Colin asked.

"Most of it." She pulled the third chair in my room closer and sat down on my other side. "Let me show you what I've found."

She lifted an eyebrow and smiled when I leaned back. Moving my laptop from its carefully aligned place on my desk, she changed windows and soon had all ten monitors filled with different pages. "It's not important now which page comes from which book, but I thought you might find this interesting."

I found it within five seconds. "All of them have it?"

"Yes. I haven't looked at all the pages in all the books, but I've found these and was going to look for more when I saw you guys."

I looked away from the monitors. "How did you see us?"

"Surveillance cameras. This whole place is rigged and I see it all in my basement."

"Aha, I see it." Colin pointed at the bottom left monitor, turning my attention back to the case and not the fact that I'd carried no knowledge of Francine's security cameras. "All of these illustrations have a ring in them."

"The same ring." Francine zoomed in on one of the illustrations. This was a female figure, her left hand resting on her right shoulder. The fine gold band with one small sapphire was subtle, but clearly visible. "It doesn't matter whether it is a male or female figure. They are all wearing the same ring."

"Did you find an insignia, a seal or something to identify it?"

"Nope. On some of the figures, the rings are on their pinkies, on others their ring finger or even index finger. I've looked for inscriptions, but it's just a simple ring. I've only looked at seven of the twelve books, so maybe I'll find something in the others."

"I doubt it," I said. "If the artist was consistent in painting the ring in every book, he or she would be consistent with an insignia or some other symbol."

"I'll look in any case."

I nodded once. It wouldn't be prudent to overlook details. "Have you found any more QR codes?"

She shook her head slowly. "I tried, girlfriend. I suppose I just don't have your eye. But it was looking for the QR codes that helped me find these rings."

"What rings?" Manny walked into the room, looking as rumpled as when I'd first met him. He was wearing clothes from his new wardrobe Francine had helped him purchase over the last few months, but they were wrinkled as if he'd slept in them. Even his coat was wrinkled. The concern and anger causing deep lines all over his face brought my mind back to the reason I hadn't slept much.

Francine briefed Manny on her findings and he grunted. "Another bloody cute clue. Doc?"

"I don't know the meaning of it. We need to look at it in the context of the books, the victims, the timeline, the websites as well as the history of this era."

"You and Frey can cover those fields. You two can also find the other rings. Supermodel, I want you to find a link between these churches or between the priests or between the churches, priests and Gasquet. There has to be something that connects them."

"I've already looked." Francine's shoulders drooped and she sighed. Manny didn't answer her, he merely stared at her, his eyebrows lifted. After almost a minute, Francine pulled her shoulders back, her lips thinning with determination. "I'll look again. I *will* find the connection."

"That's my girl." A flash of embarrassment passed over Manny's face. He shook his head and I knew the topic would be changed. "Have you heard anything from the lab?"

I frowned. "I thought you were in contact with them, with the head of the ECDC."

"Yeah, that's what they want me to think."

"But?" Colin asked.

"I can't put my finger on it. I think they're not giving me all the information. And for the life of me, I can't imagine why they would want to hide anything from me."

"A wider conspiracy?" It was a sign of Francine's state of mind when she didn't sound delighted at this prospect. "Could someone involved in this case higher up want to withhold information from us?"

I thought about all the different elements in this case, all the people involved. "It is very unlikely. I'm not saying it's impossible, just highly improbable."

"I agree with Doc. Don't jump to any conclusions. Just keep an open mind while looking for links."

"Don't preach to me about being open-minded, Mister I'm-never-wearing-cartoon-socks." Francine rolled her eyes. "You might be interested to know that I've gone through all Gasquet's clients again using the discoveries we have and didn't find any more assassinated competitors. I think my search was quite thorough, but someone might have slipped through the cracks."

"Did you find more priests?" Knowing Francine, I was convinced she had dedicated part of her sleepless night to this search.

"Yes. I widened the search to include neighbouring countries and found two similar deaths in Germany, four in Italy and three in Spain. My search is pretty well-defined now, so I'm going to widen it even more to include all European countries. At this rate, I'm sure we'll find more."

"Holy mother of all, why does anyone want to kill so many priests?" Manny rubbed his hand over his face. "Are they all paedophiles? Have they all stolen money from the Church?"

"Paedophilia was also the first thing that came to my mind, so I phoned my dad." Francine's relationship with her father was oddly accepting. She'd told me that she never told her father anything about her lifestyle and he never pressured her into being a Christian. From my observations, their love and acceptance were unique. "He looked into the names of the priests I'd found and only one of those ever had any accusations against them."

"Statistically, that would be accurate," I said. "According to the latest information, only four percent of priests have been accused of such behaviour. That makes this targeted group of priests an average group. If a higher percentage of them had been accused of paedophilia, it would be a reasonable assumption, but not now."

"You are all so frigging politically correct," Vinnie said from the door. "So I will be the one to say that someone shoulda cut those child-abusing motherfuckers' weenies off a long time ago. If Gasquet or this artist killer were targeting paedophiles, I would say good riddance. Those would be public service murders."

"On any day I would agree with you, criminal," Manny said. "The problem is when we start dealing out justice like this."

"It's not justice." Not according to the technical definition.

"Right, Doc. It's vigilante justice. As much as I would like to see bastards like this fry, we can't start taking the law into our own hands."

I inhaled to disagree. In many instances, our team had worked outside the normal and legal parameters. It had been explained to me on numerous occasions that we needed to hack into someone's system or illegally locate a phone in order to protect the public. Wasn't this taking the law into our own hands? I pushed Mozart's Oboe Quartet in F major into my mind. I didn't want to waste time with this argument.

When I reached the second line of the Adagio, I pulled my laptop back into its position and zoomed in on one of the illustrations Francine had put on the monitors. I pointed to it. "There. That's another QR code."

"Shit!" Francine leaned forward. "How on earth do you see that? I looked at these pages for hours and didn't see it."

Non-neurotypical people saw art, architecture, everything differently. Some might look at everything as a mathematical equation, others might only see the lines, others the colours. I saw patterns. Clouds that might look like the wind had whirled them around to me signified spiral fractals. In paintings, I saw the mathematics, the linear designs, the fractal patterns. That was what made it beautiful to me.

Francine went into the team room and returned with her tablet. She scanned the QR code and a few seconds later a website filled the screen. It was a beautiful illustration, similar to those we'd found yesterday for Father Clément and Father Sydney's books.

"Another victorious picture." Manny pushed his hands deep into his pockets. "Who the hell is doing this? Supermodel, what did you find out about the websites?"

"They're hosted in Bulgaria. Anyone can create a website and have it hosted there. I traced it as best I could, but these sites were set up in different countries, often in internet cafés or from using hotels' wi-fi connections."

"Which countries?" I asked.

"All European." She looked up as she thought about this. "I see where you're going with this. Give me a sec."

I didn't know how she could see what my intention was with my question, but I gave her time to work on her tablet. It also gave me time to organise my own thoughts.

"Got it! You're a genius, girlfriend." She winked at me. I'd learned that people proclaimed genius not as a statement of fact, but rather an expression of admiration. "Okay, each website was created from the country where the dead priest lived. These websites also went live within a week of the priest's death. The exceptions are the websites from the non-church books. Phillips's and Nikki's were created two months ago. Both are hosted in Bulgaria, but were registered from an IP address here in France."

"Where?" Manny pulled his smartphone from his coat pocket.

"One was from a coffee shop with wi-fi connection, the other a hotel in Lille."

"Useless. Anyone can connect there at any time." Manny's frown deepened when his phone started ringing in his hand. He glanced at the screen before swiping it. "I'm putting you on speakerphone."

"Oh. Okay. Um. Hello?" Dom sounded amused.

"Hi, Dom." Francine leaned towards the phone. "Thanks for sending those photos so quickly."

"Francine?" Dom's voice deepened. A sign of attraction. "Good morning, and it was my pleasure."

"What have you got, Dom?" Manny pulled the phone closer to him and glowered at Francine.

"We had a briefing and my guys said something that might help you. Two of the priests they spoke to said they remembered the dead priest receiving the book from a female member of their congregation."

"Female." I nodded. "This fits the profile."

"Are you sure she was part of their congregation?" Colin asked. "Or is it an assumption the priests made?"

"My guys think that it was an assumption. Especially since the two churches were over three hundred kilometres from each other."

"Do they remember anything about this woman?" Manny asked.

"My guys aren't trained interrogators, but they asked as many questions as they could. And no. The priests only remembered that it was a woman."

"Bloody hell. It would've helped if we knew whether she was young, old, white, black, anything." Manny pulled the phone even closer. "Dom. Why am I getting stonewalled by the ECDC?"

"Hold." There was a rustling and the sound of movement. A few seconds later, a door clicked shut. "Okay, this is a bit more private. You're talking about Doctor Eduard, right?"

"Yes," Manny said through his teeth. "What is she withholding?"

Dom's laugh sounded forced. "That woman is a prime bitch. She's most likely hogging all findings because she's trying to look good. God only knows how she got that position."

"I need to know the results from the tests on the books, Dom. Lives depend on it."

"Nikki's life depends on it," I said.

"I'll get that for you." Dom's tone was clipped. "This is such bullshit. She's been in this position for only four months and this is the second time she's done this."

Interdepartmental competition was not uncommon, but this sounded like it was a more complex situation. I was tempted to analyse it, but there were more pressing matters. I opened one of the books Dom had sent. I paged slowly through each photo and absently registered Francine and Manny leaving and Vinnie placing two fresh croissants in front of me.

I'd gone through half of the first book's photos when Colin insisted I had the croissants. I hated the interruption, but understood the necessity. It gave Colin time to isolate the QR code I'd found and send it to Francine. I'd also found another illustration with a young boy wearing the ring. Colin sent that page to Francine as well as to Manny.

It took us just over four hours to work through the eight books. I wanted to go through them again to make sure of my findings, but was confident that I'd located most of the rings and all of the QR codes. My increasing worry about Nikki had my concentration at its fullest. I wanted to hear her inappropriate loud singing while she was in the shower again. I wanted her to invade my personal space and tease me about it.

"Brunch, cowboys and cowgirls," Vinnie called from the team room. "A short break with some food."

"And a briefing." Manny appeared in the door. "Come on, you two. Let's take ten."

"Ten what?" I asked.

"A ten-minute break, Jenny." Colin got up. "It's a good idea. Stretch your legs a bit."

I felt very close to connecting all the different elements we'd uncovered and didn't want to interrupt my momentum. From experience I knew that short breaks often helped me come to those answers much quicker. With a final glance at the monitors, I followed Colin to the team room. The round table was laden with cold meats, breads, cheeses, fruits and salads.

Phillip was already seated at the table, talking to Manny about the case. He stopped and studied me from across the table. "How are you, Genevieve?"

I considered my answer. "Focussed."

"She'll be fine." Colin winked at me and waited for me to sit. "As soon as we have Nikki home."

"Okay, what do we have that we didn't have before?" Manny sipped his tea, his eyes closing in pleasure.

"Give me a moment." Francine took a bite from her buttered bread roll and picked up her tablet. The large screen against the wall flickered on. "This is one of the book of hours websites. Genevieve got a QR code from each book and we have websites for all of them."

"Still without trace?" Manny asked.

"Yup. They were all registered from IP addresses all over Europe, all of them hosted in Bulgaria. I cannot trace who owns the sites or which computers were used. One does not need the most complicated or technologically advanced skills to do this."

"Which means what, supermodel?"

"This person doesn't have to be a top IT expert."

"Show me the sites." I needed to see what they had in common. "Can you show them in chronological order? From the one created first to the most recent?"

Francine huffed. "Does a bear poop in the forest?"

"If the bear lives in the forest, yes." What an inane and irrelevant question. When my response elicited laughter, I knew it had been one of Francine's expressions. My lack of understanding had lightened the mood in the room. As usual.

Another website filled the screen. "This one is from a church, created eleven years ago."

"Eleven?" I had not expected such a timeframe. "Did you expand your time parameters?"

"After the first search, yes. Today I expanded the geographical parameters. This is the oldest." She handed me her tablet. "I've ordered the tabs in chronological order."

"Thank you." This was one of the benefits of allowing people to know me. Francine knew me well enough to understand that I would need to take my time looking at each website. Three years ago, I'd had no one anticipating my needs.

While I studied each site, the others speculated about the companies' involvement in this case. Francine spent at least five minutes speculating on the different ways Gasquet could be involved in the priests' deaths. Manny became annoyed and told her to eat and not talk hogwash. I hoped to remember to ask Colin about that expression, but was quite sure I wouldn't. Not with what I was seeing.

"Love?" Colin squeezed my forearm and I looked away from the screen. My plate was untouched. Everyone else had finished eating and was watching me.

"Helixes. There are rings and helixes."

"Jenny." The smile in Colin's voice reminded me to explain clearly.

I took three deep breaths and one by one showed the websites—from oldest to most recent. "Look at the people in these websites. Each one is standing next to a vine. Look at the twists of the vines."

It was quiet in the team room as I showed the twelve websites with illustrations.

I zoomed in on the last illustration. Still no one reacted. I uploaded the illustration to a design programme and carefully erased the leaves on the vines. When I was about twenty-five percent done, Colin gasped. "Shit. No way."

"What?" Manny leaned forward.

"It's a DNA double helix. Right, Jenny?"

"Yes. But that is all I know. My knowledge of DNA is far too limited to offer any opinion on what DNA this is. I am sure Dom's team in the laboratory would identify it."

"Are they all the same, Doc?"

"They look very similar, but each one has some uniqueness to it."

"And you saw this between all those leaves?" Vinnie's bottom jaw was slack. "You rock, Jen-girl."

"Doc, what the frigging hell does DNA have to do with all of this?"

"I don't know yet." This was fast becoming a fascinating riddle.

"What about the code in the back of the books? Have you figured it out yet?"

I sighed. They never listened to me. I spoke slowly. "I need the book that is the key to the cipher. If I had weeks of free time, I might be able to decrypt it, but I don't have that time."

Manny winced. "Sorry, Doc. We're asking you to figure everything out."

"No, you're not." I buttered a bread roll, suddenly hungry. "Everyone is helping. Francine was working on finding more priests. Hmm. Did you find more?"

"Sadly, yes. Widening the search has given us another seventeen names."

"Holy bleeding hell, supermodel!" Manny leaned forward. "Why didn't you say this earlier?"

"Because my computer search is not done. I can't believe someone is targeting priests."

"Have you found any common denominator?" Colin asked.

"Not between the churches, their finances, the priests or congregation members. There are some connections, but nothing that links all of them in one place or to one specific thing."

"All in Europe?" I asked.

"Yes. Eight of those new names are from France, the others from all over Europe."

In each case we investigated there was a point where I was overwhelmed with information with no discernible link between it all. A few months ago, Nikki had compared it to a puzzle and I'd liked the analogy. It felt like I was looking at a table filled with pieces of a puzzle. I didn't know where to start building the puzzle because I didn't have the final picture. I didn't have the context. All I had were countless individual pieces. It was most frustrating.

"What is the connection between the churches and the companies?" This was another question that troubled me.

"And where does Gasquet fit into this?" Vinnie asked. "Or an even better question, where the fuck is he?"

It would appear that I was not the only one frustrated at the influx of data that we had trouble joining.

"Sir?" Tim stood in the doorway. "There is a guest for you in the conference room."

"Who are you talking to?" Manny scowled at Tim.

"To you." Tim wasn't intimidated by Manny's expression. Vinnie had been the only one able to intimidate Tim and it had been pure physical intimidation. "A Monsieur Romain Proulx said you were expecting him."

Chapter THIRTEEN

I was not pleased when I followed Manny and Phillip into the conference room. Manny had neglected to tell me that he'd asked Phillip to set up a meeting with Romain Proulx, grandson of ZDP's founder. I preferred to have time to brace myself for meeting new people. Being caught unprepared like this put a lot of strain on my equilibrium. I only had the short distance between the team room and the conference room to recall all we'd learned about Romain, the fact that his investment company had had the least contact with Gasquet, yet had been one of Gasquet's most influential clients.

Standing next to the conference table was a tall, lanky man. He was studying the Turner painting on the far wall. Everything about his appearance communicated successful professional. His suit was of the highest quality and his slightly greying hair added to his appearance of experience and distinction.

A subset of salesmen were often referred to with great loathing. These individuals seemed to be trustworthy, putting their clients' interests first. They were dynamic, authoritative and well-versed in the psychology of sales. Yet they abused their knowledge and insight into their clients and frequently sold them products that were substandard or hugely overpriced.

Romain reminded me of one of those people. The difference between him and a lesser salesman was the product they sold and the price of the suits they wore. But the speculation, the calculation was embedded in his micro-expressions. This was not a man to be trusted.

"Romain, thank you so much for agreeing to meet us." Phillip extended his hand, his expression open and welcoming. But I could clearly see the social politeness he was employing. He had a certain tone of voice, smile and posture whenever he dealt with clients he was wary of.

"It sounded urgent." Romain shook Phillip's hand, but looked at Manny. "Is there some problem with my account?"

"I'm Manfred Millard." Manny also offered his hand. He was slouching, squinting intermittently to create an impression of being disinterested and absentminded. "Pleased to meet you."

"This is my colleague, Doctor Lenard." Phillip gestured towards me, but didn't encourage any closer introduction. "Please sit down, Romain. Would you like something to drink?"

Romain sat down slowly, his eyes narrowed. "Your assistant already offered to bring me coffee, thank you. What's going on?"

Tim came in with four cups on a tray—three coffees and one milky tea for Manny. No one spoke while he unloaded the tray. He glanced at the men, then at me before leaving, taking the tray with him.

"Well, Romain"—Manny sipped his tea and placed the cup back—"you are about to lose everything you've worked for. Ah, ah, ah. Wait for me to finish. If you give us enough helpful information, we will make sure the prosecutors know about your co-operation."

Romain's top lip curled. "Is this a joke? What is this, Phillip? Should I have brought my lawyer?"

"It would be better if Colonel Millard explains this to you. I'm merely here as an observer."

"Colonel Millard?" Romain took his phone from his jacket pocket. "Then I think I need to phone my lawyer."

"You're definitely going to need him in the future. Possibly a whole team. Right now, we are not arresting you, so you don't need a lawyer." Manny shrugged. "For now."

Romain pushed his coffee cup away and leaned onto the table. "What arrest? What are you talking about?"

I always found it fascinating to watch Manny work. He had a masterful sense of how to approach people in order to get the most information from them. He'd successfully taken away Romain's sense of superiority. Romain's shoulders were slightly elevated and to the front, his arms closer to his torso and he was constantly flexing the fingers on his right hand. Conversely, Manny had straightened in his chair, his chest puffed, his left elbow resting on the back of the chair next to him. His posture of confidence served to unnerve Romain even more.

"We're talking about how you established small shell companies to run an investment scam. The financial guys have all kinds of fancy terms for what you did. I will just call it committing a crime. In your case, a crime with... how much was it, Doc?"

"A hundred and ninety-three million euro."

Manny pointed his thumb at me. "Hear that? A hundred and ninety-three million euro."

The *masseter* muscles in Romain's jaw lost some of their strength, leaving his mouth slightly agape. "How... wha... who are you?"

"I am an Interpol agent, which means that any and all international connections, accounts and clients you have can easily be included in our little investigation." Manny smirked. "And this is why you're going to tell us what we need to know. Starting with Laurence Gasquet."

Romain's face lost even more colour. He closed his mouth, pressed his lips tightly together. His thought process was evident around his eyes and mouth. After a few seconds he nodded once. "What do you need to know?"

"How did you come to hire him as your security advisor?"

Romain closed his eyes and moved his jaw. On a heavy exhale, he looked at Manny. "The CEO of an elite construction company and I attend the same social functions. When his company recovered from two years of quarterly losses, I asked him about it. At first, he insisted it was careful strategy and goals. I called him on it."

"It takes a bullshitter to know a bullshitter," Manny said.

Romain's nostrils flared. "Look, I know I'm fucked. My business, my life is over. But I don't have to give you squat. An extra few years in prison won't make a difference now. It's my choice to tell you what I know, so I would appreciate some courtesy."

"You stopped qualifying for courtesy when you climbed in bed with a mass murderer."

Romain's head jerked back. "A what?"

"Tell us about your first meeting with Gasquet. How did you get in contact with him?"

"The construction guy gave my number to him. He phoned me and we set up a meeting at my home."

"Not your office?"

"At that point I didn't know the extent of Gasquet's services, but I knew that I didn't want anyone at the office to see me meeting him." Romain sighed. "I was right. The man was scary. Suave, but not in a positive way. Like he's smooching up to you to cut your throat."

I shuddered at the description. The profile I'd compiled of Gasquet supported that disturbing analogy.

"He wanted full access to my company's data. He wanted to see our client list, our financial information, everything. Naturally, I refused. Gasquet wasn't fazed by this. He left and a few hours later our system went down. Someone had breached our very secure computer software with minimal effort. Gasquet phoned me and said that this was just a taste of what he was capable of. He immediately restored our system, but used it as an example of what he could do to our competitors.

"It worked. I was interested. I met with him again and pretty much handed over my hundred-year-old family business. He had some amazing experts on his team. Within a week, he came back to me with a strategy that you obviously know about. The plan he presented to me was ingenious, too good to refuse. For the last five years, I thought we'd gotten away with it." Romain's laugh was without humour, bitter. "I got real comfortable. And then Gasquet saw his end six months ago. I've been waiting for this day since then."

The regret displayed on Romain's face was too controlled. Micro-expressions revealed his true emotions. His top lip lifting in contempt confirmed my initial impression of Romain being a calculating individual. He was attempting to present himself as remorseful. He wasn't.

His kind of personality would be planning a strategy while gaining our trust and sympathy. Phillip's nonverbal cues were still professional. Manny's bordered on arrogance. He made a point of appearing victorious.

"How did Gasquet find the right investors for you to approach?" Phillip asked.

Romain turned all his attention to Phillip. "I didn't know Gasquet was what you say—a murderer."

Phillip didn't respond.

Romain sighed heavily, slumping his shoulders. "Really, Phillip. I didn't know. Hector, the construction CEO, told me that Gasquet got rid of his competition and showed me the scandal that had destroyed that company. I only knew Gasquet to be somebody who gave me a questionable strategy that brought my company back from the brink of bankruptcy."

"How did he know who to target?" Phillip asked again.

"I don't know. He said he had a crack team that would use all the information from my company data to find the best way to manipulate the market. I left it at that. I suppose I didn't want to know."

"And look where it got you."

"Please." His contrition would have convinced me had I not been an expert in nonverbal communication. "Three hundred and seventy-two people work for ZDP. I was trying to save my company, save all those jobs. Some of those people have been working for the company longer than I have. They don't deserve this."

Manny studied Romain, then nodded slowly. "We'll try our best."

"I find it hard to believe that Zacharie's son would've resorted to such unethical action." Phillip had the correct amount of disapproval to make it seem authentic. Was no one in this room being truthful? "Your father built his business on trust, on respect and on truthfulness."

"My father?" Romain lost some of his pretence, his lips moving in a sneer. "That man didn't have an ethical bone in his body. Did you know that his first big client was Alvin Benett? Yes, *that* Alvin, the notorious mafia boss. Did you know that he also handled the finances of many other criminals? Of course, all of this was done in secret, because to everyone else, he was such a good, upstanding family man."

It was the intensity of the hatred in the last two words that caught my attention. What had Zacharie Proulx done that made his son hate him fifteen years after his death? People seldom understood the impact their behaviour and words had on their children. It was no true comfort, but at least I knew my parents' hurtful actions had always been out of self-interest, never with malicious intent. They had been—still were—too concerned with their own social standing to have any interest in the emotional state of anyone around them.

"I find that hard to believe." Phillip's head tilted to one side. "I met Zacharie at a few functions and he was highly respected among his peers."

Romain's laughter didn't reach his eyes. "Yeah. No one knew what went on behind the walls of the family mansion. To the world he was a stable family man, a leader in the community. At home he was an abusive prick. My mother never stood a chance against him. She was weak. Weak. As long as I can remember, she never stood up against him. By the time my sister was born, she left us to our father and the nannies he carefully chose. If she wasn't in a spa, she was involved in some charity organisation. Even that didn't make her happy."

I could relate to his childhood. My affluent, powerful parents had been shamed by my disorder. Money and positions of power and influence affected people in different ways. Sadly, a large percentage became terrified of losing the money and power they'd acquired and were willing to compromise their own values in order to maintain their standing in that exclusive group of people.

"At least my father approved of my gender," Romain continued. "My sister never heard the end of her weaker sex. She was always artistic and he scorned her nonstop. Our father had a fit when she quit her science or whatever studies to go into art. He always said, if you knew the bliss which resides in the taste of knowledge, and the evil and ugliness that lies in ignorance, how well you are advised to not complain of the pain and labour of learning."

I jerked. It felt almost physical, the connection my brain made. I knew that quotation had significance, but couldn't immediately place it. I didn't know whether it was the quotation itself or if it reminded me of something that was a key element in this case. What I did know was that I needed to be alone, allowing one of Mozart's complex compositions to flow through my mind and help the subconscious connection surface to my thinking brain.

Manny and Phillip continued to ask Romain Proulx questions, leading him to believe that they were accepting his answers as truth. I tried to pay attention, but my mind kept wandering back to the quotation.

"Sir?" Tim stood at the door, looking at Manny. "Daniel asked me to tell you he's here with his colleague."

Daniel pushed past Tim into the conference room, ignoring the young man's huff. A short man followed him into the room. I didn't like this distraction. I narrowed my eyes and studied the stranger. His suit, tie and shoes were elegant, but of lower quality than Phillip's tailored wardrobe. A lot of short men tried to make a larger impression by being aggressive or loud. This man was neither. He carried himself with quiet authority.

"Hi, everyone." Daniel looked at Romain, his smile almost gleeful in its insincerity. "I would like to introduce you to Detective Camille. He's from the Special Financial Crimes Unit. He'll be spending some quality time with you over the next... oh, I don't know, the next few months."

Romain blinked a few times, shrinking back into his chair. He swallowed and straightened. "I need to phone my lawyer."

"Maybe get that team we were talking about earlier." Manny stood up and shook hands with Detective Camille. "Manfred Millard. Pleased to meet you. You've been briefed?"

"On the basics, yes. I've got all the files from a Francine. She sent over a hundred and fifty documents implicating him." He nodded towards Romain. "Do you still need him, or can I take him from your hands?"

Manny looked at me and I looked back. After five seconds, he grunted. "Doc? Do you have any questions to ask Romain?"

"No." I would've asked them if I'd had any.

"Okay then. Camille, this thieving idiot is all yours. I'll get the footage of this interview to you as well." Manny glanced at one of the two cameras in the conference room. I wondered if Francine was watching us at the moment. If she were, she had already sent this to Detective Camille.

Three minutes later, only Manny, Phillip and I were in the conference room.

"What do you think about Romain's performance, Doc?"

"Your deception was successful enough for him to leave here thinking you believed everything he'd said."

The corner of Manny's mouth lifted briefly. "You got that, did you? That man was so full of shit, thinking we'd buy his sob story about his father."

"That was true." I'd seen the honesty in Romain's hatred for his father.

"Maybe. But his claim not to have known about Gasquet's methods was not. Right, Doc?"

"I don't know how much he knew, but he knows more than he said. His strongest lie was about his concern for the employees of ZDP."

"He doesn't care about his people," Phillip said. "I've heard many rumours about Romain's treatment of his workers. Apparently, he gets them to sign non-disclosure agreements after a huge payoff, so none of the rumours are ever substantiated."

"Hmm." Manny leaned back. "Get us some names, Phillip. We'll pass those on to Camille. Maybe he can get those people to talk and strengthen his case against Romain."

I didn't know why Detective Camille would need any more evidence, unless it was to try Romain for more crimes. The evidence Francine had sent him was more than sufficient to prove illegal activity.

Manny's phone rang and he took it from his jacket pocket. His eyebrows lifted when he looked at the screen and he answered immediately. "Tell me you've got something, Dom.

You're on speakerphone with Doctor Lenard and Mister Rousseau."

"It's malaria."

"What's malaria?" Manny asked.

"The lab has found an altered malaria parasite on the books. They're still doing tests, but they're saying each book's parasite is unique in some way."

I had so many questions, I didn't know which one to ask first. "Did Nikki's notebook also have a malaria parasite on it?"

A rustle of paper sounded over the phone. "Yes."

It felt as if a heavy weight lifted from my chest. If Nikki had malaria, the treatment was available and she'd get better. She would be home soon, singing and laughing.

"You said the parasite was on the books. Where?" Phillip asked.

"Everywhere." Dom cleared his throat. "Doctor Eduard told me about this. They've not been stonewalling, Manny. They just didn't believe what they found was for real."

Colin and Francine walked into the room. Colin sat down next to me and frowned.

"Nikki might have malaria," I told him before I leaned towards the phone. "What did they find that was so hard to believe?"

"The malaria on Nikki's notebook was…" Dom grunted. "I have no other way to say this. It was weaponised. The lab got a sample of Nikki's blood from the hospital and confirmed that the swabs they'd taken from the book contained not only the malaria parasite, but also Nikki's DNA. The parasite had been modified, using Nikki's DNA, to infect her and her only. Not only that, but malaria is never contracted through touch, never absorbed through the skin. As far as the lab has been able to determine, that malaria parasite found on Nikki's book had been designed especially for her and to be contracted by touching that book."

"Bleeding hell. Is that even possible?" Manny rubbed his face. "They can treat Nikki now, right?"

"Most definitely, yes. I've already contacted the hospital. We tested her blood sample and confirmed that she has malaria. The doctors will start her treatment immediately." There was a smile in Dom's voice. "If all goes well, she might be home in two days."

It all became too much for me. The explosive relief of a possible treatment for Nikki, the overwhelming concern I'd been trying to control over the last two days, the influx of data, as well as the quotation that Romain had recited. Darkness rushed towards me and for once I didn't fight it. I wanted that safety, that calm. I knew I was hiding, I was being a coward. I didn't care. I simply surrendered as the warmth of the blackness surrounded me.

Chapter FOURTEEN

It took two seconds to register my environment and remember I was in my bedroom. Last night, I'd come out of my shutdown three minutes after midnight and had realised I was in bed. I'd left Colin sleeping deeply and had gone through my nightly routine before I'd returned to bed.

I inhaled slowly, feeling rested for the first time in six days. Most often, I would come out of a shutdown exhausted. A few times, I felt invigorated because my mind had had time to reboot. But never had I felt as relaxed as I did at the moment. I turned and switched on the low light of my bedside lamp.

"You're awake." Colin opened his eyes and turned his head to look at me. "Come here."

Without giving me a chance to respond, he pulled me closer until I was flush against his side. It had taken me almost a year to enjoy what Colin referred to as 'morning cuddling'. I used to get out of bed the moment I'd woken up. Recently, we talked quietly or Colin entertained me with a dream he'd had before we would get ready for the day. I had come to enjoy the time resting my head on his chest, listening to his strong heartbeat.

"How did I get here?"

Colin kissed the top of my head. When I realised he wasn't going to answer me, I poked him. He chuckled. "I carried you."

"What do you mean you carried me?" I tried to lift my head, but he pushed it against his chest. I slapped my palm against his chest and pushed up to glare at him. "Why didn't you leave me?"

Colin sighed and kissed me on my nose. "Because it was getting late. Because Francine was talking crazy theories again. Because we were all tired. Because Millard was irritating the shit out of me. And because you allowed me to."

"Explain."

"Millard usually irritat—"

"Not about that. I want to know how I allowed you to carry me."

Again, he chuckled. "By seven o'clock, it didn't look like you were going to join us again soon, so I told you that I was going to carry you home. You didn't respond and I picked you up. I was quite prepared to be kung fu'ed or something, but you didn't react at all. It was quite the moment. We all stared at each other in shock for a few seconds before Vinnie offered to bring us home. Then I put you in bed."

I closed my eyes against the embarrassment. "Everyone saw this?"

"Only us." He wiggled his eyebrows. "Francine thought it was very romantic."

I fell back against his chest. "It's not romantic. It's... I don't know what it is."

I didn't know how I felt about this. On the one hand, it disturbed me that I'd had no control over what happened with me at that time. On the other hand, I wasn't upset by this because I trusted the people who'd taken control of the situation. Colin would never have done anything to harm me in any way.

"Hey." He rubbed my shoulder and kissed the top of my head again. "Should I not have done it?"

I thought about this. "No, you did the right thing. I don't like the loss of control—"

"I think you were in full control, love. I don't think you would've allowed anyone else to take you anywhere if you didn't want it."

"You don't know this. I don't know this. When I shut down, I'm not aware of anything around me. I don't know what my mind is doing at that time."

"It seemed like your mind was hard at work. You were rocking and counting things on your fingers."

I pushed myself up again, staring at his face. "Counting on my fingers?"

"Hm-mm. That was a first. Usually you keen, rock, tap with your fingers as if playing piano."

I wondered what I was counting. Was it related to the case? Had my subconscious worked out the key to the code in the books of hours? Or had I found the significance of the rings, the double helixes or maybe the quotation from a Gothic novel? Double helix. Gothic. This had to be it. I could feel the connection looming between my conscious and subconscious. My eyes widened. "I have to get to the office. Now. I have to go."

Colin released me and sat up when I hurried out of bed. "What is it, Jenny? What have you got?"

"I don't know yet. It's there." I tapped against my left temple. "It's so close. I just need to be in the office."

I rushed through my usual morning routine. Thirty minutes later, Colin joined me in the kitchen. "Are you leaving a note for Vinnie?"

"No." I looked at the glass in my hand. "I was drinking juice."

"Let's leave Vin a note. He'll wonder why there's no one at home when he wakes up in"—he looked at his watch—"another half an hour."

"I'm up." Vinnie walked into the kitchen, stopping to yawn and stretch. "What are y'all doing up and ready at frigging half past five in the frigging morning? The cows aren't even awake and ready to be milked yet. The damn rooster hasn't even crowed yet."

"I have to be in the office." I put the glass in the dishwasher and walked to the dining room table to collect my handbag from its usual place.

When Colin and I were in his SUV, I couldn't suppress my need to understand anymore. "What cows were Vinnie talking about? And where does he hear the rooster every morning?"

"In his cowboy dreams." Colin laughed when I made a frustrated sound. "He was just using his silly visual talk. He said he'll meet us at the office in an hour."

I turned on the radio and Colin fell silent. He once said he'd learned to interpret my choice of music while he was driving. If it was world music, I was open to conversation. If it was Mozart, he should not speak at all because I was thinking. I chose Mozart. The Clarinet Concerto in A Major filled the SUV interior all the way to the office. Once settled in my viewing room with the nine websites opened on my monitors, I was still playing the concerto mentally.

"Jenny?" Colin's gentle touch on my forearm brought me out of my thoughts. I glanced at the clock on my computer. Thirty minutes had passed. "Maybe you should talk this through with me."

"I can't access it." I pressed the tips of my fingers against my temples. "It's in here. The connection. That one element that links the deaths of the priests, Nikki's malaria, the double helixes on the websites, the Gothic… theme…" My voice tapered off when at last the connection reached my consciousness.

I waved impatiently towards Colin when he asked me to finish my thought. I moved closer to my desk and started working on the computer. I Googled the churches where the HMR teams had recovered the books of hours and looked for the best photo of each church. So far we had twelve churches in addition to the Strasbourg Cathedral and Father Sidney's church. I split the last two monitors to display four churches and sat back.

"Oh, my God, Jenny." Colin's eyes were wide, his hand over his mouth. "Why didn't I see this earlier? It's so obvious."

"What's obvious?" Manny walked into my room, followed by Vinnie and the smell of coffee. "What's with all the churches?"

"They're all Gothic structures." Colin pointed at the screens. "See their pointed arches, the rose windows? Gothic. All of them, without exception."

I didn't comment on Colin repeating himself. People tended to do this as they processed information. He continued to describe more complexities of the architecture of that era, but I was not paying full attention. My mind was racing with the implications of this new discovery. I refined my searches for each church to find more about their histories.

"But what is the meaning of all these churches being built around the same period?" Manny asked. "I get that the books of hours hail from that era and now the churches as well, but how does that help us find Gasquet? How does it help us find the person making these books, spreading malaria?"

I didn't want to interrupt my train of thought to answer Manny. I was slowly making progress and opened another window.

"Wait, Jenny." Colin stopped in the middle of describing the flying buttresses. "Go back to the previous page."

I did as he asked, knowing that he'd noticed the connection I was trying to confirm.

"What are you looking at now?" Manny tilted his head. "Speak to me, people."

"This is why I don't want you in the same room when I'm working. You're disruptive and don't allow me to follow through on my searches." I lifted my hand in a universal gesture to stop someone. "Wait until I'm ready to tell you what I have."

Manny grunted a few times, but took a step back. It took me another twenty minutes to have the new information on the monitors. All the many bits of information started coming together. I loved these moments in an investigation when separate elements connected, making sense. It was a great sense of satisfaction.

Colin sat back in his chair, shaking his head. "Didn't see that one coming."

"Doc." Manny spoke through his teeth, his voice low.

I twisted in my seat and saw Francine leaning against one of my antique-looking cabinets. She was working on her tablet, but glanced up and smiled at me. "Hey, girlfriend."

"Hey." I cleared my throat and waved at the monitors. "I couldn't find detailed history on each church, but what I have so far are three churches that have been renovated."

"This one"—Colin pointed to the second monitor on top—"was renovated during spring four years ago. Father

Ken died that summer. The church in this centre monitor was renovated in spring seven years ago. Father Claude died a week after the renovations were finished. This one here was renovated in autumn last year. Father Roul died January this year."

"Holy hell." Manny's eyes widened, his *zygomaticus* muscles lifting the corners of his mouth. His pleased expression was evidence that he was coming to some conclusions. He straightened. "Romain Proulx's sister is some artist renovator person, isn't she? She's the one who renovated the Strasbourg Cathedral. That little witch is behind all of this."

"This is not irrefutable proof that Simone Simon is the person who made or sent the books."

"Could she have made those books? Frey?"

"Absolutely, yes. She might be a leading expert in stained-glass renovation, but she's also one of the best artists to work on art from that era. That means she can easily create something that looks like it comes from that era. She would have all the scientific knowledge to recreate the kind of paper used, the kind of binding for the books, everything. She is the perfect suspect."

"Well." Francine stepped forward, glaring at Manny. She raised one eyebrow and her posture was arrogant. "If you had listened to me last night and not dismissed me as—what did you call me?—mad as a March hare, you would have a lot more knowledge about Simone right now."

Manny sighed heavily. "What do you have, supermodel?"

"Biohacking."

"For the love of all that is pure and holy. Not that again." Manny pushed his hands deep into his trouser pockets and leaned back.

"What is biohacking?" Was this Francine's crazy theory Colin had referred to earlier?

"Since you are my best friend and the only true rational one here, I'll tell you." She glanced at Manny and sniffed. "Not him."

"That doesn't make sense. Manny is here. If you tell me, he'll also hear."

"Again." Manny shook his head. "I'll hear it again."

Francine turned her back on Manny. "I hack computer systems. With my superpowers, I gain access to someone's system and can see every detail that makes up that system. Knowing how it functions, I can alter those functions, take control of it, steal everything on it, even lock out its owner."

"I did not need to know this," Manny said.

"Biohacking is roughly the same," Francine continued, ignoring Manny. "The difference is that these hackers gain access into DNA. I can go on and on and on about this, but Grumpy here will complain too much. So I'll give you a simple example. Biohackers can make plants glow in the dark. It's kinda like they're writing entirely new genetic codes on their computers and inserting them into living organisms. They got the plants to glow in the dark by engineering them with genes from bioluminescent bacteria."

"Are these biohackers trained scientists?" Excitement raised the pitch of my voice.

"Nope. Most of them aren't. Most biohackers work from their basements or garages. Very few actually work from in a lab that could qualify as professional. Nowadays, a biohacker can set up his own home lab with PCR machines and microscopes he bought on eBay for a few thousand euro."

"A polymerase chain reaction machine?" That was the equipment used to identify a specific segment of DNA and make multiple copies of it.

"Yes." She shivered. "Isn't it just too fabulous for words?"

"Okay, supermodel." Manny got up to stand next to Francine. "I'm listening. You're making a lot more sense than last night."

"I've had time to refine my theory. I learned so much. Biohacking is really cool. There are even people who install body enhancements like magnetic implants into their own bodies. Those people are called grinders."

"Bloody hell. That's just wrong."

Francine took a deep breath, her expression familiar. It was the look she got before entering a lengthy argument with Manny. I wanted to avoid that. "Have you found any evidence in her financial history to suggest that she'd bought a PCR machine or any other equipment?"

"Who are we talking about, Doc?"

"Simone Simon. The little we know about her now includes that she studied science."

"I caught that juicy little morsel when I watched the interview video." Francine's smile was proud. "So I checked little sister's course. She studied microbiology. For three years. More than enough time to build up a very healthy knowledge of DNA, parasites and how to hack biological stuff."

"Holy mother of all." Manny's eyes were wide.

"Now do you believe me, handsome?" There wasn't any mocking or arrogance in Francine's question. Only concern. "Simone Simon is a woman fully capable of slicing and dicing DNA and parasites to create some bioweapon that she paints all over the antique books she so expertly forges. Books she's also fully capable of creating. My research last night has led me to suspect that each book's malaria parasite might be uniquely created for the recipient of that book."

"She took the priests, the businessmen, Nikki's DNA and created a bloody bioweapon just for that person?" Manny's voice was tight with anger, his hands fisted.

"Malaria." Colin's head pulled back, his brow pulling low in a frown. "No wonder everyone had flu or cold symptoms."

"I checked those too," Francine said. "Typically, the malaria parasite takes seven to thirty days to incubate. The first symptoms are fever, chills, headaches. If untreated, it can result in severe organ failure. Treatment is easily available and very effective. Most drugs are active against the parasites in the blood. Over one million people do not have to die every year from malaria. The priests didn't have to die."

"The doctors treating those priests would not have tested for malaria if the priest had not travelled to Africa or some other country with malaria," I said. "We also don't know if Simone Simon altered the parasite to be resistant against quinine or other more common treatments."

Manny walked to the glass door and back, rubbing his hands hard over his head. "Fucking hell. Biological weapons. Fuck!"

"Do we have proof?" I was still waiting for Francine to answer my earlier question.

"No. It's all circumstantial so far. It makes for a strong case, but I haven't found any paper trail, any online footprints to implicate Simone."

"Well, let's find ourselves some proof then." Manny took his smartphone from his pocket and jerked when it started ringing. "Talk about the devil." I didn't care to understand his expression, but I was curious why he chuckled at himself when he answered the phone. "Father Nate. I was just about to phone you. Please hold while I put you on speakerphone."

"Good morning, Mister Millard. Um. Who else am I talking to?"

"My whole team."

"Doctor Lenard?"

I leaned towards Manny's phone. "I'm here."

"Good morning, Doctor." He sounded happy to speak to me. "Are you well?"

"I am." I sighed at the unnecessary small talk. There were much more pressing matters at hand. "When was the renovation to the cathedral done?"

There was a moment of silence. "Six years ago it started, then finished nine months later. I was told that Father Clément was quite unhappy because it lasted three months longer than they had promised. It had disrupted a lot of services, if you know what I mean."

"Six years." Manny looked at me, both eyebrows lifted. "Father Clément died a bit more than five years ago."

"Yes, that is why I phoned. I've been asking around about that book you found here. One of the students who was an altar boy five years ago remembered that book."

"Does he remember who gave it to Father Clément?" I asked.

"He does. He said it was a woman. I asked him some more questions." Concern made his voice sound strained. "He described the woman as tall, in her thirties or forties, with long brown hair, and she was wearing dirty clothes."

"Dirty?"

"He said it looked like she worked in a paint shop."

Everyone in the room tensed, including me. Colin cleared his throat and leaned towards the phone. "Is it possible that she looked like an artist, her clothes splattered with paint?"

"That was what I also thought, if you know what I mean. So I asked the boy and he said he remembered her working as part of the renovation team. The project had lasted for so long that he remembered most of the people who were working on the church." There was a short pause. "Is this helpful?"

"Immensely," Manny said. "Thank you."

"Are you feeling well? No symptoms of a cold or being tired?" I asked. This new theory was still being developed. We didn't know without any doubt that these parasites only infected those targeted or how long the parasites stayed alive.

"Nothing. I've been a little bit worried about this, so I've been keeping a close eye on my health, if you know what I mean."

Manny ended the call after a few more words of caution. For a long moment it was quiet in my viewing room. My mind was racing with this new discovery, connecting all the previously unconnected pieces of information. I was sure everyone else's minds were similarly occupied.

"Okay, Doc. What do you think?"

"About what? You should be more specific."

"About Putin's love for sport. What the hell do you think I want to know?" The supratrochlear artery on Manny's forehead became pronounced.

Colin laughed. "You should know better by now, Millard. You walked right into that one."

Manny breathed loudly through his nose, ignoring Colin. "Doc, tell me how the bleeding hell we're going to prove

Simone has done all of this. And how's she's connected to Gasquet."

"I need more data. I need to know more about her. We have no information, except that she is Romain Proulx's sister, that she is an expert in mediaeval art restoration and that, according to Romain, her father disliked her."

"We need to move on this." Manny pointed his phone at Francine. "Help Doc find as much info on Simone Simon as soon as possible. I'll get Daniel's team to find out where she is at the moment and get eyes on her. We can't bring her in on what we have. Find something, supermodel. Find the good stuff. I want her arrested before the end of the day and I want evidence that will stick."

Chapter FIFTEEN

"What's this?" Manny walked into the team room and stared at the round table. "Did you do this, criminal?"

Vinnie's chest puffed slightly. He caught himself and lifted one shoulder. "I thought everyone might function better with a good meal. You're getting on in years, so you need your nutrition, old man."

Manny lifted his middle finger and sat down in his usual chair. Vinnie had disappeared shortly after our conversation with Father Nate and had returned ten minutes ago with two large dishes with lasagne. The aroma had awakened my hunger. It was twenty-two minutes past one. Lunch time.

"We have uncovered quite a lot of juicy stuff, so we might as well do our briefing over lunch." Francine turned from Manny to look at Vinnie down her nose. "Did you remember to put turmeric in here?"

"Are you out of your God-lovin' mind, woman?" Vinnie sneered. "That stuff belongs with Indian cooking, not my Auntie Helen's sacred Italian food. Don't make me ban you from this meal, you heretic."

Francine giggled and put a large helping onto her plate. "Maybe you can try adding some lavender next time. I heard it really brings out all the flavours in food."

Vinnie grabbed the serving spoon from her hand and pulled both dishes closer to him. "I'm giving your second helping to the old man. You don't deserve my food."

Phillip joined us and seven minutes later, everyone was eating.

"Okay, let's hear it." Manny didn't look up from his plate. "What did you find, supermodel?"

"I got all the dirt. Genevieve got all the boring stuff." Francine winked at me. "You start with the main course and I'll add the dessert later."

I looked at the dishes in the centre of the table. "I am eating the main course. Why do you want to wait until dessert before telling Manny what we've found? Is there dessert?"

"Sorry, girlfriend." Francine didn't look contrite. "I meant that I will give the gossipy info after you gave the factual stuff."

"Oh." Why didn't she say that? I finished another mouthful before I rested my knife and fork on the side of my plate. "Simone Proulx or Simone Simon is forty-seven years old. She was born here in Strasbourg in the same hospital as her brother. He is fifty-three years old. Her mother committed suicide when Simone was six years old. An article reported that it was Simone who'd found her mother in the bathtub with her wrists cut."

"That's just awful." The corners of Vinnie's mouth pulled down. "Do you think that is what made her crazy?"

"We have no confirmation that Simone is… crazy. But I would posit that such an event would have devastating effects on a six-year-old's psychological health." I took a sip of the water next to my plate. "Simone Simon graduated from school also in Strasbourg, but went to Paris for her studies. Her first three years, she studied microbiology, then she changed her course to art. We checked the modules of the course she did and yes, she had sufficient knowledge to have done what we suspect."

"Holy hell." Manny scooped a large helping onto his fork. "Why did she change to art?"

"I don't know. Francine got Simone's grades from the university. She excelled in the microbiology studies. There was no reason for her to change courses."

"Unless she was unhappy," Colin said. "She has an incredible artistic talent. Her brother also said that she had always been arty. That leads me to believe that her personality was much more suited to studying art than microbiology."

"Then why did she start with that course?" I shook my head and lifted both hands. "No, don't answer that. It will be speculation and we're looking for factual evidence. More facts about Simone are that she graduated at the top of her class. She was offered employment at three museums and two universities by the time she graduated. She started working at Corbeny Atelier and has been working there for the last twenty-two years."

"Tell me more about Corbeny Atelier, Doc."

"They specialise in restoring historic buildings. They are one of the few companies registered to work on art, buildings and windows dating from the Middle Ages. Their website has an impressive portfolio of restorations."

"Now for the juicy stuff." Francine dabbed at her mouth with the thick paper napkins Vinnie had put next to our plates. She carefully folded the napkin and placed it on her empty plate. "The Proulx family has a story that reads like some soap opera. It's delicious."

"Only the facts, supermodel. No theories."

"I don't need theories to make this one good." Francine had gasped in delight a few times while she'd done the research. "Okay. Here goes. But don't ask me how I got this info."

"Just tell us." Manny glared at Francine.

"Oh, keep your tighty-whities on, handsome." She flipped her hair over her shoulder. "When Simone changed courses, old man Proulx disowned her. She's been using the same bank for the last thirty years, so it was easy enough to get her financial history. Although thirty years ago they didn't really keep good online records, but I found enough to paint a picture.

"She had saved up and had enough to pay for her first year of art studies when she was cut off. By her second year, she had no problem finding a study grant. Incidentally, it was given to her by Corbeny Atelier. Those terms were most likely that she would work off her student debt once she graduated."

"I have contacts at one of the other museums that had offered her a job," Colin said. "When I spoke to my contact, he remembered Simone, not only because of her accomplishments, but because of their history. This museum had offered to pay off all her student debt and give her a bonus, but she'd declined all the offers and had gone to work for Corbeny Atelier. She never gave them a reason, just politely declined."

"I didn't have time to get into Corbeny Atelier's system, so I can't say much about her work," Francine continued. "But her financial history tells quite a story. Or a non-story. This is one seriously boring woman. She doesn't spend money on anything but the essentials. She pays her rent, pays her utility bills, does some mundane online shopping, but doesn't spend any interesting money."

"She's renting?" Manny frowned. "A woman her age, with a permanent job and income, who hasn't bought her own apartment or home. Hmm. This is the address you sent me, right?"

Francine nodded. "Is Daniel and the team there?"

"Dom's team went with them to make sure there weren't any funny surprises waiting for them. They checked it out, but she's not home. And the place is clean. Daniel says that it looks like no one's been living there. It has minimal furniture, most likely the stuff the flat came with. There are no personal effects, no photos, no books, nothing to indicate that she's been sleeping or spending any time there."

This was an interesting insight into the woman. I wondered where she did sleep and relax. "She might be at work at the moment. It is two o'clock on a Wednesday, a workday."

"Well, let's find out." Manny took his smartphone and looked at Francine. "What's Corbeny Atelier's owner's number?"

Francine gave him a number and a short phone conversation followed. Manny was surprised by the man's co-operation. After Manny gave him his credentials, the owner said he would first confirm Manny's identity at Interpol and phone back within five minutes. He called eight minutes later. Manny swiped the phone's screen and put the device on the round table. "Monsieur Lebas, you're on speakerphone with my team."

"Oh. Okay." He cleared his throat. "Good afternoon, everyone. What can I do to help?"

"I have a few questions about Mademoiselle Simone Simon."

"Has something happened to her?" Concern was clearly audible in his voice. I wished I could see him to determine whether the concern was sincere.

"Is she not at work?" Manny asked.

"No, she hasn't been to work this whole week. She seemed distracted last week, but nothing more than usual. She's one of our stranger employees."

"What do you mean by strange?" I asked.

"That was Doctor Genevieve Lenard speaking," Manny said.

"Doctor Lenard? The nonverbal expert? Golly gosh. Now I remember where I heard your name before, Mister Millard. You are the guys investigating art crimes." There was a moment of silence. "Has Simone been involved in something illegal?"

"We don't know yet," Manny said before I could answer. He widened his eyes at me in a warning. I bit down on my lips and sat back in my chair. Manny was better with interviews and getting information from people. "Her name came up in an investigation and we're trying to determine if she has any part in it."

"What do you need to know?" There was no hesitation in his voice.

"Do you have any idea where Simone is at this moment?"

"No. She's never revealed much about her personal life. I know that a few of her colleagues joke that she doesn't have one. She works a lot." He cleared his throat again. "Except for this week. This is the first time since I've taken over as the director that she's not shown up for work without a reason. The few times she wasn't at work, it had been for valid medical reasons. We've not been able to reach her the last few days. I was thinking of reporting her missing this afternoon. I know the police usually don't pay attention to a missing person's case until seventy-two hours after the person's been missing, so I thought today would be a good time to report it."

"What else can you tell us about Simone?" Manny looked at me. "What are the opinions of her co-workers, her behaviour, what is it that makes her strange?"

"Look, I want to help, but I feel very uncomfortable speaking ill of her. She is an accomplished artist, highly respected in her field."

"We know, Monsieur Lebas," Phillip said. "I'm Phillip Rousseau."

"From Rousseau & Rousseau. We met two years ago at the Modern Art Gallery year-end ball."

"I remember. We had a very interesting conversation about the winners of that year's Turner prize." Phillip paused. "Monsieur Lebas, we need as much information as you can share with us. We can get a court order if that would make you feel more comfortable divulging what you know."

"No, no. That won't be necessary. I just don't like idle gossip."

"Is it gossip?" I asked. "Or are these opinions based on conclusions drawn from the subconscious observations of Simone Simon's colleagues?"

"Most likely the latter." He inhaled. "Okay, that makes me feel better saying that most of the people who've worked with her think she's crazy. Some call her psychotic, some say she's a sociopath. Personally, I don't think anyone really understands the real definitions of those mental disorders."

"Then give us examples of her behaviour that leads people to say such things."

"Well, she has terrible relationships with her work colleagues. She is very literal, has been caught in quite a few lies and isn't very reliable except when it comes to her craft. She is good at appearing charming, but it never lasts long. It's her expert workmanship that has held her position in this company. Socially she is hard to spend time with."

Everything he said pointed to sociopathic behaviour. "How long have you been at Corbeny Atelier?"

"I've been here nine years."

"Has there been a change in her behaviour or has she always behaved in this manner?"

There was moment of silence. "She's always been intense, egocentric, but the last year or a bit longer she's been even more… strange."

I processed this information. A timeline formed in my mind and I wished for my notebook in the viewing room. I thought more about the connection between Simone and the priests' deaths. "Monsieur Lebas, could you give us a list of the mediaeval churches your team has renovated in the last fifteen years?"

"Um… why?"

"Unfortunately, we cannot talk about an ongoing investigation. Your co-operation would help us a lot." Manny infused authority into his tone.

"Of course. Of course. I'll give you a full list." There was a second of silence. "Look, I'm not one of those people who is paranoid about the government seeing our secrets. Your team has also been building quite a respected reputation amongst the art community. Anything you need to know about our renovations, about Simone, about our company, I will freely share with you."

Francine rolled her eyes and shook her head. She would never share any information, no matter how inconsequential, with an investigator. Once I had pointed out to her the incongruity in her behaviour. She wouldn't voluntarily give information, but she hacked and took information all the time without asking for permission. She'd shrugged and smiled.

"Please email the full list and all information about your renovations to us as soon as possible."

"I will do so now. Is there anything else I can do to help?"

Manny looked at me and I shook my head. He pulled his phone closer. "Not for the moment. Thank you very much for all your help."

Manny gave him an email address to send the list to and they ended the call. For a few seconds we sat in contemplative silence. Eventually Francine put both her hands flat on the table. "I'm just going to say it. That girl is all kinds of crazy. I mean, who goes around killing priests? For such a long time? And why would she do it?"

Motives for crimes interested me only for the insight into the human psyche they offered. Sometimes the trigger for extreme actions was an almost insignificant comment, photo or book. Sometimes it was a life-changing event. While the rest of the team speculated about Simone Simon's psychological health, I thought back to all the information we'd uncovered. Something clicked and I gasped at the logical simplicity of it. "Francine, did Simone inherit anything from her father at all when he died?"

"Not a single dime."

"Who were the beneficiaries of Zacharie Proulx's last will and testament?"

Francine held up her index finger and grabbed her tablet. She uncovered overwhelming amounts of information, but never took longer than a few seconds accessing it. Nineteen seconds later, her eyebrows shot up. "Got it. Okay, Daddy gave the business and everything related to it to sonny-boy.

Then he gave forty percent of his money to Romain, ten percent to his driver and oh, my God! Wow. I did not see this coming."

"Supermodel."

Francine looked up, her eyes wide. "Daddy Proulx gave fifty percent of his seven hundred and thirty million euro fortune to the Catholic Church."

"Bloody hell."

"That's not all, handsome." Francine shook her tablet lightly. "His will stipulated that the money was to be used only for churches and priests. None of it was to benefit nuns or any other women."

"Well, that is a strong motive if ever I heard one," Manny said. "I'm not surprised Simone was pissed off about this."

"I never had the impression that Zacharie was such a sexist man." Phillip tugged on his sleeves. "The image he portrayed was one of philanthropy, generosity, charity and honesty."

"And that is why I don't trust anyone." Francine leaned towards Manny and whispered loudly. "Except you. And everyone else in this room."

"Such high praise." Manny tried for sarcasm, but I'd seen the flush of pleasure. He nodded at her tablet. "Has Monsieur Lebas sent that list yet?"

He had. It took us the next three hours to work through the list. Phillip, Manny and Francine spent most of the time phoning the churches, speaking to the priests. It required social finesse I did not excel in to convince the priests that these queries were authentic and that we were indeed looking for a Gothic book gifted by a woman, possibly the one who renovated the churches' stained-glass windows.

Manny showed his multifaceted skills by being charming, respectful and everything I'd expected from Phillip. I knew Francine wouldn't have trouble speaking to and getting information from the priests. As Phillip, Manny and Francine received confirmation of the presence of a book of hours on the premises, they immediately informed Dom.

When the last phone call had been made, it was half past four. I was in my viewing room, looking at the photos we had, hoping to see something I had not already noticed. No matter what approach I'd taken with the coded few pages in the back of each book, I had so far not found the key to decrypt it.

Manny walked into the viewing room, stretching his arms above his head. "We've found thirty-eight more books, Doc."

I turned, my eyes wide in shock. "Thirty-eight? Did each book result in the death of a priest?"

"Nope." He stretched his neck to the side and grunted. "Simone started handing out her books of death twelve years ago. The first few priests still have their books and are still in good health."

"The priests started dying nine years ago." Francine walked in, followed by Phillip. She looked at me, looked at the people in my viewing room and turned around. "Phillip, could we ask Tim to make us coffee and bring some cookies? Let's do this in the team room."

Everyone settled around the table, but I stopped at Francine's chair. "Thank you."

Her smile was genuine and filled with affection. "You're welcome, girlfriend."

I sat down and looked at Manny. "We need Dom to test the earlier books as well. I wonder if Simone had been experimenting with this delivery medium for three years before she got it right. I've been reading up about this and getting a parasite to remain viable for a period of time until it has been transferred to its host is not easy. There are too many variables. A slight change in humidity, in temperature and it could die or lose its potency."

"I'll get them to check all the books, Doc." Manny stopped when Tim entered the room with a tray. I didn't want the cookies, only the coffee.

"Where's Vinnie?" I took my mug and inhaled the aroma.

"He joined GIPN to get those books as soon as possible."

Adrenaline rushed through my system, causing my hands to instantly feel cold. I put my mug down on the table. "Are they wearing protective suits? Vinnie doesn't know how to handle hazardous materials. He should not be there. Call him back. I'll call him."

"Jenny." Colin put his hand on my forearm. "Take a deep breath. Good. Now put some logic in your argument. Do you think Vinnie would be stupid enough to handle hazardous materials?"

"No, but what if he doesn't know it is hazardous?"

"Love, he's with Daniel's team. They're looking out for each other."

"More importantly, each GIPN team going out has a HMR team professional with them, making sure nobody and nothing is contaminated." Manny took a sip of his tea. "I made sure Dom is with the criminal. He's safe, Doc."

It took a lot of control and two lines of Mozart's Clarinet Concerto in A Major to release the obsessive concern for Vinnie's health. I opened my eyes and nodded. "We know that it took Simone three years to perfect her method. How perfect was it? Have all her books in the last nine years resulted in deaths?"

"No." Francine glanced at her tablet. "She seems to have a pattern. Every year she produced around four books."

"Very doable," Colin said. "Even though these books are a lot of work, she could most definitely produce one every three months."

"Well, nine years ago, only one priest died," Francine continued. "Eight years ago, three of the four priests died. If we work on four books a year, she should've produced forty-eight books, but we only located thirty-eight. Of those, only twenty-six priests died."

"Only," I said quietly.

"Yeah, that sounded awful." Francine groaned. "Sorry for that. It's mind-blowing that she's been getting away with this for twelve years."

"Are you sure there was no one before that?" I asked.

"I've checked real thoroughly and haven't found anyone else." Francine closed her eyes briefly. "God, I really hope there aren't any more. I think twenty-six murdered priests are twenty-six too many."

"Let's not forget about the businessmen who have been murdered in the same way." I reflected on the information we had. "Knowing that Simone is the one producing the hour books as well as the gifts for the businessmen creates an interesting link."

"What's that, Doc?"

"Not what. Who. Romain is the link between Simone and Gasquet. I posit that Gasquet and Simone met through Romain's business dealings with Gasquet."

"Highly probable." Manny rubbed his jaw. "And such an odd partnership. I would not have put Simone and Gasquet in bed together."

"We have no evidence proving they are romantically involved."

Manny snorted. "Sorry, Doc. An expression for being in business together, working together."

"Hmm. A good analogy." I pressed my lips together to prevent myself from further analysing the symmetry between working partnerships and romantic relationships.

"We need to find Simone." Manny pressed his hands palms down on the table. "We've got all these teams collecting the books—"

"Will they remember to send photos of all the pages?" This was most important.

"Yes, missy. I reminded them every time you reminded me." He exhaled in annoyance. "As I was saying, we've got these teams getting the books, but we need to be out looking for Simone. Doc, where is she?"

"I don't know." I registered his growing ire and held up one hand. "Not yet. Let me think about this for a minute."

It was quiet around the table while I considered the information we'd gathered on Simone Simon. It only took me a minute to come across a thread we had not yet looked into. I turned to Francine. "Simone didn't inherit anything from her father, right?"

"Right."

"Did she inherit anything from her mother?"

"You genius woman, you. Give me a moment." Francine tapped on her tablet, biting her bottom lip. Her eyes widened and she smiled. "Gotcha! She inherited property from her maternal grandparents. Her grandparents outlived their daughter and when they died, they left their house to Simone."

Manny took out his phone. "Address?"

As soon as Francine gave it to him, Manny phoned Daniel, who reassured him that they'd be at Simone's house within twenty minutes. Daniel was going to take his GIPN team, including Vinnie, as well as four of the HMR team members. He made Manny give him his word that we would not arrive there until Dom had declared the house clear of any contaminants. Manny made the promise, but I witnessed on his face the same impatience I felt. He ended the call with a sigh.

"As soon as they've secured the house, I want to go inside." My tone held a finality that conveyed my mindset. "If she's been living there, it will give us a lot of insight into her psyche. It might even give us the key to the code in the back of the book."

"I agree, Doc." Manny sighed heavily. "Holy Mary, I hate waiting, but I suppose that is what we'll have to do now."

Colin took my hand. "Why don't we go visit Nikki for a short while? It's halfway to Simone's house. As soon as Dom phones, we'll be on the road."

"That's a fab idea." Francine got up. "I'll join you guys. I bought Nikki the cutest PJ's. She's going to love them."

There was so much more research that could be done until Dom phoned, but I wanted to reassure myself that Nikki was well taken care of. And that she was safe. The short time not analysing the case might also give my mind time to process the new information we'd found. I wondered if we would find something in Simone Simon's house to bring this case to a conclusion.

Chapter SIXTEEN

Winter nights were not a time I enjoyed being outside. Especially when I had to wait. We were outside Simone Simon's house. Dom had phoned Manny twenty-five minutes ago to tell him that they were about to finish in the house. Colin and I had left Francine with Nikki and had rushed to the house. Manny wasn't here yet and Dom's team were not completely finished. I shifted to my other foot, hoping I wouldn't have to stand in this cold for too long.

It had started snowing lightly, a thin layer of white powder covering everything. Colin had parked his SUV two houses away because of all the other vehicles, including the large, fully equipped hazardous material decontamination truck, already parked in the residential street. These areas seldom had much traffic, and I was sure that very rarely, if ever, had law enforcement descended on a neighbour's house. GIPN had taped off the area around the house and Daniel's team guarded it, making sure no one entered.

Colin and I were standing in the front yard. This was one of the larger houses on the street, the garden surrounding it beautiful, even in winter. Pine trees and other evergreen bushes made it look like a manicured wooded area. The floodlights GIPN had placed around the house gave me the opportunity to study Simone Simon's garden.

At first glance, it looked like a garden that might need a lot of time and effort to maintain. It wasn't. The trees and the plants were for maximum display, but minimum maintenance. The only thing required would be to mow the lawn once a week in summer. There were no flowerbeds, making this an undemanding garden, perfect for the busy professional to enjoy.

The outside of the house also reflected this. Everything was neatly maintained, not a thing out of place that would attract attention. I supposed that was the purpose of the garden as well. It fitted in with the neighbourhood, but didn't stand out. The perfect way to go unnoticed for many years. I wondered if Simone's car was also a nondescript sedan. I was getting impatient to get inside the house and learn more about her.

The front door opened and a figure dressed in a protective suit came towards us. Only when he removed his helmet and mask did I recognise Dom. He smiled at us. "All clear. My team went through every nook and cranny of this place and didn't pick anything up. As a precaution, we blasted the house with UV rays and fumigated it. That would destroy any biologicals hanging around on surfaces. But I would still like for you to wear gloves when you are in there."

"I wouldn't go in there without any." The thought of touching anything Simone had worked on sent a shudder through my body. "I would also prefer to wear a mask."

"Here you go, Jen-girl," Vinnie said from behind us. I turned around and accepted the plastic-wrapped mask he held out to me. "I got this specially for you."

"Where did you come from?" I hadn't seen him since we arrived.

"I was guarding the back of the house, freezing my butt off. It's cold out here." He looked at Dom. "Can we check the house out now?"

"Yes, but put on latex gloves when you're inside." Even though Dom had finished speaking, I could see there was much more he wanted to warn us against. It was in the way he swallowed, the contractions around his eyes and the way he pressed his lips together to prevent himself from speaking. I wondered about asking him for a suit, but decided against it. They had been in the house for more than five hours, securing it. Daniel's team had also checked for any explosive devices or any other delivery methods.

Colin took the latex gloves Dom offered and put them on. I didn't understand how he and Vinnie didn't wear gloves in these temperatures. I put my fleece gloves in my coat pockets and put on two pairs of latex gloves. I removed the medical mask from its plastic wrapping and secured it over my mouth and nose. I didn't want to take any chances.

Dom nodded and we followed him into the house. I stopped in the entrance and looked around. The entrance was spacious, a small built-in cupboard to the left, most likely for outer wear. A single wall unit on the right decorated this space. There were no rugs, nothing to make a visitor feel welcome. The wall unit looked antique and had a brass tray that could be used for holding keys.

Double doors opened up into the living area. They were wide open and I walked into the large open space. The kitchen was directly to the left. Two wooden steps led to a slightly lower sitting area. I marvelled at the beauty of the minimalism. There was not one ornament in sight. The sitting area had two white sofas and two white wingback chairs.

"What do you see, Jenny?" Colin was next to me, also looking around.

"It is what I don't see that is more interesting." I stepped into the living room and opened my arms. "No rugs, no ornaments, just a neutral cityscape print on the wall. There are no plants, no remote control, nothing to indicate that she's living here."

"Just like her flat," Daniel said from the kitchen. I frowned and wondered where the other door was where he'd entered the kitchen. Possibly behind the fridge. "Hi, Genevieve."

"Hello, Daniel. Tell me more about her flat."

He smiled, then looked up and left, recalling a visual memory. "It was not as richly furnished as this. But just as... impersonal. At least here you can see that she used her bedroom and especially the home office."

"Where is that?"

"Upstairs."

I turned towards the stairs on my right and looked up. "Is it safe to go there?"

"All cleared." He walked past me and led the way up the wide wooden staircase.

This house had to be at least eighty years old, yet the interior looked renovated. According to the financial information we had on Simone Simon, she could not have paid for it. Not in the last twenty years. I paid closer attention to the finishing as we walked to the last room in the hallway.

"How long ago do you think this house was renovated?" I asked.

Colin pointed towards the bathroom on the left. "Going by the tiles in there, I think the eighties. At least they kept it simple and didn't get those kitsch designs, but yes, the eighties."

"Yeah, look at the lights," Vinnie said. "My auntie Teresa renovated her home in 1984 and she has these light fittings in every room. Not one of the best things to come from the eighties."

We walked into a large bedroom, the bed facing the window. The cover was a strong red, matching the curtains in colour and design. A set. It was not a usual colour for someone to choose for a relaxing space where they could rest. Red gave energy, even aggression.

In front of the window was a dressing table, without anything on the counter. It had two drawers next to each other, a stool pushed under it. I walked closer and rested my hand on the handle of the drawer to the right. "You're sure this has been checked?"

Daniel nodded. "Very sure. They opened every drawer, cupboard, looked under every piece of furniture."

I held my breath as I opened the drawer. Inside were cosmetics one would expect in a woman's bedroom. Facial creams, body lotions, mascara, but no other makeup. I closed the drawer and exhaled. I breathed in and held my breath again. I opened the other drawer and lifted my eyebrows. The entire drawer was filled with bottles of nail polish. They were arranged according to the colour spectrum and each colour was represented.

I closed the drawer and turned to Daniel on the exhale. He was standing in the door, giving us space to explore. "Did they test the nail polish?"

Daniel's smile was the same as in the kitchen. Amusement and patience. I liked him. "Yes. It's just nail polish."

I wondered how they could've tested the nail polish in such a short time, but decided not to pursue that line of thinking. I stepped away from the dressing table and faced the bed. Above the headboard was a large painting. I was not familiar with the style. Colin was standing next to the bed, studying it.

"What is that?"

He looked over his shoulder. When he saw I was talking to him, he turned back. "Cyberpunk art. Really good cyberpunk art."

"Did she paint it?" Vinnie asked.

"It's a sketch and no, I can't see her style in here." Colin tilted his head. "See these gears? If Simone sketched this, they would be smoother. There is a roughness to this I haven't seen in any of her work."

"Tell me more about cyberpunk." I'd heard the word used for a subculture, but had not taken enough interest to research it. I now rued my decision.

"It is a subgenre of science fiction. The focus is on advanced science, cybernetics, but goes hand in hand with a breakdown in society." Vinnie shrugged. "Francine has this cool computer game that got me interested."

"*Cyberpunk 2020*?" Daniel smiled when Vinnie nodded. "Cool game."

"I would like to see the home office now." I wasn't interested in computer games and had seen enough in this room. Daniel led us to the other side of the hallway. To the right was a large room with an unused bar in one corner. The shelves designed to display bottles of liquor were used as bookshelves.

"I reckon this was the entertainment room until Simone moved in. She set herself up quite nicely here." Daniel pointed at the drafting table. "She sure had enough space for her art."

Colin walked towards the table and I resisted the urge to

hold him back. If this was where she created the books of hours, I wondered where she tainted those books.

"I'm going to check on my people." Daniel's feet were already pointing towards the door. "I'll be back in a few."

I hated that expression. Vinnie used it often and I never knew whether he meant a few seconds, minutes, hours or days. With a huff, I pushed the mask tighter against my face and followed Colin to the worktable. On the desk were a few parchment pages. "They look old."

"She could've gotten them from old books and washed them in a solution to remove the previous writing or art. Or she could've made her own parchment." Colin leaned closer, his eyes narrow. "But I think these are from old books."

"Look what I found." Vinnie pointed at a desk with various tools and I walked closer. The needles and thread brought understanding.

"Is this where she bound the books?" I was impressed with her clean workspace.

"Definitely, yes." Colin walked past us to the largest wall. "My God, just look at these."

The wall was completely covered in framed artwork. Vinnie and I followed Colin. Of all the spaces in the house, this room was the truest reflection of Simone. "Are these all her work?"

"It looks like it." Colin took his time walking along the wall, studying each painting. At the far end, he stretched his arm out to include the whole wall. "All her own art. The same style as in the books, although most of these are rather dark in mood."

I had also noticed it. The paintings in front of me had the typical vines and flowers depicting the Gothic style, but the colours were different. Like the figures in her books, these figures displayed aggressive or sad body language. The woman in the painting directly in front of me had a frown pulling her brows together, her lips were thin and the corners of her mouth turned down.

"And all of these people are wearing the ring," Vinnie said. "What's with that ring?"

"Who knows, Vin." Colin and Vinnie started speculating about the ring, so I moved towards the adjoining wall. A bookshelf covered the entire wall and it was filled with books. An initial inspection revealed many books on art, a few on biology, but nothing suspicious. I checked the books again, making sure to look at all the shelves.

On the top shelf to the far left were a row of romance novels. A woman of Simone Simon's intellect and interests would not often read such material and, when she did, would not want it to be public knowledge. She even hid those books from her own line of sight.

I recognised a few literary masterpieces as well as three Gothic novels I also had in my library. Two of the three looked well-preserved. I read my books with the utmost care, aspiring not to damage the book, only to enjoy its masterful prose and authenticity.

The third book caught my attention. It was on the fourth shelf, at eye-level. I leaned closer, but held my breath. With Simone's history, I didn't want to take any chances. The spine of this book was unharmed except for the top. I stretched slightly and looked at the top of the book.

"Whatcha got, Jen-girl?" Vinnie asked right next to my left ear.

I gasped. Vinnie had frightened me and I'd inhaled. I was even more irate when he and Colin laughed.

"Sorry, Jen-girl." He raised both hands, palms out. "Didn't mean to startle ya."

"It's not amusing at all, Vinnie." My tone was clipped.

"Sorry." He was still smiling, no sign of contrition evident.

I turned back to the book.

"What are you looking at, Jenny?" Colin pushed Vinnie away and stood next to me.

I rested the tip of my index finger on the top of the book. "See how the spine looks untouched, but the top"—I stretched again to look at the top of pages—"yes, it looks like someone frequently touched it here. Maybe like this."

I pushed down and pulled the book towards me just as Vinnie shouted, "Don't do that!"

His shout caused my hand to jerk the book even further. The moment the book tilted at a slight angle, a click sounded. Part of the bookshelf swung open with a rush of air.

Darkness rushed towards me with the possibility of what had just happened. I bit down hard on my jaw and looked into the well-lit room. Vinnie was speaking into his communication unit, ordering Daniel to get Dom and his team back in here. In their protective suits.

It would take minutes for them to reach us. My mind rushed through different scenarios. If there had been any airborne pathogens, it was no use avoiding the new room. That rush of air had touched all of us, possibly infecting us. We were wearing gloves, keeping us safe from the alternative delivery method. It took a mere three seconds to make up my mind. Colin unsuccessfully grabbed at me when I walked into the room.

"Jenny!" Colin followed and took my elbow in a firm grip. "You shouldn't be in here. Let's go."

"We will be of much more help in here. If there was something in the air, we've already been exposed to it." I pulled my arm from his hold. "I'll search this side of the room. Look on that side for anything that can give us an indication of Simone's plans, her work, anything that will help."

Colin stared at me for a second before he nodded. "Let's make it quick."

The room seemed separated into two areas, the entrance serving as the divider. On the side Colin was searching were two tables, one with laboratory equipment, the other covered in piles of papers. On the first table were two microscopes and a PCR machine—equipment needed to identify DNA and replicate it. I turned to my area.

Against the one wall were four doors. I opened one and was faced with floor-to-ceiling shelves filled with more laboratory equipment. Beakers, droppers, goggles and test tubes in racks were arranged in neat rows, all clean and appearing ready to use. The second door also opened to shelves. These were filled with books, folders and piles of papers. The books were all on the topics of genetic engineering, microbiology, virology and weaponising biologicals. I shuddered and opened the third door.

My peripheral view was immediately swamped with blackness. I blinked several times. I was looking at a tall built-in fridge with rows upon rows of vials, all carefully labelled. Most of the names I was not familiar with, but I did recognise Father Sidney Larousse, Father Clément, Rainier Lahage and Andrien Crevier. One of the shelves in the fridge held vials all labelled with priests' names. That had to be their DNA.

Panic made it feel as if my muscles were under sedation. I forced Mozart's Clarinet Concerto in A major into my mind and took a few calming breaths. It took another line of the Allegro before the darkness receded and I had the courage to open the fourth door. It too held shelves, but they were mostly empty.

"Jenny, come look here."

Since there was nothing to learn from these shelves, I walked over to the table where Colin was paging through documents.

The many papers covering the surface of this table were arranged in neat piles. On the top left of the table were hand-written notes. I guessed there were at least three hundred pages lying there. On the top right of the table were maps. I lifted one and studied it from different angles. It looked like an antique map or those found in historical novels. I paged through the top few and found mostly geographical maps. A few seemed to be of old fortresses. One definitely looked like a castle. I wondered why Simone would have this in her home laboratory.

Noises came from the doorway and the sound of plastic moving. Dom's team were on their way. We didn't have much more time in this room. I looked at the pile of papers on the left of the table, closest to us, and picked up a pile.

As I paged through them, the room fell away.

Colin putting his arm around me for support fell away. Vinnie's colourful swearing fell away. Colin telling Dom they would have to wait a while and the argument that ensued fell away.

My full, panicked attention was on the papers detailing how to make a parasite airborne.

A website address at the top of each page led me to the conclusion that Simone had downloaded this from the internet. It was a Tor website address. The underground web browser allowed people to secretly find ways to kill many people. Previously disconnected bits of information rushed together to form a clear picture. A terrifying picture.

I felt the warmth of a shutdown enveloping me and sorely wanted to give in to it. There I would be safe from all pathogens. I would be safe, but many other people wouldn't.

With an almost violent determination, I mentally wrote another page of the Allegro until I felt Colin's warmth at my back. His arms surrounded me, his hands resting lightly on my tightly folded arms. He was rocking with me. I took a few shuddering breaths and tried to open my eyes. It was hard. Not facing the next hours was tempting, but I didn't give in. I forced myself to take one deep breath and opened my eyes.

Colin and I were the only ones in the room. Vinnie was standing in the door preventing Dom and his team from entering. I couldn't see their facial expressions, but their body language was showing urgency, concern and impatience. I straightened in Colin's embrace and awkwardly patted his arm. He stepped back, but turned me until I was facing him. "You okay?"

I nodded, not yet ready to speak.

"That bad?"

I nodded again.

"Guys, we have to get you out of here and in the decontamination unit," Dom said. I only recognised the suited figure by his voice. "The quicker we get you cleaned up, the better."

Vinnie looked over his shoulder. "You good to go, Jen-girl?"

"Yes." I pointed at the papers on the table and looked at Dom. "You should study these documents. I'm convinced Simone has found a way to turn malaria into an airborne weapon."

Chapter SEVENTEEN

"Doc!" Manny's voice carried from the back of the HMR truck through the thick glass separating us from the rest of the interior. "What the holy bleeding hell is going on?"

"Aw, fuck it all to bits." Vinnie turned towards Colin and me, only to immediately turn back to face the glass door. "Why don't we just sell tickets for this show?"

The HMR team had rushed us into the only decontamination shower in the large truck. Vinnie had complained in great detail that he didn't want to share a shower with us when they'd confiscated our clothes to incinerate them. Dom hadn't given Vinnie a choice. He'd cited a few laws and had threatened to get Daniel's team to force him into the shower at gunpoint if necessary.

I was now trapped in the shower with Vinnie and Colin, all three of us naked. The water was hot, the flow strong. The liquid soap we'd been given was harsh, but smelled of camomile.

My mind was consumed with the flood of new information from the secret room. I knew that if I took my mind off the possibility of airborne malaria being released in a populated area, and focussed on my current situation, I might have a meltdown, not a shutdown.

I wasn't concerned about my state of undress. Nor was the decontamination shower causing me any distress. If only every hotel bathroom were this clean, I would travel more often. Being in this small space with Colin alone would've been tolerable with the help of some Mozart. But adding Vinnie's tattooed and scarred body to this space had increased my heart rate and breathing until I forced all my focus onto Simone and her biohacking experiments.

"Doc!" Manny's voice came closer, followed by a gasp. "Oh, for the love of all that is good and holy! I did not want to see that."

"Then you shouldn't have come in here," Vinnie said through his teeth. He held his hand over his shoulder. "Dude, give me the soap. I need to get the fuck outta here."

I closed my eyes and pushed Mozart's Clarinet Concert back into my mind. It drowned out all conversation and sounds from within the truck. I focussed on the water washing over me and making sure that I scrubbed every centimetre on my body. I had to balance myself carefully to scrub the soles of my feet and decided on a third scrubbing to ensure that I didn't miss anything.

"Jenny. Love." Colin's hand closed over mine holding the hard sponge. "We all think you are clean enough now."

I slowly opened my eyes and forced my hand to release the sponge. I nodded tightly, sending a few water drops running down my face.

"I'm turning the water off," Dom said. "There are towels and sweat suits laid out for you. The extra-large might be a bit small for you, big guy, but it will keep you covered."

The water immediately stopped flowing and Colin stepped back. Vinnie had left the shower. He wrapped a towel around his hips and handed Colin two towels. Colin gave me one. I inspected the white towel, only taking it when it looked as clean as the towels in my linen cupboard. I wrapped it around myself and took another towel Colin held out to me.

When I saw the blue and orange sweat suits still in sealed bags, I felt comfortable accepting clothes that were not mine. The thick socks would help keep my feet warm, because the plastic shoes were not going to be helpful in this weather. At least we would reach Colin's SUV without freezing.

"Oh, good." Manny stepped into the truck, bringing cold air in with him. He was wearing a protective suit, mask and gloves. "You're all dressed now. Seeing the criminal's wee willy winky took ten years off my life."

"From shock, awe or jealousy, old man?" Vinnie tried to pull the sleeves of the sweat top down, but it wouldn't reach his wrists.

Manny grunted, then turned to me. "Doc? How're you holding up?"

"Are you asking me how I am?"

He sighed. "Yes."

"I'm trying to avoid thinking about our possible malaria infection." No sooner had I said this than Vinnie sneezed. Twice. If we had not been in a truck sent out to contain biological hazards, I might have found his expression comical.

His eyes were wide and he swallowed a few times. "What does this mean? Am I sick? Did I catch this?"

"I doubt it." Dom laughed and lifted a syringe in his hand. "We'll take blood samples from each of you and test it."

"What if Simone changed the malaria?" Panic tightened around my chest. "Would this test also be able to detect a different strain?"

"We'll run full tests on your blood, Doctor Lenard. The malaria parasite takes a good seven days to show up in a blood test. But let's rather be safe than sorry."

I folded my arms tightly across my chest. I didn't want to

think about this anymore. My tendency to micro-analyse everything would lead me to create numerous worst-case scenarios and that would not be productive.

"Is your team still testing that room for viruses and toxins?" Colin held out his arm when Dom finished drawing Vinnie's blood.

"Yes. So far they've not picked up anything. Simone kept her home lab surprisingly clean." He expertly inserted the needle in Colin's arm and sat back, waiting for the vial to fill. "Three months ago, we were called to a home lab that was a biohazard nightmare. This was also one of these biohackers, but this idiot was cooking up dangerous stuff. He was fooling around with ideas of cloning and such. We had to rescue a few animals from his basement where he was testing God knows what on them. Like I said, Simone Simon's home lab is a breeze after that place."

The door to the truck opened again and another suited man stepped in. It was beginning to feel crowded. He removed his helmet to reveal a shaved head. His light blue eyes were alert and curious. "It's clean, Dom. We didn't find any bogies. All the surfaces were clean. The only place we found the bad boys was in the fridge. And all of those were malaria strains, marked and sealed. Elisa checked them under the microscope and agrees they're malaria, but we're still taking it all to be tested."

"It's a smart way to get someone really sick," Dom said. "Infect them with malaria when they haven't travelled to a malaria area and no one would think of testing them for it. They would have flu-like symptoms, but treatment for flu would not cure them. Rather brilliant."

"Sick, not brilliant." Vinnie rubbed his nose. "Do you think I have malaria?"

Dom chuckled. "There's no way to tell. As I've said before, malaria needs seven days to incubate. At least seven days."

The tight feeling around my chest returned and I took a few deep breaths. It took incredible strength to not think about the incubation process of the malaria parasite.

"Are they contagious?" Manny touched his mask. "And can I take this bloody thing off?"

Dom and his bald colleague looked at each other. The bald man lifted both shoulders. "Personally, I don't think they are. But my opinion is not a hundred percent guarantee."

"Eighty percent?" Manny asked.

"More like ninety-five," Dom said.

"That's more than enough for me." Manny pulled off his mask and took a few deep breaths. "I don't know how you people can work with masks for hours on end."

"Think of it as our guns," the bald man said. "You don't go anywhere without your gun, we don't go anywhere without our masks."

My mind started wandering again to the possibility of malaria parasites in my bloodstream. I thought of the case and what our next steps should be. "Your team must take photos of that room and email it to me. I need photos of all the documents and vials in that room as well as all the books in the cupboard and on her shelves. Photos of the rest of the house will also be helpful."

Dom's eyebrows continued to raise as I spoke. His expression conveyed offence. I didn't know why he would be offended.

"Please." Colin leaned forward. "We would appreciate these photos, please, Dom."

Dom frowned at me before looking at Colin. "Sure. I'll have them send those photos to you."

"And the maps. We need the maps on the desk too." I thought of Colin's approach and cleared my throat. "Please."

Manny and Vinnie made sounds that could've been laughter, but covered it with fake coughs. Vinnie pointed at his throat, his eyes wide with insincere concern. "Malaria."

"You should not jest." My tone was sombre. "Malaria kills a million people per year."

"Talking of which"—Dom nodded towards the three computer stations in the front of the truck—"I've notified all hospitals to be on alert. If someone comes in with flu-like symptoms, they should check for malaria. Especially priests and businessmen."

"Bet that is going to cause a lot of speculation." Manny straightened. "Okay, Doc. What's next?"

"I need to get back to the office. If Dom's team sends the photos, I can start working though those. We need to find out what Simone is planning and where she is." I lifted my hand towards Colin. "No, don't argue with me. I'm going to the office. I won't be able to sleep in any case, so I might as well make productive use of my time. You can go home if you want to."

"It might be wise to limit the number of people you come in contact with," Dom said. "At least until we are sure you have not been infected with anything."

I closed my eyes and swallowed. Panic tightened my throat muscles and caused my saliva to dry. I stood up. "Can we go?"

It took another ten minutes before we left the truck. Dom first took a blood sample from me. I had to mentally write a Mozart composition the whole time. Manny stayed behind, needing to make a few phone calls. He'd promised to meet us in the office in another hour. Vinnie had convinced Dom to give him protective gear so he could enter the house and take photos for us. I was pleased with this solution. Vinnie would know what was important enough to photograph and he would upload the pictures immediately.

The sweat suit, socks and plastic shoes weren't enough protection against the elements. It had stopped snowing, but it felt colder outside. By the time we reached Colin's SUV two houses away, I had to clench my jaw to prevent my teeth from chattering. My toes were beginning to ache from the cold as Colin opened the passenger door for me. I got into the cold SUV and couldn't control the shiver that shook my body.

Colin got it and immediately turned the heater as high as it would go. "It's going to take a few minutes to warm up. Shit, it's cold."

We sat in silence for a while. Something wasn't right. I turned to Colin. His muscle tension was too high and I didn't think it was from being cold. "What's wrong?"

He glanced at me, closed his eyes briefly and exhaled. "Nothing, love. This case is just hard."

"You're lying." It was not easy to detect. Colin was an accomplished liar.

He closed his eyes again and rested his head against the seat. "Sometimes I wish you didn't see so much."

"Why? What do you want to hide from me?"

He looked at me, his expression serious. "Nothing, Jenny. I have nothing to hide from you."

I crossed my arms. "Then what is the problem? You seem angry."

"I'm tired." He shook his head. "Let's get home, get dressed and go to the office."

He pulled the car into the road and we drove in silence for a few kilometres. I'd known Colin for more than two years and had been intimately involved with him for eighteen months. His current nonverbal cues were not those I usually observed when he was tired. It was more than this. I didn't like the feeling of powerlessness from not knowing what had caused his distress. I thought back to the last hour and couldn't determine what might have happened to upset him.

"Let it go, Jenny." Even the *masseter* muscles in his jaw were tense. "Put on some music. We'll be home soon."

Telling me to let something go was counterproductive. "I need to know why you are upset."

"Aw, love." Colin sighed heavily. "You're not going to let this go, are you?"

"I can't." Literally.

"Okay." He took a few deep breaths. "You know I love you, right?"

"Yes. Are you angry about that?"

He laughed softly. "No. I'm not angry. I don't really know what I am. This case is hard. Nikki in the hospital. This malaria thing. It's all a bit much to deal with. I feel much more comfortable chasing Gasquet and other suspects we can see. Chasing a parasite is driving me crazy."

"But that is not what is upsetting you."

"As always you are right." His laugh held no humour. "You are often right. Very often. And the manner which you communicate your rightness has the ability to cut right to the bone, love."

"You're using analogies." Which meant he was more upset than I had thought.

"That I am. I sometimes wish I could use more euphemisms. It would make what I want to say so much gentler."

"Why does it need to be gentle?"

He huffed. "Why indeed."

We turned into one of the main roads. The streets were quiet at two o'clock in the morning. Colin didn't seem keen to continue this discussion, but I needed to know. From his avoidance, I was surmising that I'd been the cause of his emotional state. "Colin?"

He was quiet for a few seconds before his nostrils flared. Subconscious preparation for a confrontation. "Fine. I'll just say it straight then. When you correct me—well, any of us—in public, it often comes across as chastisement. In the truck, in front of strangers, you talked to me in a tone that was condescending and disrespectful."

I gasped. "When?"

"Telling me that you're going to the office and I can go home if I want to. Of course it wasn't what you said, but the delivery."

I thought about that. I hadn't spent a moment thinking about my tone of voice, just getting the message across in the clearest and most concise manner possible. My words came out in a whisper. "I could never disrespect you."

"I know that, love. Vinnie and Manny know that, but those other guys don't know you like we do." His lips pressed together. He didn't want to talk about this. "Like I said, I'm tired, so it got to me when it usually doesn't."

"Usually?" My voice raised a pitch. "Do I do this often?"

He nodded. "It's okay when it's within the family, but it doesn't feel good to be treated like a naughty schoolboy when there are other people around."

I pressed both hands over my chest. "Colin, I…"

My heartfelt apology was cut off by a violent collision. It felt as if my body was being pulled in several different directions at once. I registered the crunch of metal a moment before the SUV started spinning. Screaming filled the car and I realised it was me. I grabbed my head as a lamppost rushed towards me. It was all too much. This case, the realisation that I had been treating my friends and the man I love with disrespect, the possibility of being infected. It was all too much. Not even trying to prevent it, I surrendered to the warm safety of a shutdown.

Chapter EIGHTEEN

"Jen-girl. Aw, fuck. We need you. Colin needs you." Vinnie's voice trembled. "Please, just come back. I don't know what to do with you."

It was the fear in Vinnie's voice that brought me back into the present. I opened my eyes to find myself curled up on the passenger seat, hugging my knees tightly to my chest. I looked out of the front windscreen and was surprised to find no visible damage to the vehicle. The deflated airbag hung limply in front of me, the other one dangling from the steering wheel.

Apart from my sternum hurting, most likely from the seatbelt, I didn't have any indication of serious injuries. I lowered my legs to the floor, becoming aware of how cold I was. The driver's door was open and Vinnie was leaning into the SUV, his body blocking my view. The driver's seat was empty.

"Oh, thank God." Vinnie turned his head and called over his shoulder, "She's with us, old man."

"Colin." Sudden and intense panic made it feel as if someone had their hands around my throat. "Where's Colin?"

"He's out here, Jen-girl. The paramedics are looking after him."

"Paramedics?" The word came out high and strangled. I tried to move, but the seatbelt was still locking me against the seat. When I reached down, my fingers were clumsy from the shock and the cold. I groaned in despair when I couldn't unlock the seatbelt.

"Here, let me help you." Vinnie leaned closer and with one press freed me. I tried to open my door, but it didn't move. Vinnie's nonverbal cues worried me, especially when he attempted schooling his features. "You connected with a lamppost on that side. It just missed your door, but I think it fucked up the lock. We couldn't open that door either. Do you think you'll be able to climb out this side?"

I didn't answer, just scrambled over the centre and the driver's seat. It was done without much agility and grace. Numerous places on my body were sending pain signals. I let my legs dangle from the driver's seat for a moment to reassess my physical state. I didn't see any blood and I hadn't broken anything, so I slid down and stood in front of Vinnie.

He was still shielding me. Cold seeped through the thin soles of my plastic shoes and I shivered. I hugged myself tightly. I was not going to surrender to the tempting darkness again. Even though my heart was racing with concern, I needed answers. "Vinnie, where is Colin?"

Vinnie swallowed. Then he pulled his shoulders back and stepped aside. "He's over there. The paramedics say that it looks like he's only lost consciousness. They are stabilising him to transport him to the hospital."

I stared with wide eyes at Colin's prone body on the white snow. Two EMT's were kneeling next to him. One held a compress against Colin's forearm, the other was adjusting the flow of an intravenous drip that Manny held in the air. Even though the snow was trampled around Colin, red dots were visible all around his body. I ran on unsteady legs to Colin, falling onto my knees next to his head.

"Colin? Colin!" I reached out, but didn't know where to touch him. The entire surface of his face was injured. His left cheek was terribly swollen and had a cut that had stopped bleeding. "I'm sorry. I'm sorry. I'm sorry."

He didn't hear my apology. I needed him to know that I never intended for any of my communication to come across as condescending. I loved him. And as I looked at his unconscious form, I realised exactly how much I'd come to depend on him. He brought a balance into my life, into my world that I'd never experienced before. His acceptance and tolerance of me and my ways put my behaviour, my habit of not considering my words before I spoke, to shame. I continued to apologise, eventually letting my hand rest on his hair. It was sticky with his blood. Tears burned my throat and eyes.

"Doc." Manny's voice was quiet.

I couldn't look up. I didn't want to look away from Colin. He needed to know how contrite I was that I'd made him feel bad. All he'd ever done was made me feel accepted. How could I repay him with thoughtless words? With an inconsiderate tone of voice? "I'm so sorry. Please don't leave me. I'm sorry."

A hand touched my shoulder lightly. "Genevieve."

I shook my head. Manny seldom called me by my name. I didn't want to shift my attention to analysing why he would do so now.

"Genevieve," Manny said again, squeezing my shoulder. "We need to let the medics take Colin to the hospital."

My whole body jerked when Manny used Colin's name. He had never done it before. Never. I looked up at Manny, hot tears streaming down my cheeks. "Why did you call him Colin? Why? He's not going to die! He's not!"

I hated the desperation, the near-hysteria in my voice, but couldn't prevent it. The shock on Manny's face was severe enough for me to take notice. He shook his head emphatically. "No, no, Doc. Frey's just out for the count. Um, he's unconscious. He's not going to die. Right?"

Both paramedics looked over at Manny's demanding tone. The man closest to me spoke. "No, sir. The patient's vital signs are normal and apart from the facial injuries and the laceration on his arm, he has no obvious serious injuries. He should wake up any moment."

"Then why are you taking him to the hospital?"

"Jen-girl." Vinnie knelt next to me. "Colin needs stitches. They need to make sure that there really are no serious injuries and clean his wounds."

One of the paramedics leaned closer to me. I leaned away.

"We need to check you as well, miss."

"Doctor," Vinnie and Manny said at the same time. To my relief, Manny took his hand from my shoulder. Unlike Colin's touch that calmed me, grounded me, Manny's had exacerbated my concerns and my panic. He tilted his head towards me. "She's Doctor Lenard—not a medical doctor—and I agree that she has to be checked. After that collision, who knows what was rattled loose."

"No. Don't touch me. Not now." My control was far too fragile at the moment. "I didn't break anything. I'm uninjured."

"You were unconscious for more than an hour," the paramedic said.

"I wasn't unconscious." I wasn't going to justify my shut-down to a stranger. A strong shiver shook my body.

"Jesus, Doc. We need to get you dressed." Manny started taking his coat off, but stopped when I jerked back.

"I won't wear anyone else's clothes."

"You really need to be checked for injuries… Doctor." The paramedic's eyes shifted between us, clearly not understanding the situation.

"No." I looked at Colin. "I'm not injured. I need to be with Colin."

"Then you can join us in the ambulance."

The thought of being in a moving, enclosed space with this stranger sent a fresh flood of panic through my system. I stared at Colin's swollen eye and wondered how I could leave him. Why could I disregard everything and get into the ambulance with Nikki, but not now? Not with Colin? All I knew was that I would have another shutdown if I were to get into that ambulance.

"Jen-girl." Vinnie touched me with the tip of his index finger on my thigh. As soon as I looked at him, he pulled his hand back. "We need to get Colin to the hospital and you somewhere warm right now. How can we do that? Help me. Tell me what you need."

I studied him. Had I also made him feel like a naughty schoolboy? Here, this large man was taking care to work around my cognitive and behavioural limitations and I seldom, if ever, thought about the effect of my words on him. I had studied psychology to understand the strange world of neurotypicals. It had been important for me to make sense of their irrational behaviour. I had done it to help me function in their world, to aid me in understanding their manners of communication. Not once had I considered the possibility of adjusting my own set ways of communicating and behaving to allow them into my world.

"Jen-girl?" Vinnie pressed his fingertip against my thigh again. "It's real cold out here. We don't want anyone to get hypothermia on top of all the other boo-boos. How about the old man goes with Colin and you come with me in my pickup truck? Will that work for you?"

I studied his face. All I saw was sincere concern. "I don't know what a boo-boo is."

He laughed. "Will you let me tell you in my truck?"

"Will we follow the ambulance? Will we be at the hospital at the same time as Colin?"

"Yes." There was no doubt on his face.

I nodded. A flurry of activity ensued around me. One of the paramedics left to fetch the gurney. Vinnie stood up and held out his gloved hand to help me. I noticed shiny smears on it and knew it to be blood. I swallowed hard and got up without taking his hand. Manny stepped closer and for the first time I paid attention to his expression. I had never seen him this distressed. We'd shared many stressful situations in the last two years and I'd seen his reactions to those. This was different.

The way he rubbed his hands against his hips and his body leaned towards me, I got the impression he wanted to hug me. Vinnie was the hugger in the group. Not Manny. Another shiver went through me. I was going to have to spend a lot of time re-evaluating my behaviour. Especially if one of my friends needed comfort, reassurance. Now I did the only thing I thought I could cope with. I put my cold hand against Manny's stubbly cheek.

He blinked a few times in shock. Then he reached up and pressed my hand hard against his face. He looked into my eyes with such intensity it brought more tears to my eyes. When he spoke, his voice was hoarse from emotion. "Don't ever do this to me again, Doc."

From experience, I knew this strange expression. I nodded, pulled my hand back and glanced at the two paramedics as they carefully lifted Colin onto the gurney. Vinnie was standing to the side, watching us. When he caught me looking at him, he smiled gently and turned to his pickup truck.

"Go with the criminal, Doc. I'll go with Frey. We'll see you at the hospital."

I was suffering from internal conflict about this situation. I breathed in deeply, feeling the pain in my sternum. This was an opportunity for me to change my previous behavioural patterns. Making a decision about what was the best for everyone, not just for me, I nodded tightly and followed Vinnie to his pickup truck.

This was far too much emotion for me. I longed to withdraw into safe rationality where feelings had little control over decisions, words and actions. But it would appear that this safe place caused other people harm. I didn't know if there was a balance. Or how I was going to reach it. How did neurotypical people live with this constant bombardment of emotions?

Vinnie held the passenger door of his truck open for me and waited while I carefully got in. I was sure there was a huge bruise on my right thigh, possibly from being thrown against the door during the impact. Many other places were also hurting as I settled in the seat and fastened the belt around me. Vinnie got in and started his truck, turning the heat as high as it would go.

Only then did I notice all the emergency and law enforcement vehicles. I pointed at a man coming out of the GIPN response truck. "Is that Daniel?"

"Yup. As soon as the old man got worried, we left a few guys behind with Dom's team and started looking for you." Vinnie pulled onto the street behind the ambulance. "What the fuck happened, Jen-girl?"

"I'm not sure. I heard a crash and then…"

"You blacked out?"

"I saw that lamppost coming towards me." That image was imprinted on my memory. "How long were we there before you came?"

"We calculated that you guys must have had that crash five to eight minutes after you left Simone's house. We came looking for you twenty minutes after you left."

I had been in a shutdown and Colin had been lying on the cold ground for twelve to fifteen minutes. It was a short amount of time for me, but very long for an injured person to be exposed to such cold temperatures. I pressed deeper into my seat, frowning. "This doesn't make sense at all. Look at me. I'm hardly injured, but Colin looks like the impact was on his side of the car. The windscreen wasn't broken, I… I didn't see any blood on his side of the car."

"Yeah." Vinnie's *depressor anguli oris* muscles pulled the corners of his mouth down. "Colin was beaten up, Jen-girl."

I gasped and immediately pressed my palm against my sternum. "Who did that?"

"We don't know. Since you were shut down when it happened, we're hoping my man will tell us as soon as he wakes up." Vinnie hands tightened around the steering wheel. "I'm going to kill those motherfuckers."

"There was more than one?"

Vinnie glanced at me. "I don't know, Jen-girl. At the moment, all we know is that it looks like a car hit you from behind. It was at a smart angle too, that is why you spun out of control. The old man and I reckon that Colin was immediately pulled from the car and beaten."

"Do you think it's Gasquet?"

"Of course. The old man thinks so too." Vinnie turned left into the street leading to the same hospital Nikki was in. I hadn't even thought of asking where they were taking Colin. Clearly Manny and Vinnie had everything under control. Vinnie looked at me. "Are you warming up?"

I nodded. My fingers and toes were still cold, but I was no longer shivering. "How long was I out?"

"Well, we got there almost thirty minutes after you left, then it was another half an hour while the paramedics were working their magic."

"Colin…" I shook my head. "It's not a good sign when someone is unconscious for such a long period."

Vinnie took a deep breath. "I know. But I'm thinking that if Gasquet got the jump on Colin, he could've killed him. He has the specialised training. But he didn't kill Colin. He used the pressure points he knows that will put a man to sleep for a while."

For the next two minutes we sat in silence. The ambulance hadn't turned its sirens on, only the flashing lights. It slowed and turned into the driveway of the hospital. I'd been here far too often in the last two years. Once again I thought about desensitisation and how it seemed to be easier to ignore the bad memories I held. The childhood trauma of constant tests and doctors trying to make me 'normal' had left me with a powerful aversion to hospitals. The emotional pain of worrying about my friends' health was proving powerful enough to override my previous memories.

We parked behind the ambulance just as the doors flew open. Manny got out, his face pulled in a familiar scowl. I got out of the SUV and shivered. It was cold.

"For the love of Mary and Joseph, Frey! Just let them do their job." Manny shook his index finger at me. "You deal with him. He's driving me bonkers."

Another car screeched to a halt behind Vinnie's truck. Francine jumped out, dressed in the same clothes as last night. She ran towards us. "Is he okay? Girlfriend, are you okay?"

"Deal with him, missy!" Manny walked past me and grabbed Francine's arm, pulling her back towards her car. "She's fine and he's a pain in my bloody arse."

Francine walked backwards on her high-heeled boots, her eyes wide. As they reached her car, she called out, "I've got clothes for you, Genevieve. For Colin too."

"Jenny?"

I swung around and ran to the ambulance. The gurney was standing next to the vehicle and Colin was leaning on his elbows. The paramedics pushed the gurney towards the brightly lit hospital entrance. Colin fell back, closed his eyes and groaned. "Jenny."

I reached the gurney as they pushed him into the hospital. As soon as the glass sliding doors closed and left the cold outside, the paramedics stopped moving the gurney.

"You people are difficult." The tallest paramedic looked more curious than angry about this. They walked to the reception counter, leaving me with Colin.

He opened his eyes and lifted his hand towards me. "Are you okay? I wasn't going to let him get to you. I fought hard."

I grabbed his hand between both of mine. "I'm sorry. I'm sorry. I'm sorry."

Colin's *corrugator supercilii* muscle pulled his brows into a frown. "What are you talking about, love? You didn't cause the crash."

"I'm sorry for making you feel like a naughty schoolboy. I'm sorry that I only ever think about myself. I'm sorry that you are the one making all the sacrifices for me." My voice broke. "I'm sorry."

"Aw, Jenny-love." Colin pulled me closer until I had to lean over him. He reached up to touch my face, but saw how dirty his hands were and froze for a moment. Then he smiled slightly and put both hands on my shoulders, squeezing hard. "I'm the selfish one. I've never done anything I didn't want to. I haven't gone anywhere I didn't want to and I certainly never stayed with anyone I didn't want to. This bad moment we had is just one small moment in a lake of many beautiful moments."

"You're using analogies."

His smile widened, but then he winced. "My cheek hurts. And that is not an analogy."

"It's cut."

He pulled me closer. "I'm using analogies because when it comes to you, I'm all out of rational thinking. That one little bad moment was just that."

"I want to change." I shook my head when he lifted one eyebrow. I tried to straighten, but his grip on my shoulders held me close to him. "I don't want to make you feel bad."

"Okay, Frey." Manny walked towards us, followed by Vinnie and Francine. "You've seen she's in one piece. Now tell us what the bleeding hell happened."

Colin ignored Manny, his full focus on me. "I love you as you are, Jenny. We all do. Use that rational brain of yours. Do you really think any of us would've stayed if you were a horrible person?"

"What the fuck?" Vinnie stepped closer and leaned down to look at me. "I don't know what is happening between you two, but it better not be anything bad. I love my room and don't want to move out because Mom and Dad are having a fight."

This time when I tried to straighten, Colin let go of my shoulders. I blinked at Vinnie. "How do your mother and father's arguments have any relation to your room, moving out and my apology to Colin?"

Francine and Colin chuckled and Vinnie sighed in relief. "Nothin', Jen-girl. Nothin'."

"Enough of this crap." Manny pushed Vinnie out of the way. "Frey, who did this?"

"Gasquet."

Manny's nostrils flared, his brows pulled together in a scowl. He turned around and walked towards the paramedics who were watching us in bemusement. He noticed their interest, grunted, turned around again and walked towards us, shaking his fist. "Why didn't you tell me this in the ambulance, you good-for-nothing thief?"

"Because I prefer you when you're angry and not looking like someone stole your kitten." Even though Colin's response was said in a tone indicating sarcasm, I saw the full truth behind it. He must have seen Manny's extreme distress and did what he could to refocus the older man. I took Colin's dirty hand and he held it tightly.

"I'm gonna kill that motherfu—"

"Vin, you're scaring the natives." Francine leaned against Vinnie and whispered loudly, "I'll find him. You'll make him regret the day he was born."

"It will have to wait." Colin pushed himself onto his elbows again, his mouth tightening in pain, but not letting go of my hand. "First, we need to find out what the hell he and Simone are planning."

"Why? What happened?" I couldn't read his facial expressions as clearly because of the injuries, but I knew him well enough to have caught the grave concern.

"That's just the thing." Colin shook his head. "I'm not sure what happened. It looked like Gasquet was out of his mind. He looked high or psychotic or something."

"Care to be a bit clearer there, Frey?" Manny pushed his fists in his trouser pockets.

"Seriously, Millard. I can't." Colin looked at me. "His pupils were like pinpricks, his breathing was erratic and he... he looked wild, like a trapped animal."

"That could be many different things." I thought about this. "The information we have on him does not indicate any drug use."

"Well, he was out of control. The way he was hitting me was not very co-ordinated. He also kept muttering about how he's going to be remembered. How they are going to be remembered. He said this over and over again."

"Who's this they?" Vinnie asked.

"And what are they going to be remembered for?" Manny asked.

"Well, I think it is safe to say the 'they' are Simone and Gasquet." Francine folded her arms. "The real question is what they would consider memorable."

"Okay, people." Paul walked towards us, settling a stethoscope around his neck. "This party is over."

I narrowed my eyes. "We're not having a party. Colin is injured."

"Ah, Doctor Lenard." His expression showed more concern as he came closer. "Are you also in need of medical attention?"

"I'm not injured."

"You have blood in your hair." He pointed to the left of my head.

I touched my head and flinched. "It's a small cut."

"Have it checked out." Colin squeezed my hand. "It will be like couple's massage. Only this will be couple's ER."

"I don't know what you're talking about." But I didn't care. He was conscious and had heard and accepted my apology.

"Please, Jenny. For me?"

I looked at Paul. "Only you are allowed to touch me."

"Well, then." He turned to the others. "Is it even worth asking you to wait here?"

"Not on your life, mate." Vinnie's shoulders moved back, broadening his chest, his arms also moving away from his body. He was ready for a physical altercation.

Paul sighed. "Just stay out of my staff's way. Let's get *Colin* to a room."

As we made our way to a room large enough to host everyone, I wondered how I was going to cope. Too many people, too many intense emotions and too many strangers. My throat felt like it was starting to close and my breathing stuttered. I was walking next to the gurney, still holding Colin's hand, which tightened around mine.

"I'm here, love." Colin looked at me, allowing me to study his expression. "We're going to get checked out, stitched up and then we're putting a stop to Gasquet and Simone."

He seemed so sure of it. I marvelled at his trust in our abilities. Thinking about how we could find Simone and Gasquet and if they'd organised something to make them memorable would keep my mind occupied. That and the fact that I had used Colin's real name in front of Paul.

Chapter NINETEEN

"Genevieve, are you sure you are well enough to be here?" Phillip inspected me from my feet to my head for the third time.

"The X-rays and ultrasound tests prove that I'm uninjured." It had been most distressing to allow all those tests, but it had appeased everyone else, so I considered it a small price to pay. "I have a small cut under my hair, but it didn't need stitches. And I have a lot of bruises."

Phillip's expression remained sceptical and I understood his reasoning. We'd been at the hospital for six hours. Colin and I had both been thoroughly X-rayed. Then there had been ultrasound examinations to ensure we had no internal injuries. At Manny's insistence, Paul had sent us both for MRI scans. Colin had gone first, giving me time to prepare for entering that tunnel. I hadn't been able to.

It had taken a few other less distressing tests to convince Manny that I was indeed uninjured. By that time, Colin had been cleared of any internal injuries as well as head injuries. Paul had recommended he stayed in hospital for the day, but Colin had immediately refused and got off the bed. We'd decided it wise not to visit Nikki while looking as if we'd been in a car accident. Manny and Francine had visited her before we'd left and reported that she'd looked better.

I'd preferred to go home to change before coming to the office. Going through my cleaning ritual in my own space had done a lot to calm my mind. It had taken Colin longer than me to get ready, his injuries slowing his movements. He'd tried to hide his discomfort, but it was clear he was in pain. Fifteen minutes after we'd entered Rousseau & Rousseau, Phillip had walked into my viewing room and asked for a private moment with me.

"What about Colin?" Phillip looked at Colin sitting at the round table in the team room. Colin was talking to Manny and shifted in his chair, his lips thinning from the pain. "He doesn't look like he should be out of a hospital bed."

"He has three broken ribs, a hairline fracture on his zygomatic bone—"

"His cheekbone?"

"Yes." The swelling on his cheek had gone down a bit after treatment at the hospital, but it still looked painful. "He also has many bruises from the initial impact and has nine stitches in his arm."

"Genevieve, this job..." Phillip tugged on the sleeves of his suit jacket, every micro-expression communicating concern. "It's getting too dangerous. I think we might have made a mistake getting involved in these cases."

"While waiting for the radiologist to finish taking X-rays, I thought about this as well. Then I put it into context of all the other cases we do. In the last twelve months, we've investigated and closed seventy-three cases. Of those, only three led to these kind of situations."

"Those are three too many." Phillip shifted until his feet were a bit further apart, his body straightened into the posture he employed when he was making final demands. "I want you to consider withdrawing from these investigations."

"Philip, now is not the time." Manny walked into my viewing room. "I thought we agreed on this."

"Agreed on what?" Colin asked from the team room. He got up carefully and walked towards us.

"Nothing." Manny's tone indicated no openness to arguments. "Doc, what do you have?"

"I asked Vinnie to—"

"Got it!" Vinnie ran into the team room, holding up a book. "Hey, where's everyone? Oh, there y'all are. What's up?"

He stopped at the door, his eyebrows lifted. My room was getting crowded again, my mind too fragile to cope with it. I clutched the arms of my chair and closed my eyes to focus on my breathing. My mind was torn between the desire to order everyone to leave me alone with what I thought could lead us to many answers and the mindfulness of how my words had affected Colin.

"Jenny?" Colin's warm hand rested on my forearm. "They're all in the team room ready for you."

I opened my eyes. Colin was sitting next to me, everyone else in the team room, looking at us. Once again, everyone had to work around my neurological needs. I knew that if I started analysing how I felt about it, it would lead me into a spiral that I might not return from. Instead, I got up and looked at Colin. "Don't get up. Please."

His eyes widened briefly at my last word. He nodded and relaxed into his chair when I walked into the team room.

"I got the book, Jen-girl." Vinnie pointed to the antique book lying in the centre of the table. "I hope this is the right one."

"What is this?" Manny frowned at the book. "Don't tell me this is one of Simone's books. It should be handled by Dom's team."

"It's my book." I walked to the table and took it. "I'd forgotten to take it when Colin and I came to the office, so I asked Vinnie to get it from my library. It's Christine de Pisan's *The Treasure of the City of Ladies*."

"Why do you need it?" Phillip asked.

"Who needs what?" Francine walked into the team room, dressed in turquoise suede pants and a turquoise crocheted top worn over the same colour silk camisole. Even her boots were turquoise. She put a large carton with a local chocolatier's logo on the table and opened it. "I think we all need chocolate. Lots of it. And I got us lots of it. Now tell me what else we need."

She took two pralines, sat down next to Manny and held one for him. He glared at her hand, then took it and popped it into his mouth. "Doc is going to tell us about her book."

"Simone had this on her shelf." It took tremendous control not to comment on the time Francine had wasted buying the chocolates. I held the book up. "This was the book used to weigh down and release the lock to her laboratory. I was thinking about this book and wondering if she used this book as a key to her laboratory—"

"It might also be the key to the code in the back of the other books." Francine licked chocolate off her thumb. "Genius. Do you want help with it, girlfriend?"

"No." My hand tightened on the book. "No, thank you. It shouldn't take too long if this is indeed the key to the book cipher."

I ignored the confused and concerned looks on everyone's faces and walked back to my viewing room. I hit the button to close and seal the glass door behind me.

Colin hadn't moved. He waited until I sat down and opened the book before he put his hands over mine. Only then did I realise they were shaking. "Jenny?"

"We first need to see if this will decrypt the last three pages of all the books of hours as well as the coded texts in the other books."

He didn't release my hands. "Jenny, look at me."

"No."

He chuckled. Then he cupped my cheek and gently turned my head until I looked at him. "We all love you as you are."

"I really need to work." I didn't like the broken sound in my voice.

Colin must have seen my desperate need for the neutrality of work. He leaned closer, grunted in pain, but smiled as he kissed me on my nose. "What do I need to do?"

It took us an hour to decipher the last three pages of the books of hours as well as the two pages in Nikki's book and three pages in the book of hours sent to Phillip.

"This is so sad." Colin shook his head and frowned. "She's really screwed up."

I got up. "Come. We need to tell the others."

Colin followed me into the team room. Vinnie was sitting at the round table, as usual paging through a magazine. Manny and Francine were both working on their computers. Everyone looked up when we entered the room and Manny got up. "What have you got, Doc?"

"Letters." I looked at Francine. "I put the decrypted texts on the server."

"I'll have it up in two seconds." It took her eleven seconds to have the text on the large screen against the wall. "Oh, my God. That's heartbreaking."

"The first letter is in all the books of hours from the churches." Even though it had taken up three pages in the books of hours, once I'd deciphered it, there were only four paragraphs.

"'Dear Dad,'" Manny started reading from the screen. "'This is my tribute to you. To your double standards. To the day that you told me you wished I'd never been born. To the day you told me that I, and all other women, were a waste of precious oxygen. To your declaration that women were only good for producing more sons.

"'This is in honour of the day you ordered me to dress to hide my personality, to hide my gender, to hide myself. Of that day you told me you'd registered me at the university to study microbiology. Of the day I overheard you boasting of your son and when asked about me, you'd said I was a nonentity.

"'This is to commemorate the day I changed my studies to art. The day you found out about it and disinherited me. The day you died and I cried, not because I was sad, but because the years of hearing of my worthlessness had ended. The day of your funeral when I discovered the part of the estate that would've gone to me you'd left to the Church.

"'This is to leave my mark. To tell you that your precious priests are easy targets and that you'd painted that bull's eye on their back. And to say that I wish you'd loved me. But you didn't. So fuck you, Dad. You and your priests.'"

It was silent in the team room. Even in Manny's professional tone, the reading had come across emotional. This woman had been suffering and no one had noticed.

"It's horrible." Francine held a forgotten praline in front of her mouth. Melted chocolate stained her fingers. "So sad."

"Don't forget she's killed twenty-six priests that we know of." Manny nodded at the screen. "Put the next one up, supermodel."

"Huh? Oh. Okay." She popped the praline in her mouth and licked her fingers clean.

I winced and turned my attention to the screen. "This one was in Nikki's notebook."

"'Dearest Dad.'" Manny started reading again. "'My time is running out. My time to hate you. My time to prove to you that I can be the best in something you would never approve of. My time to do all the things you tried to beat out of me. My time to make a name for myself. My time to show you that Romain is not the good little boy you thought he was. My time to hope the world will see you as you really were.

"'This is the time for me to take action. Time for me to enjoy my life's achievements. Time for me to reminisce on every moment that was a fuck you to you. Time for me to enjoy being me.'"

"It sounds like she's saying goodbye," Vinnie said. "The chick sure carries a lot of hate around."

"Read the next one." This one caused me the most concern. "It was in Phillip's book of hours."

Francine brought it onto the screen and Manny cleared his throat. "'Daddy dearest, this is the end. The end of your hold over me. The end of your hatred of my gender, my personality, my way of walking, talking, thinking. The end of my pain. The end of trying to prove to myself that I am worthy. The end of hoping for change, hoping for love, hoping for peace. Fuck you, Daddy dearest.'"

"Okay, I changed my mind. *This* one sounds like she's saying goodbye." Vinnie took a handful of pralines from the carton. "What do you think it means, Jen-girl?"

"I don't want to speculate."

Manny put both hands on the table. "Okay, then tell me if you can agree with the criminal that her last two letters sound like she's saying goodbye."

"I can agree with that."

Manny was quiet for a moment. "Do you think it is a suicide note, Doc?"

"I don't know. Suicide notes usually are apologetic, assuring their family that they were loved, or even confessing to something they think they can't change or fix. This has a lot of traits of a suicide note, but it is not definitive."

"It could also be that she got herself sorted out and is moving to the Caribbean to get herself a cabana boy and enjoy life." Francine reached for the carton, paused, thought about it for a second, then took another praline.

"I don't know." Vinnie tilted his head, looking at the screen. "It's much more suicide-y to me."

"Doc, let's assume this is a suicide note. What implications does that have?" Manny lifted one hand. "And before you complain, we need to find out what this means, so indulge me and speculate."

I hated it when he asked me to speculate, but I knew Manny needed it for his investigative process. I didn't have the type of mind to give in to imagined situations, so I worked with what I had. Rationality. "If we work on this hypothesis, I would posit that she would do it in private. She's been killing priests for the last twelve years and not once has it been a public action. She's never tried to attract attention. The coded letters confirm this. Her revenge, emotions, suffering were private. She would not die publicly."

"So we can rule out a suicide mission?" Manny looked relieved.

"No. I'm not comfortable doing anything more than hypothesise."

"Of course." Manny grunted and slouched in his chair. "Then what do you... *hypothesise* her next step to be, Doc?"

I contemplated my answer. After a minute, Francine teased Manny with an outrageous theory. Irritation was evident in his voice and they started arguing. I let this familiar sound recede into the background and recalled everything we'd discovered so far in the case. I thought about Gasquet's connection to this case, the businessmen he'd targeted using Simone's books. I thought about Simone's laboratory, the photos Vinnie had taken of Simone's house, the strange things Gasquet had said to Colin.

"The maps." I straightened and looked at Francine. Her mouth was open in an unfinished sentence, Manny's supratrochlear artery was visible on his forehead and Vinnie was smiling. "There were maps on Simone Simon's worktable together with all the documentation detailing her work with the malaria parasite."

"Let me ask Daniel if they've been looking at those maps." Manny took out his smartphone and walked to his desk.

"What are we looking for, girlfriend?" Francine tapped on her tablet and the photos Vinnie had taken appeared on the screen.

"Logic dictates that those maps had importance. If they didn't, they wouldn't have been on the top of all the documents on that table. They wouldn't have been on the table at all." I looked at the map on the screen and asked Colin, "Do you think she created these maps?"

He narrowed his eyes. "Could be. These map have elements of Gothic art. But this work is very generic, not like her unique style in the books."

"Daniel says they haven't looked at those maps, but he'll get Pink on it now." Pink was Francine's counterpart on the GIPN team. "Okay, Doc, talk to me about the maps. Let's hypothesise again."

"Why are you sarcastic?" I'd been trying hard to pay attention to my wording and tone.

"Ignore the old man, Jen-girl." Vinnie took a praline, bit off half and held the remaining half out to Manny. "Need something to sweeten your sour old self?"

Manny bit down on his jaw, sighed heavily and turned to me. "Without sarcasm, Doc. Would you please hypothesise."

"In a moment." I turned to Francine. "Can you cross-reference these maps with modern maps of buildings in Strasbourg?"

"All buildings or anything in particular?"

"Start with historic buildings."

"Aha. From the Gothic era." Francine tapped on her tablet, her one eyebrow raised. "Seriously, this girl is totally Gothic-obsessed. Give me a minute or three, girlfriend."

I frowned when Colin got up and went into the viewing room. He came back with his computer and a few seconds later the large printer in the corner whirred to life. I looked at Manny. "I will not speculate about what plan Simone's letters might imply. But I do think that the maps will help us find where it might take place."

"Let's see what they look like." Colin put the printed photos on the table. There were nine maps. This was the first time I had paid close attention to them. Colin didn't sit down, but leaned forward and rested his hands on the table. He chewed the inside of his lip as he studied the photos. "Hmm."

"Hmm what, Frey?" Manny looked at the photos, but the lack of comprehension was clear on his face.

Colin took one photo and put it in the place of another. He did this a few times until all nine photos were rearranged in rows of three. "This is one map, not nine."

"Ooh, let me see." Francine straightened and looked at the photos. "I see it."

She put her tablet on the table and worked while glancing up every now and then to look at the arrangement of the photos. On the screen I could see her rearranging the photos in the same order. She used a design programme to remove the ornate frames and combine the maps to form one complete map.

"Compare that to registered blueprints, supermodel."

Francine glanced at Manny. "Look at you, telling me how to do my job. Flirting with me like that will get you in trouble, handsome."

Manny grunted. "Just do it."

"How sure are we that the building is in Strasbourg?" Vinnie asked.

"Nothing is sure." And that was why I hated speculation. "But it is more probable than being anywhere else. Both Simone and Gasquet's business and family roots are in Strasbourg. We can widen the search if nothing comes up in Strasbourg—"

"It's here." Manny's face and tone held conviction. "You might not say it, Doc, but I'm sure of it."

Manny's phone rang and after a quick glance at the screen he answered. It was mostly a one-sided conversation. He didn't say much, just a few responses, but the wariness in his controlled movements revealed Manny's concern. I caught myself leaning back in my seat and crossing my arms, trying to move away from and block the bad news. Manny ended the call and put the phone on the table, glaring at it.

"What happened, Millard?" Colin took my hand. "Who was that?"

"Dom. They've been working through the evidence in Simone's laboratory." His lips thinned even more, almost disappearing. "Simone Simon's notes show that she has successfully created an airborne malaria parasite."

"Malaria." This bothered me. "It seems such an unlikely biological weapon."

"That's some screwed-up shit." Vinnie tilted the carton, disappointment pulling his mouth into a straight line. There were no more pralines. "So what is she planning with a malaria parasite that she can send into a crowd?"

"This parasite was not designed for one specific person, was it?" It wouldn't make sense. "Not designed to one person's DNA?"

"No." Manny pushed his hands deep into his pockets. "It's generic and will affect anyone taking a breath. Who did she make this for? Gasquet or herself?"

I assumed his questions were rhetorical, so I didn't answer. "We need to find her. Did Daniel say anything about their search for her?"

"She's turned off anything trackable," Manny said. "They've put out alerts to all the law enforcement agencies. Bloody hell. We also need to find Gasquet."

"She's more important." It was obvious to me. "Gasquet knows law enforcement techniques. Even if we found him now, we wouldn't get any information from him. She would be much easier to interview, easier to get the truth from."

Manny snorted. "What? You think she wants to confess?"

I thought about her letters. "That is a possibility."

"Well, if only we could get her to come to us."

"Doctor Lenard?" Tim stepped into the room. He fluctuated between calling me by my name and by my qualifications. "There is someone here to see you."

"I'm not expecting anyone."

Manny and Vinnie straightened in their chairs, their expressions suspicious. "Who is he?" Manny stood up, his tone bringing a disapproving look to Tim's face.

He turned to me. "It's a she and she says you are expecting her. Her name is Simone Simon."

Chapter TWENTY

I was not comfortable. Wearing the stiff, plastic protective suit Dom had provided gave me a lot of respect for people who worked in biologically hazardous environments.

As soon as Tim had announced Simone Simon's presence in Rousseau & Rousseau, Manny had summoned Dom and his team. It had taken an hour and forty-five minutes for them to declare the room and Simone free of any discernible contaminants.

Still, Dom had insisted that anyone who came within ten feet of Simone was to wear a protective suit. I didn't mind, even though I moved with difficulty and the suit crinkled when I walked.

I was standing outside the conference room where Simone was currently contained. Manny was arguing with Colin and Vinnie. The rest of Rousseau & Rousseau's offices had been evacuated. Only my team remained. And Phillip. He'd refused to leave and was currently in his office with Daniel.

Colin and Vinnie didn't want me to go into the conference room. In the last hour and forty-six minutes their arguments with Manny had twice almost turned physical. If I were to go into the room, they wanted to be there with me. Manny had refused. Dom had refused. Manny had called Daniel to keep Colin and Vinnie away with force if needed. I had not joined the arguments.

While Dom and his team had been busy in the conference room, I had watched Simone Simon on the monitors in my viewing room. Francine had immediately turned on the security video in that room and sent the feed to my computer. Then she'd left to calm Tim down. He'd had a panic attack when he realised that he had been so close to someone responsible for dozens of deaths.

One of the things that had fascinated me while observing Simone had been the pleasure she'd gleaned from the attention she'd gotten. People who had suffered from neglect or abuse in their childhood were prone to enjoying such attention. It didn't matter that it was negative attention. The more Manny and Dom attempted to gain her co-operation, the more she enjoyed herself. Her shoulders had straightened, her chin had lifted and frequent micro-smiles confirmed that.

But it was the six times she licked her lips or when her tongue protruded slightly that made me realise she felt victorious. This was what she wanted. What concerned me was that I didn't know whether she only wanted the attention or whether there was more to her strategy. As soon as Manny stopped arguing with Colin and Vinnie, and we could enter the room, I would be able to find out.

"You might as well give us suits, Dom." Vinnie stood close to Dom, glaring down at him. "If I hear as much as a squeak from Jen-girl, I'm busting this door and entering. With or without a suit."

"I don't squeak."

"Dom." Vinnie stared at Dom, his gaze fierce.

I sighed. I knew that most neurotypical people enjoyed protectiveness. I found it to be a hindrance. But in light of the recent insights I'd had into my friendship skills, I took a deep breath and took a step closer to Vinnie. I put my double-gloved hand on his sleeve. I felt the tension in his muscles even through the layers of material and latex.

"Vinnie." I waited until he looked at me. "I've been watching Simone. She's not a threat to me. I'll be safe. Manny will be with me."

"Hear that, criminal? Doc trusts me. Maybe you will listen to her if you don't want to listen to me."

"Jen-girl." Vinnie stepped away from Dom and lowered his head to look at me. "Are you sure?"

"I don't like this, Jenny." Colin's body language and micro-expressions indicated that he was understating.

I took my hand from Vinnie's arm and stepped closer to Colin. "I know. But she's asking for me. She's agreed to have Manny there, but no one else. She's playing a game and it would give her more pleasure to delay her true purpose for being here by refusing to talk."

Colin touched the plastic helmet covering my head. "Be careful."

"Do not touch her." Vinnie glared at me. "Don't sit near her. Don't breathe too deeply. As a matter of fact, don't breathe at all."

"You're being hyperbolic. I'll be careful."

"Let's do this, Doc." Manny pulled at his protective suit and grunted. "I hate this shit."

"Suck it up, old man." Vinnie's lips thinned. "You make sure Jen-girl is safe in there. And stay away from that viper. You're toxic enough as it is. Can't have you full of parasites as well."

Manny's head jerked slightly, the surprise visible around his eyes only for a millisecond. "Don't pretend you care, criminal. You're just brown-nosing so I won't lock you up."

They stared at each other for two seconds before they both nodded stiffly. This display of antagonism was ridiculous. I didn't know why people, why men, couldn't be more honest about caring for and about each other. Before I could mention it, Manny turned around and walked through the first plastic covering Dom's team had set up to seal off the conference room door. The heavy plastic closed behind him and he unzipped the second covering against the door.

Colin touched my forearm, preventing me from following Manny. "Please take care."

"I will." I suppressed a shudder as the plastic suit crinkled when I walked through the first covering. I waited until it closed behind me before I walked into the conference room. I zipped the door cover and closed the door, looking at Colin and Vinnie's concerned faces.

"What a delight. The genius is here." Simone's voice was gravelly, as if she'd damaged her vocal cords either smoking too much or screaming too much. Considering what I'd learned about her in the last week, I wouldn't be surprised if it had been the latter. I turned around and found her sitting in the same chair she'd occupied the whole time—in the far corner of the conference room. I studied her like I'd done on my monitors.

Seeing her through the security camera in this room hadn't revealed her true beauty. I didn't often notice women's physical appearance unless it was pertinent. Simone Simon's beauty was so unexpected that I'd taken notice the moment Francine had the footage showing on my monitors. Her long brown hair was straight. One side was flipped over her shoulder, the other half flowed down to below her breast.

Whether formed by the media or evolution, we as humans had certain criteria for what constituted beauty. Simone had it all. The high cheekbones, the full red lips, the flawless skin, the long eyelashes. I estimated her to be around ten kilograms overweight. The extra weight softened her beauty, it didn't take away from it. Unlike Francine's exotic beauty, Simone's was classic.

It was easy to mistake beauty for sanity.

I walked deeper into the room and sat down four chairs away from her. My eyes were on the fine gold band with one small sapphire on the ring finger of her left hand. Manny waited until I was seated before he sat down next to me. Between me and Simone. Her brow lowered in a quick display of sadness before she lifted her chin. "Look at the brave man protecting you."

"You wish you had someone protecting you." I had seen not only sadness, but also envy.

Simone twisted the ring around her finger in what looked like an old habit. Her left hand was mostly covered by her right hand. A soothing gesture. She was holding her own hand. She straightened a bit more, trying to hide her anguish. "Yes. Men have only ever berated and belittled me."

My eye's widened slightly when I registered what she'd revealed. It was there. On her face. Not only her pain, but also what she'd done about that. "Is that why you killed your father?"

Her smile was genuine. And happy. "I wondered if anyone was ever going to find out. Trust it to be a woman. I've been surrounded by idiots all my life. My idiot father. My idiot brother. My idiot co-workers. I can't tell you how happy it makes me to meet someone who is on the same level as me."

It took all my control not to correct her. We were not on the same level. Instead I watched her twist the ring around her finger six times. "You didn't answer my question."

"Your quest... Oh, yes. I mean no. There were so many reasons why I wanted Daddy dearest dead." Her cheeks lifted with a smile. "Who would have thought the malaria would weaken his heart so much that his sick little sex game made his ticker stop. Did you know that dominatrix woman told the police it was the flu that killed him? Hah! Flu. Even the medical examiner thought his heart gave out because of the flu. Another idiot man. So, the full answer to your question is no. Daddy dearest treating me like an imbecile was only one of the many reasons I made sure he kicked the bucket."

Manny half-turned to me. "Died."

Simone frowned. "I thought you were English-speaking. Should I speak French?"

"English is fine." I was not going to explain to her that I didn't understand many metaphors. "Tell me about your ring."

She froze. The fingers that had been twisting the ring were now covering it, protecting it. "The ring is not important."

"You briefly bit down on your lips to prevent yourself from talking. Then you swallowed, because your throat had gone dry from the stress. When you spoke, your voice trembled. These are all indicators of deception. It leads me to believe that the ring is indeed very important to you."

Simone stared at me for almost a minute. I took this time to further study her. Manny had slumped in his chair. I didn't have a full view of his face, but I knew he was watching Simone closely. He was allowing me to lead this conversation.

Another genuine smile lifted Simone's cheeks. "Laurence

told me you are good. I didn't really believe him, so I Googled you. I honestly thought they were exaggerating. They weren't."

I nodded once in acknowledgement. "The ring?"

Again her brow displayed sorrow, the corners of her mouth turning down. Her fluctuation between strong emotions was something to monitor. "It belonged to my mother."

So much of what I'd learned about Simone made sense. Since the day Simone had found her mother dead, she'd been mourning the woman who had abandoned her through death. For the last fifteen years, she'd carried the secret of murdering her father as well as all the consequent murders. It didn't take much to realise she had indeed come to Rousseau & Rousseau to confess.

"Did she give you the ring?"

Simone nodded. "For my sixth birthday."

I did a quick calculation. "That was four days before she committed suicide. Before you found her."

Her eyes flashed open before they filled with tears.

"That makes the ring very valuable to you." I watched as she swallowed a few times and gained control over her emotions. "Your mother also gave you Christine de Pisan's *The Treasure of the City of Ladies.*"

The muscle tension in Simone's entire body lessened. Her shoulders lowered, her smile grateful. "You really get it. You get me."

"I understand the impact a difficult childhood has on an individual no matter their age." It was fascinating to watch the transformation in Simone's nonverbal cues. Her expression was similar to what I witnessed on Francine's face the many times we went for lunch. Simone was regarding me as her friend, if not her best friend. I might very well be the first person in her life to validate her feelings, to listen to her, to show understanding.

"*The Treasure* is my favourite of her books. What do you know about Christine de Pisan?"

I realised that I would glean much from Simone if she continued to regard me as her friend. Small talk about interests was what friends did. I schooled my features not to reveal my inner sigh. "She wrote poetry, epistles and political treatises in the early fourteen hundreds. In that period the literary field was dominated by men, yet as a woman she left a very strong influence, especially with her *The Book of the City of Ladies* and the one you were talking about, *The Treasure of the City of Ladies*. Some even considered her the first feminist."

Manny shifted in his chair, his protective suit noisy. Without looking at his face, I knew he was growing impatient. He wanted to ask Simone about her research and possible success in creating an airborne version of malaria. But we needed her to trust me. She might unwittingly reveal something of importance.

"Isn't it amazing how she managed to educate women of that time of their worth? All the examples in her book she gives of notable and virtuous women of that time. She encouraged women to learn as much as possible." Simone closed her eyes and smiled. "She said that women in higher positions in life should know as much as possible so that even a philosopher could say of them, 'No one is wise who does not know some part of everything'."

"She also said, 'Ah, child and youth, if you knew the bliss which resides in the taste of knowledge, and the evil and ugliness that lies in ignorance, how well you are advised to not complain of the pain and labour of learning.'"

Simone's eyes flew open, her expression one of horror, her right hand furiously twisting her ring. "Why did you quote that?"

"Romaine said your father always quoted that specific part."

"Don't use his name!" She hunched over, her arms tucked tightly against her body. "He's as evil as his father."

"You mean your father?"

"Only by birth. That man did nothing to be a true father to me. He even took the only things I loved and mocked me with it. After my mother died, I only had this ring"—she shook her hand towards us—"and I had the book my mother left me. He took great pleasure quoting parts to see which would get the strongest reaction from me."

"Did your mother use the quote about the labour of learning?"

She wrapped her arms around her torso. "I didn't want to go to school. I cried every morning until my mother started quoting that to me. She told me that learning would make me formidable and open the world to me. She was wonderful. Strong and wonderful."

"But she committed suicide. Isn't that a sign of weakness?" I wasn't surprised by the strong reaction my controversial statement elicited.

"No!" She slammed her fist on the table. "My mother wasn't weak. She was trapped. You don't know my father, my brother. Once they have you in their web, it is impossible to escape."

"You escaped. You removed yourself from your family when you studied art."

If Francine had been in the room, she would've called Simone's expression evil. Her nostrils flared, her sneer vicious.

"My brother paid me. He wanted me out of their lives. Daddy never knew about this, but my brother opened a secret account for me and made me promise to live modestly so there would be no suspicion. It was easy with all that blood money he kept putting into the account."

That explained the beautifully maintained house in the affluent area and the equipment in her laboratory.

"Then how did you manage to get back into his life, killing his opposition? And working for Gasquet?"

Her expression intensified, hatred unmistaken around her mouth and eyes. "Gasquet is a monster. You should be very careful. He wants to kill you too."

"You should know." Manny's voice was neutral, but I'd seen his hands tightening around the armrests. "You made the book that your brother sent here."

"I didn't know any of Gasquet's targets. He would provide me with the DNA and I would make the books."

I leaned a bit forward, schooling my features to be engaging, sympathetic. "Why did you approach him? Why work with someone you consider a monster?"

"Oh, I did not approach that man. He came to me. Almost destroyed the windows I was restoring." A strong shudder shook her body. Her eyes shifted up and to the left. "I was working on a church in the south of France when he appeared next to me, a golf club in his hand. Those windows are five hundred and seventy years old. When I refused to do what he'd asked, he broke one and told me he would break all of them."

"What did he ask you to do?" Manny held his index finger up. "No, first tell us how he knew about your books."

"He is a horrible human being, but he is very smart." She looked at me. "Not as intelligent as you. But he figured out what happened with the priests. You know about the priests, right?"

"The priests you tried to infect and those you successfully infected and killed?"

"Not all of them died." Her mouth twisted in regret. "It took me a bit more than three years to have success and another two years to perfect the delivery method."

"How did Gasquet figure it out?" Manny asked.

"The priest in his father's old village died and another priest that he'd been confessing to." She snorted. "Idiot. Confessing? What a moron. Anyway. Laurence thought someone was after him, so he looked into it and figured out that I had worked on both churches during renovations. He looked further and connected three other deaths to me. Hey, how many did you find?"

Her eyes were wide in excitement. She was enjoying being found out. It became harder for me to school my own features, not to reveal the depth of my loathing for her actions. I inhaled deeply, deciding how specific to be. "We found many more than just three or five priests. Last count was almost two dozen."

"Oh, wow. That's so close." Her expression became more serious. "Thirty-nine priests succumbed to the effects of malaria. There are dozens more who only became really ill, but I'm sure you won't find them. Not all of them were in churches I worked at."

"Will you give us the names of all the priests you sent books to?"

"You already have them." She shrugged. That small gesture caught my attention. If she no longer cared about being caught, having her secret revealed, what did she care about? People with nothing to lose were at their most dangerous. "All the names are on the vials that your people took from my lab. I also kept a detailed ledger. It is taped under the second shelf in my bedroom cupboard. The one with my panties."

"Why are you here, Simone?" I made sure the tone of my voice was inviting, friendly.

She answered without hesitation. "To meet you, of course."

"You're telling the truth, but there is more." Since she enjoyed the attention, I considered my next words. "You are a beautiful, very intelligent woman. I posit that you became tired of being used by yet another man and have come here to take revenge on him."

Manny tensed in his chair. His jaw tightened.

Tears filled Simone's eyes. "I wish I'd known you a very long time ago. Before everything went so wrong in my life."

I pressed my lips tightly together to prevent myself from responding. Simone's psychosis had started at a very young age, most likely triggered the day she found her mother in the bathtub. Her delusional belief that meeting me would've changed something in her life was incorrect.

"Does that mean that Doctor Lenard is correct?" Manny seldom used my title, but in this case I suspected he wanted to assert distance between Simone and me.

"Yes, she is." She wiped the tears that had run down her cheeks and returned to twisting her ring. "That idiot Laurence thought he could make me do whatever he wants. Well, he sure didn't see me coming here and telling you everything."

"You haven't told us everything yet." The muscles in my torso tightened in concern over her true intention. And over the man she'd been working with. If she was here, where was Laurence Gasquet? Where did she plan her revenge?

"I will tell you everything. I know today is my last day of freedom." Her laugh was sad. "No. Actually, today is my first day of freedom. I've always known that someday this will end. I just didn't want an idiot man to end it. When Laurence told me about you, I hoped you'd be the one."

"The one to do what?"

"To discover me." Her expression revealed she sincerely thought she was being discovered, not apprehended. "I think I'll be quite happy in jail. I like structure. I'll have a lot of time to read. But first I just want to chat with you. It's so... refreshing to speak to someone who talks my language, who gets everything I say. Don't you also feel that you constantly have to talk down when you're around people like him?" She nodded towards Manny, her top lip curled. "They really are beneath us."

It took three seconds to formulate my response. "I do indeed find it frustrating to have to explain my conclusions in layman's terms. Sometimes I even have to explain twice. The service industry is the worst. I hate phoning a service centre when I need assistance. They need even more simplistic explanations. Right?" I forced scorn into my tone and rolled my eyes in the manner Francine and Nikki always did.

"I know!" She shifted in her chair to move closer to the table, closer to me. "You know who's even worse? All those idiot businesspeople who always think they know better. Just because I'm an artist doesn't mean I'm stupid. They take one look at my paint-splattered clothes and start talking to me as if I have an IQ of eighty. A few weeks ago, that idiot Laurence spoke to me just like Daddy used to. That's when I had enough. Enough."

Manny stilled. I didn't want Simone to stop her diatribe, so I needed Manny not to interfere. I stretched my leg and kicked his calf. He jerked very slightly and slumped deeper into his chair.

I placed both hands on the table, reaching towards her, strengthening our connection. "I truly understand. That man most likely underestimates you because you are a woman as well. Men tend to do that. He is most likely of the opinion that you could never do his job."

"As if I want to be a security expert. Really! But you know what?"

After two seconds, I realised she required a response. "What?"

"He used 'irregardless' as if it were a word. Then he used 'penultimate' when he meant super-ultimate. And I stopped counting the number of times he said, 'um'." She snorted twice. "Bumbling idiot. As if he would ever be anyone important. I bet he will 'um' his way all the way to jail. Especially with his plan. Hah! At least *my* revenge plans have real motivation. His is just sour grapes. Hey, maybe your team could help him go to jail faster. It would give me great pleasure to see him locked up. Hey, you could lock him up! Right?"

"Oh, we would love to lock him up for you." Despite Manny's sarcasm, he was being truthful. "But we'll need to know about his plan."

She stared at Manny and I saw the moment she decided not to answer him. She turned to me. "Want to know how I got the priests' DNA?"

I leaned forward, my interest real. "Yes."

"At first I would look through their trash. That wasn't fun. Then I got smart. I watched them to see what drinks they liked. I started buying them tea, coffee, hot chocolate and made sure it was in disposable cups. It's amazing how much DNA people leave on the rims of such cups. It wasn't difficult to isolate and multiply it."

"You made impressive progress with your biohacking."

She lifted one shoulder and looked down. Her display of shyness was contradicted by the smile she tried to hide. "Thank you. It took a while, but I got it right."

A few things bothered me and I decided to take advantage of her openness. "You infected your dad in the very early days. How did you manage that?"

The corners of her mouth turned down. "It's a bit embarrassing how primitive my delivery method was. I broke into the house when Daddy dearest was in one of his drunken stupors and used a dropper to put the parasites onto his tongue. The idiot didn't even wake up. He always drank himself into a coma."

I didn't know how to respond. Manny bumped my foot with his. When I glared at him, he mouthed, 'Gasquet'. I looked at Simone. She was looking at her ring. "I don't think Laurence will enjoy prison like you will."

She looked up. "God, no. He'll hate it. That's why you should put him there."

"Before or after he executes his plan?"

"Plan." She snorted. "His little revenge plan. Yeah, right."

It was becoming increasingly more difficult, but I continued my deception. "I'm sure his plan was immature. Did you offer him something better?"

"Of course I did. That idiot just wanted to blow the place up." She was so focussed on me, she didn't see Manny tense. "But I told him those idiots would suffer so much more if they all got malaria. But you know what?"

By now I knew to respond immediately. "What?"

She leaned back in her chair, pulled her shoulders back and lifted her chin. "It's not malaria."

"It's not?" I hoped my admiration looked genuine. "Very smart, Simone."

"Right? That idiot even believed the paperwork I showed him that I'd managed to get the malaria airborne. Hah!"

I tilted my head. "Either you developed something much more lethal or you gave him a placebo. Hmm. I see. You gave him a placebo."

"Ah, you really get it."

"Your revenge on Laurence Gasquet for treating you badly is to make his plan fail."

"Idiot. He would never guess. Not in a million years."

"There is more." It was written all over her face. "What else did you do?"

Her expression shut down and she gripped her hands together. "Nothing."

She was not a successful liar, but her expression prevented me from pursuing this. It would lead to her closing down completely. I took a moment to relax my throat so my voice would remain even. "Do you know where he is? The place where he intends to execute his plan? If we found him now, we could put him in prison. If you want, I could recommend a specific prison for him. One where he'll suffer the most discomfort."

"You would do that? For me?"

"Yes." The word came out strained.

Her shoulders dropped. "But what if I don't know where he is?"

I studied her. She was easy to read. "You don't know where he is, do you? You came here out of fear of him. You couldn't find him and you think he's going to kill you."

She nodded.

"Thank you for your honesty, Simone." I got up. Manny looked at me and got up too. "If you wait here, my team will look for Laurence and we'll let you know when we find him."

"Great. You're really a good... friend. Wait. You are my friend, aren't you?" Her eyes widened and she jumped up from her chair, her face twisted in hatred. "You played me. You bitch! You're not my friend. You're just like all of them. You're using me."

Manny grabbed my elbow and pushed me towards the door. "Get out of here, Doc."

"You bitch!" Simone ran around the table, her fists raised in front of her. "I trusted you!"

I opened the door to find the plastic covering already unzipped. Colin grabbed my hand and pulled me out of the room and into his arms. I turned around to see Manny locking the door. The sound of fists hitting the door were accompanied by Simone's screaming. I didn't know if she would calm down soon. The tone of her voice indicated an increase in hysteria. I had been right about the origins of her damaged vocal cords.

"What the fuck is happening with that chick?" Vinnie looked stunned. "We were all watching from the viewing room. She was fine one minute."

I stepped out of Colin's arms. "I need to get out of all this plastic."

"Are you okay, Jenny?"

I nodded. "I'm fine."

His eyes narrowed and he stared at me for a few seconds. "Okay. Get changed. We'll be in the viewing room."

I walked towards the washroom, thinking about everything Simone had revealed. I stared at the latex gloves covering my hands and couldn't wait to wash my hands. The realisation of Simone's hidden agenda came upon me so quickly I gasped.

I turned around, still looking at my hands. "I know what Simone is planning."

"Well, that's mighty good, little Genevieve. Do tell us. We all want to know." Laurence Gasquet held a gun against the back of Colin's head. Behind them, two men dressed in black had their guns trained on Vinnie and Manny. Gasquet pulled another gun from a side holster and pointed it at me. "What *is* that crazy bitch planning?"

Chapter TWENTY-ONE

I couldn't speak. I had completely frozen. Again. I had never considered myself neurotypical or any other definition of 'normal'. But having a gun pointed at myself and at my team three times in one year would never be categorised as standard. All I could do right now was mentally write Mozart's Violin Concerto No. 4 in D Major and hope it would push the overwhelming darkness away.

"Yoohoo?" Gasquet pushed his gun harder against Colin's skull, causing Colin to lean forward.

Simone had not stopped banging on the locked door, her screaming growing more frantic. It did nothing to ease the tense situation. Despite seeing the micro-expression of decision around Gasquet's eyes, I was not prepared when he suddenly swung the gun he'd had trained on me towards the conference door and shot three times into it.

The report left a shocked silence in its wake, broken only by the sickening thud of Simone's body hitting the floor. Not a single sound came from the conference room. Considering the placing of the three bullet holes in the door, it would be a great unlikelihood that she was still alive.

"At last." Gasquet's smile held triumph as he returned the aim of the second gun to my face. "That bitch was asking for it. So… little Genevieve. Speak. What did she plan?"

I closed my eyes and shook my head. The sound of footsteps had me opening my eyes in fear. I didn't want Francine, Phillip or Tim to put their lives in danger by coming here.

It wasn't them. Another three armed men came into the hallway. One was pushing Daniel in front of him. Daniel's cheekbone was cut, a line of blood moving down his cheek, pooling at his chin and dripping onto his dark uniform.

"Is everyone oka…"

The man hit Daniel on the head with the butt of his weapon—hard enough for Daniel to collapse onto his hands and knees. The way he moved his head indicated that he was disoriented, very likely suffering from concussion.

"Let's understand each other very well." Gasquet's calm tone belied the tension in his body. "Only the good doctor and I will speak. Anyone else say another word and I kill this one for real this time."

I gasped when he moved the gun to Colin's temple. "Please don't shoot. They won't talk."

Manny stared at me from behind the protective mask he was still wearing. Vinnie was glaring at Gasquet, murderous intention clear on his face. I could not look at Colin. I didn't want to see his expression for fear of tumbling into the darkness.

"Good. Now, tell me, little Genevieve, what was the bitch planning?"

I felt powerless, helpless. I didn't know whether I should tell him what I'd concluded. I'd come to rely on my team to guide me in such situations. I recalled the books I'd read on dealing with neurotypicals. I'd read four books on negotiations and three of those had made reference to hostage negotiations. I straightened my shoulders.

"First tell me where the rest of my team is."

Gasquet lifted an eyebrow. Without taking his eyes off me, he moved his head to the side and asked, "Did you find anyone else in the building?"

"No, sir," the one who'd hit Daniel said. "We searched everywhere and only got this one."

Gasquet smiled and my stomach muscles tightened so severely I thought I would throw up. "Well, our little doctor thinks there are more people. Rob, Victor, search the premises. They must be here."

I vowed to myself to never attempt negotiations again. I had just given Gasquet more information than he'd had before. I could only hope that Francine, Dom, Phillip and Tim had escaped to Francine's basement.

I should use the skills I was proficient in. The best of which was observing and analysing people.

Gasquet's complexion did not appear healthy. His skin was clammy and pale, his breathing harder than it should've been. His blinking was far above the average eleven blinks per minute.

"You are not well."

"Damn straight I'm not well." Gasquet waved his gun towards the conference room. "That bitch poisoned me with fucking mercury. I knew she was up to something when she tried to make me believe her lies last month. When I started feeling sick, I knew she'd done something to me. But I know her, so I got the doctors to check for all kinds of toxins and what do you know? I had proof the bitch needed killing. Do you need killing, little Genevieve? Or are you going to tell me what she had planned?"

No more negotiations. I thought about chess and considered my strategy. I was working on the assumption, the hope, that Francine, Dom and Phillip were in the basement, that Francine was monitoring this situation, listening in and reporting all of this to Daniel's team. And I hoped they were already working on a strategy to save the four men being held at gunpoint.

I took a deep breath. "She lied about making malaria airborne. Whatever she's given you is harmless."

He snorted. "I know that. Stupid bitch thought I bought her little notes as proof."

"When was this?"

"Like I said, a month ago. She changed after she made the last two books for me."

"Nikki and Phillip's?" The ones with the suicide-type letters.

"Yup." He wiped his brow with the back of his forearm and immediately pointed the gun at me again.

"Why did you target them?" Maybe if I engaged him in conversation, Daniel's team would have more time to get here. If they knew about this situation.

"I did it to play with you, little Genevieve. I've been studying you. I know how much you care about the student and Monsieur Rousseau." He nodded at Colin. "This one here and the others are also close to you. I wanted you to feel what it's like to have everything important ripped from you."

"You're referring to the farm."

Manny shifted, but I didn't look at him. I couldn't.

"You took that away from me. You took my business away from me." Gasquet's breathing became more erratic and he frowned as if struggling to focus. "Then all those businessmen turned their backs on me because of you. I'd helped those guys be the successes they are today and now I'm the pariah?"

By leaving a traceable footprint with his cash withdrawals, he had hoped to terrorise me with the knowledge that he was coming to Strasbourg. It had worked. He had manipulated Romain to become Rousseau & Rousseau's client to gain access to Phillip and to me. It had worked. But spending the same attention on taking revenge on each business who had rejected him was impractical. His plan had to include many of his previous clients at once.

"You want to destroy them."

His smile horrified me. "Yes. Simone mocked my original plan, but in an hour, I'll be the one laughing. That mansion will be gone. I thought it quite poetic that I'll not only get most of the traitors who turned their backs on me, I'll also rob that crazy bitch of the pleasure of slowly killing more priests. It won't be slow. Not this time."

"You planted a bomb." My suspicion that he'd reverted to his original plan was confirmed when a smirk pulled at his mouth. It was hard to not glance at the security camera in the ceiling. If Francine was hearing this, she would use the map and might already have determined where this place was. Hopefully Dom and his team were already on their way there. I pushed away any doubts that Francine was not currently watching us on one of her basement computers.

Gasquet's agitation was growing by the second while he glared at me. His nostrils flared and his lips tightened. "You're coming with me."

"No." No sooner had Colin spoken than Gasquet hit him hard against the side of his head.

"You really want to die, don't you?"

"He doesn't." I stepped forward. Colin was folded over, blood dripping from where the butt of the gun had made contact. Gasquet pointed both guns at Colin, his face drawn in disgust. I needed his attention away from Colin. "Why do you want me to go with you?"

"You're going to watch. But mostly, you're going as insurance. And you're going to get me off this friggin' continent." His strategy wasn't well thought through. Mercury poisoning caused skin rashes, abnormal perspiration and decreased cognitive functions. Clearly his medication was not working yet.

"I don't have the power to help you leave Europe."

He smiled smugly and looked at the gun pointed at Colin. "You will find a way."

My breathing stuttered. What if Francine wasn't watching? What if the lives of Colin, Vinnie, Manny and Daniel depended on my ability to communicate with Gasquet? We were negotiating and I had no knowledge or power. Except... "Do you know that I have autism?"

"Yes."

"Do you know what a shutdown is?" I was seconds away from one.

His expression became suspicious. "I read about this when I researched you."

"So you know that I'll be useless for hours."

"What are you getting at?"

"I can control my shutdowns." Most of the time. "At the moment I am fighting very hard not to shut down. Let them go and I will help you."

"Jenny."

The two guards returning spared Colin from Gasquet punishing him again for speaking.

"Clear, boss. There's no one here but us. The perimeter is also secure."

Did that mean there were more of Gasquet's men outside? Was Francine seeing this? Was Daniel's team coming? Would she be able to warn them about the men outside the building? Manny and Vinnie shifted their positions, but I refused to look at them. I needed them to be safe. Looking at them would shut me down. I needed to stay alert to keep them alive.

Gasquet grunted a response and stared at me. "I'll lock them in the room with the dead bitch."

His lie was unmistakeable. "No. Let them walk out of here."

"I'll kill them."

It took all my focus not to react and keep my voice firm, steady. "Then I'll shut down and be useless to you. Let them go."

I watched as he calculated the risks.

"Can't do that, little Genevieve. They'll rush out of here and get all their heroes together and fuck up my plans."

"Your plan is flawed." Immediate regret for my thoughtless response made me wince. I had infuriated Gasquet.

"I have a plan." His lips were thin, his words clipped. "You are my plan."

"If I'm not shut down." I needed to get Colin and everyone else freed.

"I'm not wasting any more time with you on this. I will tie them up, lock them in this room and leave them alive and you come willingly with us." His smile sent cold adrenaline rushing through my veins. "Or I kill them right now."

Each of his men altered their position slightly in readiness to shoot. I lifted both hands again. "On the condition that none of your men stay behind to kill them, I agree."

I had no guarantee that Gasquet would keep his word. By willingly leaving with him, I was agreeing to my own death. The moment Gasquet had no more use for me, he would dispose of me as easily as he'd shot through the conference room door. But I had no other ideas. The only thing I could offer in return for the lives of my friends was myself.

Gasquet blinked once, then half-turned his head, still looking at me. "Tie them all up. Don't make it easy for them to break free. Little Genevieve and I will watch. Then we'll all leave together."

"Don't do this, Jenny." Colin's plea forced my eyes to his. The anguish visible on his features stole my breath.

I cried out when Gasquet hit him in the kidneys. Colin fell to the ground with a groan and one of Gasquet's men walked to him with several large zip ties in his hand. I heard the sound of a plastic tie closing and looked up to see the anger in Manny's expression as his arms were held behind him. His rage was directed at me.

This was the first time since Daniel had been brought in that I looked at them. Really looked at them. Something wasn't right with their nonverbal cues. Colin was closest to me and hadn't had any eye contact with Daniel, Manny and Vinnie. That could be why his micro-expressions were more relevant to the direness of this situation. He might not have seen whatever had passed between the other three.

For someone who'd been on his knees, groaning in pain, Daniel's expression was surprisingly clear. He kept his eyes lowered, his shoulders hunched, but he was not as good as disguising his alertness as Manny and Vinnie. Only now that I was studying them while they put up enough struggle to make it difficult for Gasquet's men to tie them up did I notice the incongruity in their body language.

I frowned, realising that Manny, Vinnie and Daniel should already have overpowered these men. Why hadn't they? Daniel was an expert in responding to emergency situations, in hostage negotiations. And how was it possible that Gasquet's team had captured him, but not Phillip? They'd both been in Phillip's office. Surely Daniel would've been able to evade them much better than Phillip?

They had a strategy. I was not going to have to leave with Gasquet. Manny's anger had to be from the frustration of waiting for me to look at him so he could communicate nonverbally with me. The elation of knowing that I was no longer the only one working on a plan made me feel light-headed. I waited for Manny to look at me again, but the hallway was plunged in darkness.

For a moment I thought I was shutting down, but the shouts in the room proved otherwise. Above all the other shouts, Manny's stood out. "Down, Doc! Get down!"

It was easy to allow my legs to collapse under me. The moment I hit the floor I curled into myself to make as small a target as possible, covering my head. A loud bang stopped Gasquet's furious shouts. Even though my arms were pressed tightly over my ears, the sound still caused a ringing in my ears. The bright light penetrating my closed eyelids made me think of the flash grenade I'd once used to help Vinnie.

Suddenly, the hallway was filled with the sound of many footsteps, men shouting and then gunshots. I curled even tighter into myself, thinking that this had to end. I could not continue living like this. My life had been safe until two and half years ago. Had it been then, I would have given in to the shutdown that was looming. Now I couldn't. I needed to know Colin was okay. I needed to know that Vinnie and Manny was well, that Francine and Philip had truly escaped unharmed.

A rush of wind passed through my hair and a thud slammed into the floor next to me. I didn't want to think of the possibility of a bullet having missed me by such a small margin. Instead I shut out gunshots and listened for Colin's voice. Only when the shooting stopped did I hear him. He sounded angry. "Let me up. Jenny? Jenny!"

I tried to relax my muscles to get out of the foetal position I had curled into, but couldn't. Someone fell onto their knees next to me and a familiar hand rested on my shoulder.

"Love, are you okay? Jenny? Please speak to me."

I focussed on his hand gripping my shoulder tightly and mentally wrote three lines of Mozart's Minuet in D major. Slowly, I lowered my arms and stretched out my body.

"Oh, thank God." Colin leaned over me, his face drawn in concern. "Are you okay?"

"I'm unharmed." I moved to sit up and Colin held out his hand. I took it and settled with my back against the wall. The lights were back on. Daniel's team was busy handcuffing Gasquet's men. The hallway looked like it had suffered extensive damage from the gunfire. I shook my head and couldn't stop. "This is wrong. This isn't right. This should not happen. I don't want this."

Colin rubbed my arms as if I was cold. After a few seconds, his hands raised and held my head until I managed to stop shaking it in denial of what my life had become.

Flesh hitting flesh turned my attention back to the men in the hallway. Vinnie had punched Gasquet so hard the murderer was on the floor unconscious and Vinnie was shaking out his hand.

I searched the hallway for Manny, but couldn't see him. I only saw Daniel's team towering over Gasquet's men. Darkness crept closer until I saw the familiar posture opposite Daniel. For a moment I'd forgotten Manny was still wearing his protective suit. He was well. Vinnie and Colin was well. Gasquet and his men were captured.

"Where is Francine?"

"In her basement with Phillip." Vinnie walked towards us and hunched down next to Colin. "She's sent Dom and his team to some place to save a bunch of priests and businessmen."

Despite Vinnie's positive report, the darkness didn't want to recede. I clutched Colin's hand, feeling as if I were in an uncontrolled free fall into a deep, dark, enveloping warmth. As I surrendered to the one place where I didn't have to worry, I whispered, "I can't do this anymore."

Chapter TWENTY-TWO

"Maybe you should put some sugar with this stew." Francine lifted the lid of one of the pots on the stove and inhaled deeply. "Oh, yes, this smells like it needs sugar."

"Sugar? Are you out of your mind?" Vinnie pulled the dishtowel from his shoulder and used it to grab the lid from her and put it back on the simmering dish. "This is a traditional recipe without any sugar in the meat. I will not let you destroy Nikki's favourite."

Not even their usual bickering could draw me out of the malaise that had been affecting my mood since I had been ready to surrender myself to Gasquet. It had been three days ago. The first day no one questioned my mood. We'd all been troubled that the security at Rousseau & Rousseau had been breached so effortlessly. Not that the security had been worthy of a top-secret organisation, but the measures Vinnie had put in place should've warned us of Gasquet's entrance.

Yesterday, Vinnie, Daniel, Phillip and Manny had met to discuss security for Rousseau & Rousseau and our team. I had been invited to take part, but had declined. I had not reaffirmed my decision to stop all investigations into art crimes. I was struggling with it. By yesterday evening, it was clear on everyone's faces that they were becoming concerned about me, about my silence.

A beep sounded from the security system.

"They're here!" Vinnie rushed to the dining room table. Since I'd settled on the sofa with a book, this was the ninth time he'd inspected the table and the decorations. Vinnie, Francine and Colin had spent two hours this afternoon decorating the apartment to welcome Nikki back. I hadn't even had it in me to be concerned about the confetti that had spilled from the table onto the floor. I still didn't.

Vinnie rushed back to the kitchen and lifted the lids of the three pots on the stove one by one. Francine was watching this with obvious amusement. She pulled him away from the stove towards the door. "Come on, big guy. We'll wait for them at the door."

I also got up, but stayed in the sitting area. Colin and Manny had left earlier to fetch Nikki from the hospital. Paul had insisted she stayed for a few more days of observation once they'd started the malaria medication. We'd been tested daily and so far none of us had malaria. Dom and his team of experts were doubtful that any of us were infected. It was good news. Today, Paul had declared Nikki fit to be released and that had started the frantic cooking and decorating.

A key turned in the door, but Vinnie was already unlocking the other locks. He swung the door open and grabbed Nikki. He pulled her into one of his crushing hugs, her feet dangling as he lifted her off the floor. She laughed and hugged him back tightly. I envied that emotional openness. Colin pushed them deeper into the apartment so he and Manny could enter.

Manny looked relaxed. Nikki had that effect on him. On all of us. She softened the roughness in the men's characters. Colin walked towards me and kissed me lightly on the lips. "Hi."

"Hi."

He studied me and I saw the same expression of concern he'd had for three days. He lowered his head, resting his forehead against mine. "What can I do?"

I knew what he was referring to. "I need time."

"Take all the time you need." He kissed me again.

"Oh, get a room." Manny walked past us and fell onto the sofa.

I turned around just as Francine stepped back from hugging Nikki. She tucked Nikki's hair behind her ear. "We are totes going to have a hair and makeup session. You and I, chickadee. And then I'm going to beat you at Deus Ex."

"You can try." Nikki was happy. Her complexion looked healthy, her smiles were genuine and I could see she knew Francine had been allowing her to win their computer game. She turned and looked at me. "Hi, Doc G. I missed you."

"I missed you too." I hadn't gone to visit her in the last three days. I hadn't thought my state of mind would be good for her recovery. We had talked on the phone though. It wasn't the same. As I looked at her and noticed the weight loss, I realised exactly how much I had missed her.

She walked towards me, her intention clear. "I'm going to hug you."

"I know." I had prepared myself for the physical contact. What surprised me was the small burst of happiness I felt at the emotional contact that hug would bring.

I opened my arms. Nikki stepped into my embrace and wrapped her arms around me. She rested her head on my shoulder and sighed deeply. "I'm so glad to be home. I never want to leave again."

"That doesn't make sense. How will you finish your studies if you don't go to university?"

Her body shook against mine as she laughed. She lifted her head and looked at me, happiness and contentment in her face. "I was being dramatic. Like very dramatic. I'm just really happy to be back."

"Good." I patted her back, never knowing when would be the appropriate moment to step out of a hug. I leaned a bit back, giving her the space to let go when she felt ready.

"I'm not done hugging you yet." She pulled me closer again and returned her head to my shoulder, her lips close to my ear. After three seconds, she quietly said, "Manny is worried about you. Vinnie and Francine too. They say there is something very wrong with you. You're, like, not eating and talking and correcting their grammar and stuff. What's wrong, Doc G?"

I didn't want to burden Nikki with any of it. I didn't want her to know how, for the first time in two and a half years, I simply could not imagine myself going into the office tomorrow morning to work on another case. Instead I rested my hand lightly on her head.

"This was a difficult case, Nikki. I need time to process what had happened."

She thought about this for a short while. "Okay."

"Food is on the table!" Vinnie's announcement boomed through the apartment.

"At bloody last. I'm starving." Manny got into an argument with Vinnie for taking so long to serve dinner.

Nikki tightened her arms around me briefly and stepped back. She looked at me, affection unmistakable on her face. "You have to eat with us, okay? Else Vin is going to bitch about it, then Manny is going to shout at him and Francine is going to tease Manny. And it will just get worse from there."

"I'll eat." Having Nikki home alleviated some of the tension that had removed my appetite. Seeing her happy relieved even more of the tightness around my chest.

As Colin followed us to the table, the doorbell rang. Vinnie and Manny stopped their argument, glanced at the door and walked towards it while reaching for their weapons. Vinnie looked through the peephole, his posture immediately relaxing. He opened the door and Phillip stepped through. A look passed between the three men that caught my attention. I wondered if it had to do with Gasquet or with the security plans they'd been discussing.

Nikki got up and hugged Phillip as soon as he reached the table. The contrast between Nikki's messy ponytail, sweat suit and Phillip's immaculate appearance was juxtaposed to their almost identical expressions of fondness as Nikki disappeared in Phillip's embrace. As soon as he was seated, he turned to me. "How are you, Genevieve?"

"Well." Physically, I was.

"Are you sure?" He was not convinced.

I sighed. "This is not about me. This is Nikki's dinner. Let's focus on her."

"Yes." Nikki leaned back as Vinnie spooned stew onto her plate. "This is all about me. Let's not forget that. That means you have to tell me everything. No one's been telling me anything in the last few days."

"That's a lie." Francine leaned forward to see past Vinnie. "I've been telling you all the office gossip, including the accountant and the…"

"What about the accountant?" Phillip asked when she stopped. "Are you talking about Cecile? From Rousseau & Rousseau?"

Francine cleared her throat. "Um, yes. She, um, well, I saw her and one of the delivery guys getting it on in the kitchen."

"Me! This is about me, remember?" Nikki's reminder interrupted Phillip's growing concern. He smiled and nodded for Nikki to continue. "I want to know what happened with the malaria case. Just FYI, I've totally been Googling biohacking and it's supercool. But now I want to know why you were all so upset when you caught the bad guys."

"What's an FYI?" I asked and moved to the side to allow Vinnie to pour wine into my glass.

"For your information," Francine said.

"Why not say that?" I'd heard Nikki use abbreviations before and didn't understand why people chose to talk like that.

"Me! Me! It's about me!" Nikki dipped a piece of bread into her stew. "Tell me about malaria guy."

"That would be malaria girl," Francine said. "She's no longer with us."

"What about the gas guy?"

"Gasquet?" Vinnie's top lip curled. "He's going away for a very long time. He and all his buddies."

"Cool." Nikki frowned. "So why were you so upset?"

It was quiet around the table for a short while.

"Gasquet managed to get past Vinnie's security and our lives were in danger."

The tension filling Nikki's features made me regret my answer. She lowered her fork. "Is that why you're so upset?"

"Not all our lives were in danger." Francine's answer was an obvious attempt to get Nikki's attention away from me. I appreciated it. "As soon as they got in, Dom, Phillip and I escaped to my basement."

"Dom is the hazmat guy, right?"

"Right. Daniel made sure we were safe and then got caught."

"OMG."

"Nikki, please." I could not bear it any longer. "OMG is not a word. Please use your words."

She giggled. "Okay, Doc G." She paused dramatically. "Oh, my God. There. I've said it."

Francine shook her head. "Anyway. Daniel had his comms on, so he was communicating with his team while Gasquet's guys took him to where they had Genevieve and the others."

I had commended Daniel for his ingenuity when I'd learned of this after I'd come out of my shutdown.

"So, like, you guys knew all the time that Daniel's team was coming for you? That's so cool."

"Not all of us." Manny glared at me. "You still haven't told me why you didn't look at us, Doc."

"She always looks, don't you, Doc G?" Nikki turned to me. "You're like the queen of observation."

I froze. My appetite disappeared and I resisted the urge to push my plate away.

Francine tapped her spoon on her wine glass. "I want to make a toast. Come on, lift your glasses."

"Don't take too long." Manny lifted his glass. "I'm hungry."

Francine winked at him. "Then my first toast will be to you. To the man who makes my heart go pitter-pat. To the grumpy smurf with the body of a—"

"Supermodel!"

Everyone burst out laughing. Francine mimed a kiss towards Manny and he rolled his eyes.

"Secondly, to Nikki." Francine blew a kiss to Nikki. "It's good have you home, chickadee. Then to us. We are the bestest team ever. But especially to Genevieve." Her expression sobered up a bit. "Without you, we would not be here. You are what holds us together. You are what makes this team. And you make us smart."

The more she spoke, the more frozen I felt. The glass was shaking slightly in my hand and I gripped it tighter. The responsibility of her words felt like a heavy weight that settled on my shoulders. My breathing grew erratic and I called up a short Mozart minuet to calm down.

Colin took my free hand in his and squeezed. I held onto his hand and focussed on the solid feel of it. He cleared his throat. "But let's not forget the one who organised two teams at once. Francine, you outdid yourself by getting Daniel's team mobilised and at the same time monitoring what was happening in the hallway."

"It was nothing compared to what you guys were dealing with. Once Genevieve got Gasquet talking, it was easy to take the info about the mansion, search for that using the map we had and get the location. Getting Daniel's team and the bomb squad out there was a phone call. I didn't have to keep my calm like you guys did."

"Can we drink the bloody toast now?" Manny looked pointedly at his raised glass. "My food is getting cold."

"To us," Vinnie said, followed by everyone repeating it. I couldn't.

"So what happened at the mansion?" Nikki asked when everyone got back to their meals.

"The bomb squad evacuated the building, then found and disabled the bomb," Manny said. "There were fifty-seven priests and seventy-three businessmen, including some government guys. They were there for a highly valued exhibition of Gothic books, art and statues. It will be in the mansion only for three days before moving to the National Museum. It was supposed to be an exclusive event attempting to build stronger ties between the Church and businesses."

"Instead they got some excitement mingling with law enforcement," Vinnie said.

"At least they weren't blown to pieces." Manny took a bread roll and reached for the butter. "Daniel said there were enough explosives to have levelled that place."

"That would've destroyed priceless artworks." Colin lifted his glass again. "We should toast that. Here's to a successful ending."

"Hear, hear!" Again glasses were raised and dinner continued. Nikki entertained us with stories about the different nurses at the hospital. They'd been telling her about their patients and she took great enjoyment relaying those tales.

After dessert, we settled in the sitting area with coffee and cookies. Nikki was sitting on the sofa next to me, Colin on my other side. As usual, Vinnie had brought a dining room chair for himself, the other three sharing the second sofa.

Throughout the conversation about summer holiday destinations, I noticed the change in Colin's muscle tension. He was not distressed. After a few seconds I realised it was anticipation. The moment there was a lull in the conversation, he leaned sideways and picked up a thick envelope from the floor next to the sofa. "I have something for us."

"What did you steal this time, thief?" Manny leaned a bit forward to look at the envelope.

Colin ignored him and turned to me. "I know we only briefly discussed this. With all that's been happening, I didn't have time to talk to you again. I went ahead and got this done, so I hope you don't mind."

"What are you talking about?" I tried to recall any brief conversation we'd had that could relate to his muddled explanation.

He pulled documents from the envelope and held it out to me. "Our family agreement."

The conversation we had in Nikki's hospital room came rushing back at me. I took the documents from him and counted seven copies. One for each of us in the room.

"What the hell are you talking about?" Manny held out his hand. "Let me see what that is, Doc. You shouldn't just sign anything this thief gives you."

"Ooh!" Nikki shifted closer until our thighs touched. "We're going to be a family."

"Dude?" Vinnie folded his arms and stared at Colin. "A contract?"

"Don't look at me like that, Vin. We are a family. A strange one, but we need to take responsibility for each other on a more legal level. This agreement gives us all power of attorney for each other. It doesn't give us access to each other's assets. I wanted us to have this agreement in case one of us needs medical attention. I don't want us to be in the same situation as when Nikki was in hospital and we weren't allowed to make important decisions because we're not legally kin."

"You want power of attorney over me?" Manny glared at the document. "You want me to trust you with my life?"

"This agreement gives you options for who you would give

this power to, Millard. If you don't want me on that list, then just list Jenny and Phillip."

"And me." Francine dragged her manicured nail down Manny's sleeve. "You have to have me as your power."

"Hmph." Manny pushed her hand off his sleeve, a light blush adding colour to his cheeks. She gave him an exaggerated wink when he scowled and took the document from me.

I opened one and Colin handed the rest out. For eight minutes it was quiet, pages being turned the only sound in the apartment. I read through it twice. The legal document was simple yet thorough. I could not find any point to dispute.

Nikki got up and walked towards her room. Less than a minute later she returned with pens. She held one out to me and I took it. She put the rest of the pens on the coffee table separating the sofas and sat down next to me. Carefully placing the document on the coffee table, she leaned over and signed it. "There. Now I'm your family. You have to look out for me."

"I didn't need a fuc… stupid document to make you my family, little punk. You were family long ago."

Nikki smiled when Vinnie didn't use the swearword. She turned to me. "Are you going to sign it, Doc G?"

"Is this dependent upon my participation in cases?" My question caught attention.

"What the bloody hell does that mean, Doc?"

"Genevieve?"

"No." Colin's firm answer overrode the others' expressions of confusion. "We are a family even if we don't work another case together. Right?"

Manny's reaction to Colin's statement was the strongest. His eyes flashed wide in shock before he lowered his chin to stare at me.

"Right." Francine leaned against Manny and looked pointedly at the document in his hands. "We are family. Give me a pen, handsome. I'm signing this."

"Dude, you know I'm not a contract person."

Colin straightened, the look he gave Vinnie serious. "You're the brother I never had. Sign the fucking agreement, Vin."

Vinnie hid the emotional effect Colin's words had quickly, but not fast enough. He'd been deeply touched. He took the contract and looked at me. "Only if you also sign, Jen-girl. You and I, we're twins. Like those twins who feel each other's pain and fun and shit. You sign and I'll sign."

I looked around the room at these people who had become so deeply entwined in my life. Phillip signing the contract on his thigh surprised me. Despite not having a family of his own, he'd never mentioned considering us as family. And he always consulted with his lawyers before signing anything. Francine and Manny were also signing it. Colin's was already signed. He put his hand over mine and waited until I looked at him.

"We love you, Jenny. If you need to take a break from the cases, it's fine. If you need a holiday, I'll gladly take you. But do this for me. For all of us. We want to take care of you the same way you care about us. The same way you do everything you can to keep us safe and happy."

"But I insult you." I had accepted his forgiveness, but not the flaw in my communication.

"No. You speak your mind. It's never anything but the truth and that is more important than anything else to me and to us all." He leaned closer. "Sign this, give us that gift and we can worry about cases and work tomorrow."

I turned away and saw the expectation on all the faces looking at me. It was so easy to become entirely focussed on myself and lose sight of the larger implications. Signing this agreement didn't just give me responsibility for all their lives. It gave them responsibility for mine. The looks of concern I'd received the last three days and Nikki's affection for me were proof that they cared as deeply about me as I did them.

I opened the document on the last page and signed my name.

"Yay!" Nikki threw her arms in the air. "I'm going to hug you again."

I didn't have time to prepare myself. Nikki gave me a long sideways hug. Then she jumped up to hug everyone. When she got to Vinnie, he lifted her off her feet and walked with her to the kitchen. "Come, little punk. We need tiramisu ice-cream to celebrate this."

I could see the questions in Phillip and Manny's eyes, but they didn't say anything. Francine winked at me and continued to bait Manny until he blushed. Colin gathered the papers and put them back into the envelope. He dropped it back on the floor and took both my hands. "Thank you."

"I didn't do anything. You did all this work."

He shook his head. "No, thank you for giving me peace of mind. I feel better knowing that I'll be able to care for you if ever I need to."

I stared into his eyes for a long time, gathering the courage and words to express my emotions. "You already take care of me. I feel as if I'm losing power over my own life. As if you, all of you, are absorbing that power by... loving me."

"Not power, love. Isolation. We've taken your isolation away from you. You're not alone. No matter what, we are all here. I'm here." The corners of his eyes and mouth lifted in a smile. "And by 'here', I'm not referring to physically being present, but rather supporting you."

"Oh." I didn't know what else to say. I didn't know if I could say anything past the tightness in my throat and the tears burning my eyes. Francine had stopped tormenting Manny and they were quietly watching us. On their faces was confirmation of what Colin had said. I cleared my throat and nodded tightly. "Thank you."

Vinnie and Nikki brought two trays with large helpings of ice-cream. Nikki's exuberance not only lifted the solemn atmosphere, but also my mood. I knew I would not be able to face the bullet-damaged hallway of Rousseau & Rousseau soon. I also knew that I would not be able to look into another case tomorrow. I didn't know what the day thereafter would bring.

But as hard as it was for me to dissociate from a plaguing concern, I took the firm decision to focus on the present. To enjoy Nikki's happiness to be home, Francine's attempts to draw attention away from me by irritating Manny, Phillip's quiet presence, Vinnie's contentment as long as everyone was eating and Colin's warm strength next to me.

Later, when everyone had settled for the night, I would lose myself in a Mozart concerto and analyse the dread that filled me thinking about work. I could only hope my micro-analytical mind would allow me to find a solution to the conundrum leaving me breathless with anxiety.

Tomorrow I would search for books on how neurotypical people balanced a stressful work environment and a family life. Nothing in my past had prepared me for either. Maybe those books might give me some insight into how I, as a non-neurotypical person, could deal with my current life.

But now, I was determined to enjoy my ice-cream.

~ ~ ~ ~ ~

Be first to find out when Genevieve's next adventure will be published.
Sign up for the newsletter at http://estelleryan.com/contact.html

~ ~ ~ ~ ~

Listen to the Mozart pieces,
look at the paintings from this book
and read more about *biohacking, malaria* and *Gothic art* at:
http://estelleryan.com/the-pucelle-connection.html

The Gauguin Connection
First in the Genevieve Lenard series

Murdered artists. Masterful forgeries. Art crime at its worst.

A straightforward murder investigation quickly turns into a quagmire of stolen Eurocorps weapons, a money-laundering charity, forged art and high-ranking EU officials abusing their power.

As an insurance investigator and world renowned expert in nonverbal communication, Dr Genevieve Lenard faces the daily challenge of living a successful, independent life. Particularly because she has to deal with her high functioning Autism. Nothing—not her studies, her high IQ or her astounding analytical skills—prepared her for the changes about to take place in her life.

It started as a favour to help her boss' acerbic friend look into the murder of a young artist, but soon it proves to be far more complex. Forced out of her predictable routines, safe environment and limited social interaction, Genevieve is thrown into exploring the meaning of friendship, expanding her social definitions, and for the first time in her life be part of a team in a race to stop more artists from being murdered.

The Gauguin Connection *is available as paperback and ebook.*

The Dante Connection
Second in the Genevieve Lenard series

Art theft. Coded messages. A high-level threat.

Despite her initial disbelief, Doctor Genevieve Lenard discovers that she is the key that connects stolen works of art, ciphers and sinister threats.

Betrayed by the people who called themselves her friends, Genevieve throws herself into her insurance investigation job with autistic single-mindedness. When hacker Francine appears beaten and bloodied on her doorstep, begging for her help, Genevieve is forced to get past the hurt of her friends' abandonment and team up with them to find the perpetrators. Little does she know that it will take her on a journey through not one, but two twisted minds to discover the true target of their mysterious messages. It will take all her personal strength and knowledge as a nonverbal communications expert to overcome fears that could cost not only her life, but the lives of many others.

The Dante Connection *available as paperback and ebook.*

The Braque Connection
Third in the Genevieve Lenard series

Forged masterpieces. Hidden messages. A desperate swan song.

World-renowned nonverbal communication expert Doctor Genevieve Lenard wakes up drugged in an unknown location after being kidnapped. As someone with high-functioning autism, this pushes the limits of her coping skills.

For the last year, Russian philanthropist and psychopath Tomasz Kubanov has been studying Genevieve just as she and her team have been studying him. Now forged paintings and mysterious murders are surfacing around her team, with evidence pointing to one of them as the killer.

Genevieve knows Kubanov is behind these senseless acts of violence. What she doesn't understand are the inconsistencies between his actions and the cryptic messages he sends. Something has triggered his unpredictable behaviour, something that might result in many more deaths, including those she cares for. Because this time, Kubanov has nothing to lose.

The Braque Connection *is available as paperback and ebook.*

The Flick Connection
Third in the Genevieve Lenard series

A murdered politician. An unsolved art heist. An international conspiracy.

A cryptic online message leads nonverbal communications expert Doctor Genevieve Lenard to the body of a brutally murdered politician. Despite being ordered not to investigate, Genevieve and her team look into this vicious crime. More online messages follow, leading them down a path lined with corruption, a sadistic assassin, an oil scandal and one of the biggest heists in history—the still unsolved 1990 Boston museum art theft worth $500m.

The deeper they delve, the more evidence they unearth of a conspiracy implicating someone close to them, someone they hold in high regard. With a deadline looming, Genevieve has to cope with past and present dangers, an attack on one of her team members and her own limitations if she is to expose the real threat and protect those in her inner circle.

The Flinck Connection *is available as paperback and ebook.*

Find out more about Estelle and her books at
www.estelleryan.com
Or visit her Facebook page to chat with her:
www.facebook.com/EstelleRyanAuthor

CPSIA information can be obtained at www.ICGtesting.com
Printed in the USA
LVOW07s2220020415

433051LV00003B/359/P

9 781505 626131